DANGEROUS TO LOVE USA

EVELYN A. CROWE
TWICE SHY

D1398760

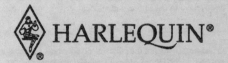

HARLEQUIN®

TORONTO • NEW YORK • LONDON
AMSTERDAM • PARIS • SYDNEY • HAMBURG
STOCKHOLM • ATHENS • TOKYO • MILAN • MADRID
PRAGUE • WARSAW • BUDAPEST • AUCKLAND

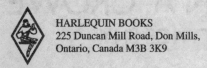

HARLEQUIN BOOKS
225 Duncan Mill Road, Don Mills,
Ontario, Canada M3B 3K9

ISBN 0-373-82341-X

TWICE SHY

Copyright © 1987 by Evelyn A. Crowe

Visit us at www.eHarlequin.com

Printed in U.S.A.

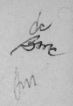

TEXAS

OFFICIAL STATS

NAME: Cord Lowell

VITALS: Age: Mid 30s
Height: 6'3"
Eye Color: Navy blue
Hair: Chestnut, short

OCCUPATION: Owner and publisher of
the *International News
Review*. Also an award-
winning photojournalist.

OBJECTIVE: To solve the mystery of
his brother's death, help
clear Shelley Morgan's
name of treason and
convince the woman
he's fallen in love with to
realize that though he is
her ex-husband's twin,
they are nothing alike.

DANGEROUS
TO
LOVE

EVELYN A. CROWE

Life sure changes. Evelyn A. Crowe went from media director for an advertising agency, to writer, with a few odd jobs in between, then back to college to finish her degree. Yet, it seems like only yesterday that her first Harlequin Superromance novel came out in 1984. Since then she's written thirteen (thirteen is a lucky number). One of those novels, *So Hard To Forget*, was made into a movie and aired several times on The Movie Channel. Even after all this time, it's still a thrill for her to see one of her books on the bookshelf, or to hear from a fan. She looks forward to writing many more novels and hopes readers enjoy reading them as much as she does writing them.

Books by Evelyn A. Crowe

Harlequin Superromance

Summer Ballad #112
Charade #160
Moment of Madness #186
Final Payment #233
Twice Shy #262
A Wild Wind #294
Word of Honor #362
Reunited #570
Legacy of Fear #646
Fathers & Other Strangers #667
A Family of His Own #704
So Hard To Forget #745
Safe Haven #850

Dear Reader,

I couldn't be happier that Harlequin has chosen *Twice Shy*
for their DANGEROUS TO LOVE reprint. *Twice Shy* is
one of my very favorite stories. It's full of laughter, tears,
a few surprises and lots of adventure. Cord Lowell and
Shelley Morgan both have a past they'd like to forget. Yet,
thrown together to solve a mystery, they find more than
answers to their troubles. They discover the surprise of
their life—they find love.

Evelyn A. Crowe

Please address questions and book requests to:
Harlequin Reader Service
U.S.: 3010 Walden Ave., P.O. Box 1325, Buffalo, NY 14269
Canadian: P.O. Box 609, Fort Erie, Ont. L2A 5X3

CHAPTER ONE

THE SUN MADE ITS EASTERLY RISE, pushing the last thin veil of darkness away from the land. With its upward swing, the sizzling globe seemed to burn brighter, hotter, as it splashed the already brown, parched Texas landscape in an eerie bloodred. Heat waves began to waft along the rain-starved ground in a never-ending sea of rolling motion.

Shelley Morgan threw a quick, frightened look over her shoulder, her heart hammering in rhythm with her running feet. She stumbled, cursed and steadied herself. *Don't look back—don't think,* her panic-stricken mind screamed. *Just move.* Small puffs of dust rose and trailed her with each pounding step.

The sound came again. A hiss. Then the rustle and snapping of dry twigs in the bushes alongside the deserted road. Terror pushed her harder, faster, yet it also reminded her that if she let go of her sanity now and ran blindly on, she would surely trip and fall in the badly rutted road. Then the evil thing would pounce on her.

Sweat slid down her sides like slithering snakes and she clenched her teeth; her clothes were drenched. There wasn't even a hint of a breeze to cool her, and she felt as if she would suffocate in the stifling June heat. In her panicked state, her breathing became labored and each gasp sounded like the harsh noise of a bellows, yet she forced her trembling legs to keep moving. Her pulse thundered in her ears, but she could still hear him behind her, never faltering, never slowing, just coming faster and faster.

How long? She struggled for air, her mouth bone-dry and the metallic taste of fear so strong she felt she might gag. *How much longer before I reach the back porch and the safe haven of the house?* Shelley pulled her dazed attention from the treacherous road long enough to spot the entrance to the lane. A few seconds later the smooth surface of the blacktop let her pick up speed. Almost there! Just two hundred yards. If only she could make it. She'd done it before, she told herself. Every morning now for two weeks she'd outsmarted, outmaneuvered and outrun this devil.

The wild flapping of strong wings behind her seemed to thunder in her ears and rocketed her heart to her throat. *Too close. Too damn close.* Her growing fear freed her caution and she started running full-out, terror pushing each frantic step. Passing the fence post that marked the halfway point, the ungodly noise came louder and closer than ever. She stumbled, gasped in dread then automatically righted herself. The white clapboard Victorian farmhouse was in sight now as the trees lining the lane began to thin out. Sweat stung her eyes, blurring her vision, yet her gaze stayed glued to the porch steps ahead.

She forced her body past the invisible wall of pain and managed to speed up even more, but the thing was gaining on her. Finally her toe touched the first step on the porch. Without a thought for life or limb, she vaulted up the remaining four steps, grasped the door handle and yanked, but it slipped from her sweaty fingers. Almost hysterical now with dread and anger, she cursed wildly.

Her heart felt as if it would burst and her lungs as if they would explode. She grabbed once more for the handle. Clutching the hot metal, ignoring the pain to her flesh, she gave a yank and the screen door flew open. She fell through the opening, collapsed onto her knees on the cool wood floor and pulled the door shut with a solid, comforting bang. Gasping for breath, her head pounding with each heartbeat, she lay her forehead against the doorframe, her eyes on the big, randy gander as he hissed, honked, flapped his wings and snaked out his thick long neck at her from the bottom of the steps.

Shelley raised a trembling fist and shook it at the farm's protector, self-appointed guard and *her* nemesis—Napoleon. ''I swear you'll end up Sunday fare yet,'' she panted. ''Goose à l'orange, if I have my way.'' She pushed the screen door open a fraction of an inch so she could peer out and down the trail that veered off toward the foreman's house. ''Lee!'' she screamed, and waited. When nothing happened she yelled again, louder and more desperately. In a few seconds a small-framed, middle-aged Vietnamese man dashed around the corner of the house brandishing a long wooden staff.

Napoleon, his daily ritual of dictatorship accomplished, hissed and honked again, flapped his wings, then marched off, his head held proudly high, his tail feathers pointed upward and twitching arrogantly.

Shelley watched in disgust as her victorious tormentor waddled away. How, she wondered, did she think she could survive life on a farm when the animals, not her, ruled supreme? After all, the only thing close to an animal she'd ever owned was an aquarium filled with tropical fish. She snorted tiredly, remembering the fate of those poor creatures after a week in her care.

The sound of the foreman's staff impatiently tapping the dry, hard-packed ground gained her attention, and she pushed the door open a little wider to get a good look at his expressionless face. Her jade-green eyes glittered as she took in his slanted black eyes, almost shut now with some suppressed emotion. "Are you laughing at me, Lee?" She searched his inscrutable face under the shade of his straw hat.

"No, Miss Sherrey." Lee spun around and as quietly as he'd arrived, headed back toward the dusty trail edged in dying grass. "You must rearn not show fear to rowry goose."

"You're a poor liar, Lee Duc Tho. You want to know how I know?" She was yelling now, her head stuck farther out the open screen door. "I'll tell you! Your English is always impeccable until you get excited or find something immensely funny. Hah!" She'd gotten the last word this time. Shelley slumped back against the frame and closed her eyes. How had she managed to get herself into this mess?

How had a respected businesswoman, assistant to the president of Martin Aviation, ended up on a small Texas farm in the middle of nowhere? She should be spending her days at the beach, basking in the cool temperatures of Seattle, Washington, or lounging at home with her friends and husband. The thought of Anthony brought a stinging rush of tears. He was the very reason she was here in this hot, dying hell of a place. Her husband—ex-husband—had ruined her life and subsequently forced her to give up everything she'd worked for and held dear.

She could never go back, and that realization brought

such a fierce shaft of fear and hate that she pulled herself up from the cold floor and ran through the house to her bedroom. There, she kicked off her running shoes with only a few broken hops in her stride before stepping into the shower fully clothed and turning on the water. The shock of the cold spray helped to take some of the pain away. But bad memories were treacherous devils. The harder you tried to forget, the more they reared their ugly heads to whisper those unwanted past happenings in your ear.

Shelley gritted her teeth and stripped off her wet jogging shorts and top. She leaned back against the cold tiles and let the now-tepid water beat her body. After a few minutes of unsuccessfully trying to forget, she moaned. What was she going to do? If she asked for help there was the possibility of implicating herself as well as Anthony and ending up in jail. Her life was a shambles with little hope of recovery. "Damn you, Anthony. I hope you burn in hell for what you've done to me."

Unbidden, a barrage of questions assaulted her from every direction. Questions with no answers, which succeeded only in causing more pain. She cringed, remembering what a naive fool she'd been and realizing how Anthony must be laughing at her now. But by God, if it was the last thing she did she'd figure out some way to get even. A way that wouldn't find her ending up in jail along with him. Suddenly, over the sound of the water, her stomach growled fiercely, loudly and so unexpectedly after weeks of skipping meals that she laughed. Leaning down, she picked up her soaked clothes and wrung them out before she stepped out of the shower.

Twenty minutes later, dressed in cutoffs and a bright

apple-red tank top, she stood before the open refrigerator trying to decide what to fix from her meager supplies. A dark, damp swag of hair fell across one eye
and she pushed it out of the way with the back of her
hand, careful not to crack the two eggs she was holding.

With the thought of food uppermost in her mind, she
didn't hear the first staccato knocks at the front door.
But when the sharp, frame-rattling noise finally pene-
trated her ravenous inventory taking, she froze. Her eyes
traveled from the depths of the refrigerator to the far
wall and she stared in wide-eyed alarm. *Surely Anthony
wouldn't have the nerve to show his face here?*

She relaxed, doubting if he even remembered she'd
inherited the farm a year ago. They'd been having one
of their usual arguments over his infidelities when she'd
received the letter from the lawyer after the deaths of
her aunt and uncle informing her of her inheritance. She
scolded herself for being afraid of her own shadow
these days. So much had happened in the past month
that her nerves were a frazzle. She straightened slowly
and absently pushed the fridge door shut with her hip.
It was too early in the day for neighborly visitors. A
frown began to etch its way across her brow as the
knocking became louder, more insistent, a commanding
sound that startled her into movement.

Shelley made her way to the front door and slipped
the bolt, being careful not to break the awkwardly held
eggs. As she opened the door with her left hand, her
attention was still on the two delicate objects so she
didn't immediately notice the three grim-faced men
waiting on the front porch. When she did glance up,
dismay and anguish twisted her mouth into a parody of
a smile. Her hand tightened automatically around the
eggs, and a slow cracking sound drew everyone's at-

tention. "Mr. Martin!" Cold, thick liquid began to ooze through her fingers, and she cupped her other hand under her fist to catch the mess.

"May we come in, Shelley?" Lloyd Martin asked, his voice as hoarse with strain as his expression.

Shelley looked down at her hands rather stupidly, wondering how she came to have two broken eggs. Then she stepped back, allowing the men to enter as she spun around and headed for the kitchen. Her boss of seven years appeared as though he had a great weight on his bowed shoulders. She knew if he'd found out what had happened that the dejection and his gray pallor were all her fault.

She stuck her slimy fingers under the faucet and washed her hands, all the while studying the other two men out of the corner of her eye. She'd met Admiral Stanford Marshall in his office at the Pentagon numerous times. Even now, despite the lack of uniform with its impressive array of ribbons pinned to his chest, he still made a commanding presence. The other man she recognized strictly by his nondescript appearance. Over the years, while working for Martin Aviation, she'd been thoroughly screened and at times followed by one of his kind.

"Shelley, this is Agent Roger Higgins with the FBI." Lloyd sighed deeply, his faded brown eyes sad with disillusionment. "May we sit? And a cup of hot coffee would be welcome."

While she made the coffee they took their places around the long, well-worn oak table.

"This is all very upsetting, Shelley. But first of all I must ask you why you left so suddenly two weeks ago. I was deeply upset that you felt you couldn't come to me with your troubles."

Shelley swallowed the huge lump in her throat. Lloyd Martin had been more than her boss and president of Martin Aviation; he and his wife had been her friends. She snapped the top on the pot and plugged it in while frantically trying to figure out what to say. How much did they know? How much would she have to tell? Spinning around, she was about to answer Lloyd when Admiral Marshall spoke.

"Mrs. Rayburn…" He paused, clearing his throat as if undecided where to begin. "Mrs.—"

"Morgan, Admiral."

"Pardon, Mrs. Rayburn?"

"Rayburn was my husband's name. I divorced him in Haiti three weeks ago and am now using my maiden name." By the way the men exchanged mute looks, she could tell she'd shocked them. A heavy silence permeated the airy kitchen, broken only by the rhythmic bubbling of perking coffee. Suddenly the front door opened, then slammed shut, shattering the tableau. Shelley stepped away from the counter and made a move toward the doorway but was immediately stopped by the FBI agent.

"That will only be a couple of my men, Mrs. Ray…Morgan."

"Shelley—" Lloyd Martin reclaimed her attention "—I don't understand any of this. Three weeks ago you were at your desk, happy, in love with your husband, and now you tell me you're divorced. I—"

"I'm sorry, Lloyd. Believe me, I never wanted any of this to happen." She was beginning to babble and knew it, but his bewilderment and obvious exhaustion tore at her heart. She bit her lip to keep from going on and quickly closed the distance to a nearby chair and sat down. "Do you remember the weekend I asked for

Thursday and Friday off?'' He nodded. ''I'd previously made my arrangements, Anthony had signed all the necessary papers prepared by my lawyer, then I flew to Haiti, stayed thirty-six hours, obtained my divorce and flew home.''

''Now you've taken an extended leave of absence—without notifying your superior, I might add—in the middle of a top secret project, to heal your broken heart?'' the agent asked sarcastically. ''You cleared your apartment of your belongings, withdrew your money from your checking and savings accounts, then left town, giving no forwarding address. You didn't tell your husband...excuse me, your ex-husband...your boss, your closest friend, Dee Radford, or your family in California where you were going. That seems a little extreme to me, *Miss Morgan*, even to mend a broken heart.''

Shelley looked down at her hands and slowly unclasped them, watching as, one by one, each white knuckle regained its color.

''You knew there'd been a leak of the VS-1 jet design didn't you, Miss Morgan? Did you also know the Russians were in the process of making a major purchase of information on the design? We need to ascertain what they know, how much they've learned of the project. Did you sell the Russians the plans? Did you sell your country along with your soul for a few dollars, Miss Morgan?''

The agent's blue eyes, eyes she'd thought were so nondescript, were merciless now. ''No,'' she whispered, once she was able to speak. ''I wouldn't, couldn't have done anything so...so...''

''Unspeakable, Shelley?'' the admiral asked out of the corner of his mouth, his lips clamped tightly on a thick cigar. "If not you, then who? Someone is a traitor to this country, and I believe you know that person. Who, young lady, are you protecting?"

"I…" Her voice trailed away as her mind skipped back to those nights she'd spent going through her own private hell. No longer could she protect herself by keeping quiet. Yet, if she told the truth she'd implicate herself in a crime so incomprehensible that she couldn't even begin to imagine the ramifications.

"Please, Shelley," Lloyd begged softly, "help us."

Defeated and weary of the waiting and worry, she nodded. It took several deep breaths to find the courage to speak. Her eyes, dark with humiliation and shame, swung from one man to the other before she gazed back at her boss. His eyes were the only ones with a spark of sympathy, and he was the only one she'd address herself to. "It was…Anthony." She could see disbelief and disappointment in the frown that pleated his deeply lined brow. "It's true, Lloyd!"

"But, my dear, Anthony was our test pilot. He didn't have access to my office or the designs. He just couldn't—" He broke off as he watched Shelley shaking her head.

"I was such a fool," she whispered wretchedly, struggling to get control of her emotions. Finally being able to say it out loud didn't ease the pain as she'd thought it would. Instead she felt as if a hand was trying to tear her heart out. "He would come up to the office sometimes when you weren't there. He used the excuse that since we planned to go out right after work there was no use in taking two cars, so he'd pick me up. One evening I left him in my office while I went to the ladies' room to freshen up." She squeezed her eyes tightly shut, wanting only to block out the memory of that day a month ago. But it was all too fresh, like an open wound that refused to heal.

She remembered Anthony standing over Lloyd's desk with a tiny camera in his hand, so totally engrossed in quickly photographing the plans of the prototype VS-1 jet that he never heard her call his name or enter the office. The sight had so stunned her it had taken a few endless seconds before the wave of betrayal and anger overtook her. In those long seconds she'd come to realize that Anthony had only married her because of her job and her proximity to Lloyd's files. "Anthony was a charmer, a con man, but worst of all he was a traitor to his country. We'd only been married a little more than a year. Maybe I could have forgiven him for his infidelities, but the truth of what he was—of what he'd become—killed every feeling I ever had for him. It was as if someone had suddenly wiped the slate clean, erasing my love for him and leaving me numb but clearheaded enough to know what I had to do."

"What happened after you found him in Mr. Martin's office and saw that he'd broken into the locked files and was photographing top secret naval defense designs?"

Shelley wasn't even aware that she'd been speaking her thoughts out loud, and she was a little dazed when her attention was forced back to Roger Higgins's question. The agent's grim expression had faded some, but there was still a glimmer of suspicion in his eyes. "I took the camera from Anthony and destroyed it."

Admiral Marshall snorted in disbelief. "He just handed it over to you as though his life didn't depend on the film?"

"Why, yes, admiral, he did, after I told him he could walk away free, but with certain stipulations." She saw their questions forming and immediately explained.

"First, he was to resign from Martin Aviation, then he was to sign a confession my attorney would draw up, a confession I promised to keep locked away as long as he never worked with another aviation company and stayed away from me. He also had to agree to a quick divorce. I did allow him one concession. I left the company before he did so it would seem we were separating." She cleared her throat. "You see, I wanted to make it appear that our split up was the result of domestic problems, so that if there was ever any hint of treason or theft it would never reflect on me." She dropped her gaze to the tabletop. "I had destroyed the film, and I'd hoped that was going to be the end of the whole mess. I guess I'm a bigger coward than Anthony, but I just couldn't have stood the notoriety if everything was made public."

Shelley rubbed her forehead, trying to block out her last argument with Anthony once they'd driven home. The screaming, the accusations, her total loss of control as he'd confessed the truth as to why he'd married her, the way he'd used her. But what had finally broken her spirit was his complete lack of consideration for his deceit and the danger he'd put her in. Anthony cared for no one but Anthony, and she'd finally accepted his worthlessness and her own weakness. Now she wanted only to forget and be left alone, but that was not to be.

They thought her the worst kind of fool. How could she expect them to understand the attraction she'd felt for Anthony? She could never make these hardened men comprehend the pleasure of a young girl's dreams come true. Anthony had fulfilled all her childhood fantasies of her very own Prince Charming. When he'd walked into her office for the first time with his good looks and overabundance of charm, she'd been lost. The fact that she was then almost twenty-six, and her biological clock was ticking away, had made her blind to the evil under that handsome veneer. "I tried to stay after the divorce, but I couldn't, knowing what I'd let happen. I should never have left Anthony alone in our offices. It was all my fault."

"Miss Morgan, were you aware that after you left Martin, Anthony asked to extend his departure to allow him to do one last test on the project he'd been involved with?"

"No, admiral, I wasn't."

"He didn't give you any indication that he was planning to finish his testing?"

"No."

"You're sure?"

"Yes."

For the next two hours she was put through a grueling interrogation. A thin gray veil of cigar smoke hung over their heads, making the room stuffy and even hotter. Her mouth was bone-dry from answering question after question, only to have each one repeated again and again as though they were trying to trap her in a lie.

A cup of hot coffee was finally pressed into her cold, clammy hands and she gulped it down, letting the scalding liquid jolt her back to awareness. She'd told them everything, or everything she felt they were entitled to know. But she refused to disclose the intimate details of her marriage. She just couldn't humiliate herself further by telling them that only two weeks after her wedding she'd discovered that Anthony was having an affair. And it hadn't taken her long to realize that there wasn't just one woman who kept her husband unfaithful, but a continually growing number. Those were her secrets, and no amount of interrogation and bullying would make her recount those details.

"Shelley, are you absolutely sure Anthony had no family or close friends?" asked the admiral, a little more kindly now that he was convinced she wasn't the traitor they were looking for.

"No, he was an orphan. We'd discussed his childhood many times because he always felt so uncomfortable around my family. Before he joined the navy he was shuffled from one foster home to another. He always said the navy was his home and his family. He never did tell me why he left the service. But I do know that after his discharge he worked for only one other aviation company before he came to Martin. As to friends, Anthony was always withdrawn and a little remote. Oh, we had friends, but he would never form close relationships with any of them. He didn't even get along with Dee Radford. She and I have been close since she started to work at Martin about six months before Anthony started there. As a matter-of-fact, Dee introduced me to him."

"You're absolutely sure there wasn't a family—no brothers, sisters or a long-lost mother tucked away whom he might have been ashamed of?"

"No!" She let her gaze shift to the half-empty coffee cup and studied the lukewarm liquid, wondering why a sudden charged silence filled the room.

"Miss Morgan...Shelley." The agent started, then stopped, his voice carrying a rough edge to it. "Anthony Rayburn died a week ago while running a routine test on a new radar system. The jet he piloted alone exploded in midair five miles over the Pacific."

Shelley looked from the agent to the admiral, then back again, as though testing the truth of the agent's words in his expression. What did they expect of her—tears? She'd shed buckets full over the past month. Anthony dead! She was sorry and mourned the loss of a human life, but her love for the man had long since died. Maybe later, when the wounds he'd inflicted had healed, she could forgive him enough to cry for him, herself and the lost fantasy of a little girl and her dream man. "I'm sorry, but…" She clamped her lips together, doubting if they could understand her feelings even if she tried to explain.

The sound of a few harsh words and a chair scraping against wood in the adjoining room brought her drifting attention back sharply. She watched as the agent lunged to his feet and rushed toward the doorway, his voice tight as he called, "Nick?"

Shelley's gaze followed his violent movements toward the two men now filling the space between the kitchen and den. Her attention was suddenly riveted on one man. Her world tilted sickly. She shoved back her chair, knocking it over as she surged shakily to her feet. Chestnut hair tumbled over the man's forehead. Familiar navy blue eyes locked with her horrified gaze and a hot shaft of pain burned a pain through her head.

A loud bell seemed to be ringing insistently. She brought her hands up to cover her ears, then dropped her arms limply to her sides as black dots danced crazily before her eyes. "Anthony? Anthony!" She spoke his name through numb lips. He was dead! His plane a ball of fire extinguished by the Pacific, his body lost. It must have been. "Gone," she murmured. "Gone forever."

She felt the floor buck and rock under her feet. Then she was sliding downward into the very depths of blackness she imagined had claimed her husband. Anthony was suddenly shouting, shoving men out of his way and reaching for her before she hit the floor. Her last clear thought before the darkness finally sucked her into a void was that a dead man held her in his arms. Then why, she puzzled, was he so warm and strong, his touch so comforting? "Anthony," she whispered his name on a sigh.

CHAPTER TWO

HE SAT IMPATIENTLY beside his guard. That was the only way he could perceive the naval intelligence officer, Nicholas Harper. All the blond, boyish handsomeness hadn't disguised the merciless green eyes that could analyze people in a flash. Nick Harper had seen too much of the seamier side of life and his fathomless stare revealed that he'd dispensed his share of death.

He took his gaze from the officer and closed his eyes. Leaning his head back, he tried to block out the interrogation going on in the kitchen. God, he was tired, absolutely bone weary, and still feeling the lingering effects of the Central American jungle and his pitiful attempts to survive among people who were immune to inadequate food and stagnant water. All he wanted were a hot shower, a bed with clean sheets smelling of sunshine instead of mildew and thirty-six hours of undisturbed sleep. He sighed heavily and Nick moved beside him. A grim sense of pleasure washed over him at the man's discomfort. Nick was not accustomed to being idle for very long.

His enjoyment was soon disrupted as his attention was caught again by what was happening in the other room. He listened in growing disbelief as Roger Higgins dropped his cruel bomb. "You sorry bastards!" He spit the words out and climbed rapidly to his feet despite his exhaustion.

"No!" Nick's hand shot out, but he administered a savage chop to his wrist and shoved him out of the way. His strength not only staggered Nicholas Harper backward but momentarily shocked him, too.

Higgins and Nick tried to hold him, but he was the one to pull up short when he saw Shelley's expression slip from confusion to growing horror as her gaze locked with his. In those fleeting seconds before he lunged from his human restraints, he realized how young and pretty she was, all mink-brown hair, jade-green eyes and pale skin tinged with pink. Tall, lithe and full breasted, she was a woman to love, not hurt. As he stared, she began slipping to the floor, her body rag-doll limp. He shouldered his way past the agent and Nick and gathered her in his arms, all the while bellowing at the four stunned men, calling them every despicable name he could think of.

A DEEP, VIBRATING RUMBLE next to her ear caused Shelley's eyelids to flicker open. Seeing Anthony's face so close to hers, she moaned, wishing she could sink into the black hole she'd just emerged from. Why were they doing this to her? Why tell her Anthony was dead when he was obviously alive? How could he be holding her so tightly if he were dead? With her gaze glued to his face, she began to squirm in his arms, wanting only to get as far away from his touch as possible. Suddenly he turned his head away from the others and looked straight into her eyes. She recoiled, then went perfectly still in his hold.

Shelley blinked hard several times trying to clear away his image, doubting what she was seeing. Dark blue eyes gazed into hers, but where Anthony's lacked depth and expression, these virtually churned with hidden emotions. She sucked in a strangling breath, her eyes moving frantically over his face, touching each feature. Anthony didn't have a thin white scar running diagonally through his right eyebrow. Nor did he have a small hump in his nose as if it had been broken at some time as this nose had. The face above hers was Anthony's, yet it was tougher, stronger, showing a character Anthony's could never have. Her chest ached and she realized she'd been holding her breath. She slowly exhaled. "Anthony?" she whispered, her voice cracking under the emotional strain of the past weeks and, yes, the fear that seemed to paralyze her every thought.

"No, Shelley. I'm Cord Lowell, Anthony's... brother." Hating to admit the relationship, the reference to kinship stuck in Cord's throat.

"But he doesn't have a brother." The contradiction to her statement gazed down at her compassionately.

She stared at him, this stranger with Anthony's face, and glimpsed the brief flash of desire smoldering in his eyes. She felt her own traitorous response unbidden and unwanted, to that look. A ripple of hunger slid over her skin like a chill wind and she shivered. This was crazy and somehow morbid, wanting a man who was Anthony's double.

"Do you feel able to stand up, Shelley? Then maybe we can answer all your questions." Cord flicked away Nick's offered hand and managed to help her to her feet before he collapsed on the nearest chair.

She couldn't keep her eyes off him, and when his weary eyelids lifted and once again they stared at each other, she flinched noticeably. This time the tightening of muscles was not from shock but from the jolt of electric awareness that tingled along her nerve endings.

Cord misinterpreted her reaction and scowled

fiercely. He didn't like being compared with another man and wondered how he could convince her that he was Cord Lowell and not his brother. His frown deepened as he berated himself. What the hell did he care what this woman thought of him, anyway? He was only doing a job. But, damn it all, he could never, *would* never, condone the way she was being treated. Turning his icy gaze on the four men now taking their seats, he demanded, "You bunch of coldhearted bastards. You better have a good reason for pulling a stunt like this. I'm tempted to walk out of here and forget any debt I might owe my government."

"Will someone *please* tell me what's happening?" Shelley begged, her temper simmering as she realized just how she'd been set up. She had the feeling that her role as victim wasn't over, either. These men had looks of determination on their faces. She choked back another stream of questions and waited.

Admiral Marshall relit his cigar, leaned back in the chair, folded his hands over the rounded mound of his stomach and puffed a few thick clouds into the already stuffy kitchen before he began to speak. "Might as well start at the beginning." He cleared his throat noisily and turned to Shelley. "About six months ago naval intelligence—" he nodded, acknowledging Nick "—came across a leak in top secret data on the VS-1 infraray radar system. A frantic investigation ensued. You're well aware of the importance of that design, Shelley. No other country has a system capable of totally obliterating its own image from enemy radar."

Caught up in his own words and enthusiasm for his subject, the admiral abruptly realized what he was saying and broke off, looking for guidance from Nick. "Has Lowell been cleared for briefing on the VS-1?"

When the man nodded he went on. "What it all narrows down to is, after some extensive backtracking, we discovered that at the other aviation company Anthony Rayburn worked for there'd been some kind of a breach of security. Nick searched—" he waved the thick cigar, disregarding the falling ashes "—your apartment one day while you were both away. That's how he found out about Lowell here. Seems your husband had known he had a twin brother for years. Lowell was adopted by a San Francisco couple when he was a baby."

Shelley was absolutely stunned. "Why wouldn't he tell me?" she asked of no one in particular.

Roger Higgins shrugged. "Maybe he planned to use the twin angle to his own advantage some way. Who knows the workings of a traitor's mind?"

Shelley winced and looked at Cord Lowell. He was staring at her so intently she felt the blood rush to her cheeks, then could have kicked herself as she noticed the satisfied smile on his lips.

"Your husband," the admiral reclaimed her attention, "kept an extensive file on Cord—copies of articles he'd written, clippings of his award-winning photographs." He noticed Shelley's puzzled expression and hurriedly explained. "Cord Lowell is publisher and owner of *International News Review*, based in Frisco. But prior to that he was an ace photojournalist."

Her eyes clashed with Cord's once more, and she wondered if she was losing her mind. He looked exactly like Anthony, yet now, after the shock had begun to wear off, she could see the differences. She shook her head at the inconsistencies of her thoughts and the frightening emotions his presence resurrected.

"With the delivery of the completed plans for the VS-1 to Martin Aviation, we knew it wouldn't be long before your husband made his move. But you intercepted him and foiled his plans, Shelley. Then his plane exploded. That left us with a problem. How much of the radar design did he already have, and had he passed it on to his contact?''

Her hands clenched together in her lap as she thought of what Anthony had done. Shame washed over her in great suffocating waves as she realized just how gullible she'd been. She dropped her gaze to her fists and blinked the stinging tears away.

"Are you all right, Shelley?" Cord asked softly, and from under the cover of the table his hand touched her thigh, giving it a reassuring pat.

"Admiral, I don't want to hear any more." Turning her head slightly, she looked at her boss. "I'm sorry, Mr. Martin. I guess you realize I never planned to come back to work. I don't understand what you're all doing here or why you brought *him*—" she threw a sharp glance at Cord "—but I wish you'd all go now." She pulled her knotted fists apart, dropped a hand to her lap and pushed Cord's disturbing touch away, relieved when her breathing returned to normal.

"We don't intend to leave, Shelley. Not till you agree to help us. I think you owe us that much."

She glared at Nicholas Harper as he spoke, then quickly looked away from his cold eyes.

"Once we realized Anthony's involvement, we began to set up our operations, but you ruined things by leaving him and moving out. Then everything happened too fast for us to control."

Nick's soft voice sent a chill up her spine. She didn't like this dangerous man and his lifeless eyes.

"But we had one stroke of good luck. About the time of the plane crash, someone tore your apartment apart.

All of Anthony's possessions were destroyed, but not out of malice. They were looking for something and we don't think they found it. I believe whoever your husband was dealing with will try to find you.''

Roger interrupted Nick. ''Tell her what else you found, Nick.'' But he didn't give the man a chance. ''Nick found burnt pieces of Cord's file in the fireplace and concluded that, for whatever reason, Anthony burned his brother's file before he went up that last time. Whether he knew his cohorts wouldn't trust him and suspected they'd make their own search or...'' He let the second half of Nicholas's theory trail away.

Shelley gasped at the possibilities. Was Anthony's death murder, suicide or a malfunction in the jet?

''There're two things in our favor.'' Nick went on in his quiet voice as if Roger had never spoken. ''One, no one knows Anthony is dead. We managed to hush it up. Two, when you left Seattle without telling anyone where you were going, you provided us with the time we needed to put our new operation into action.''

''Wait a minute! What operation? For heaven's sake, just go away and leave me alone. No one's going to come looking for me. For what? I didn't steal any plans.'' Shelley jumped to her feet, then immediately sat back down as a wave of fear swept over her. Surely they didn't mean to use her as bait? She stared at Nick. The man didn't seem to have heard a word she'd said.

''Once I was in your home it didn't take me long to realize that your husband—'' her scowl made Nick rephrase his words ''—your *ex-husband* was a meticulous record keeper. I'm positive that whoever searched his belongings after I did came to the same realization. It stands to reason that he may have kept notes and records on the sale of top secret information—dates, amounts, places of drops and pickups, and most importantly…maybe the boss himself. I believe they'll soon put together your missing belongings and Anthony's disappearance and draw their own conclusions. That's when they'll come after you and Anthony to find out what he knows and to retrieve his records. Do you think Anthony hid a notebook or folder of some sort among the things you packed without you knowing?''

''No.'' She looked from one hopeful face to the other, thinking of the boxes stacked shoulder-deep in another room along with her furniture. Automatically her eyes traveled to Cord and she quickly glanced away. The very fact that he sat so silently listening to her every word, watching her every gesture and expression, unnerved her. She rubbed her hands together under the table's edge, then glared at him, wondering why his stare was so damn disturbing. ''Anthony was very particular about his records and wouldn't let me interfere or help. I don't believe he would have hidden something as important as you say where I might come across it.''

''You're wrong, Shelley.'' Nick's flat voice challenged her. ''It's exactly what he would do. He knew the dangers and would try to protect himself at all costs—including throwing you to the wolves. Think about what would have happened if we had found those records among your belongings on our first search? The accusations and confusion would have afforded him the time he needed to disappear.'' He reached into the FBI agent's briefcase and threw two passports across the table.

Shelley fingered the rough covers, then pushed them away without looking at their contents. She felt sick to her stomach.

''False passports, Shelley. One identifies Anthony as

a Swiss citizen, the other as a Russian. You see, he was covering all bases.''

She propped her elbows on the table and covered her face with shaky hands. This wasn't happening, she told herself. She'd wake up soon, her heart pounding in fear, but she'd be in bed and not sitting at her kitchen table with five men. She peeked through her fingers and stifled a groan—it was all too real. Numbly accepting the cup of hot coffee Cord pressed into her hands, she asked, "What do you want? You're free to go through everything I possess to look for Anthony's record book…if there is one, but that's all I can think of to help.''

The total silence that greeted her anguished reply troubled her, and she set down the cup with a thump. The first gaze she met was Cord's and the glimmer there increased her uneasiness. "Mr. Martin—" she broke off at his peculiar expression. "What is it?"

"They want this man—" Lloyd Martin waved toward Cord "—to stay here and pose as Anthony to draw out his contacts.''

"No." She wouldn't look in Cord's direction, telling herself he'd go away if she ignored him. It was an old trick dredged up from her childhood, but this time she knew simply wishing him away wouldn't work.

Nick picked up where Lloyd left off. "We want you to act like a couple working out their marital problems, reconciling their marriage.''

"No!" But no one paid the least attention to her.

"Anthony's contacts are going to want to know why he ran out on them without delivering the designs. They'll be worried that he's trying to make a deal with another interested party. Someone will try to find you and Anthony—Cord. We want those agents, Shelley, and believe me, it's also imperative you find Anthony's records.''

She was about to answer when the admiral butted in. ''Intelligence is a subtle, secretive business, where our enemies are only shadows. We have to bring them out into the light, make them show themselves. Easy pickings, my girl, are always suspect in our world, so don't make their path to you a smooth one. Force the bastards to show themselves so we can identify, follow and catch them red-handed.'' He snorted, and a gush of cigar smoke streamed out of his nostrils, making him look like an enraged bull. Then his snort turned into a belly laugh. ''Red-handed!'' He chuckled again. ''No pun intended.'' When only strained smiles met his joke, he harrumphed and went on. ''You follow Nick's orders, Shelley, even if you don't agree. The man knows what he's about. He wants to catch these people, but he also wants to keep you and Lowell safe. Be visible, but not too visible. Know what I mean?'' She shook her head. ''Damn it! Visible, young lady, but not accessible. Keep a low profile. Don't answer the telephone and announce your whereabouts. If Nick says jump, don't argue, just ask how high.'' He gave Shelley a hard look. ''You see how important it is for this man to pose as Anthony now, don't you?''

''No! Absolutely not. You must know it's totally crazy? He can't pose as Anthony. I'm…I'm divorced.'' She was grabbing at straws and knew it. They all just stared at her. Her angry gaze swung to Cord, and she almost screamed in frustration. She didn't want any man living with her, much less a man who was the spitting image of Anthony.

Shelley surged to her feet as what they were asking

of her finally sunk in. "You're using me to bait your goddamn trap, and I won't have any part of it."

Nick Harper cleared the distance between them and took her arms in a painful grip, pulling her to her toes. "You listen to me, baby." His eyes darkened to pinpoints of anger as they stood level with each other. "The VS-1 is a matter of national security and worth doing anything to protect. You'll do what you're damn well told and keep your mouth shut, or I'll see to it that you're charged—" He got no further as he suddenly found himself lying on the hard kitchen floor, nursing his jaw.

"You forgot yourself, Nicholas." After a moment Cord held out a hand and pulled the surprised man to his feet. "Don't *ever* touch or threaten her again. Do you understand?" They stared at each other for what seemed an eternity. Then as Nick nodded, Cord slowly released his breath and turned to Shelley. "I apologize for Nick. He's used to dealing with scum." Cord's lips twitched, fighting the grin that fought to emerge at Shelley's suddenly haughty expression. His next words wiped her face clean. "Maybe you can teach him some much-needed manners. You see, he's going to be our hired hand and will be staying with us till someone shows up or our government decides to call off their plans."

"Now wait just one damn minute." Her hands balled into fists and she jammed them on her hips, her chin thrust out angrily.

Cord's eyelids drooped heavily as he realized Shelley was the most magnificent woman he'd ever seen. His gaze dropped, surveying the long, shapely legs, smooth and tanned. His eyes roamed to the trim, narrow waist, then on upward till he felt his muscles tighten at the sight of her full bosom. He could discern the outline of her nipples against the soft fabric of her top, and the heat seemed to sing through his veins. Cord smiled. As tired and sick as he felt, he wanted her with a fierceness that surprised him.

Shelley watched Cord's eyes play over her hungrily and steeled herself as they came to rest on her breast. *This is just wonderful,* she told herself grimly. She was about to be pushed into living with an oversexed man she knew nothing about. She glared at him, refusing to back down from the suggestion in his eyes. "What about your job?" Belatedly, she remembered what they had told her of him and rephrased her question. "Don't you have a business to run?" She wished her voice wasn't so breathless and managed a deeper scowl, showing her disapproval of the absurd plan.

"My company's being managed just fine while I'm away."

The beginnings of a headache tapped lightly against her temples, alternating its pressure with each heartbeat. She rose, wandered to the bay window over the kitchen sink and stared out mindlessly. The Texas sky, a cloudless blue, mocked any hopes of rain. Shrubs and trees had wilted in the relentless heat and the grass was dying of thirst.

Her eyes traveled to the only spot of green and she smiled. Lee's strawberry crop resembled a brilliant emerald surrounded by the dark topaz of the dry earth. He had explained, in depth, his completed irrigation system, but she still hadn't a clue as to how he could make water run uphill or what the various pipes, ditches and gates did.

A far-off movement caught her attention. She squinted, trying to make out the object. A precisely

spaced line of white dots moved toward the drying
creek bed, and her mouth twisted as she recognized Napoleon. The little dictator was marching his harem of
females, searching for the few puddles left for their
morning swim.

She sighed. Her world had come to a stop a month
ago, and she'd been forced to blank out her feelings in
order to cope. Now she was starting to feel again, to
respond to Cord, and the painful return of emotions
made her angry. How could she let *that man* pose as
Anthony when she only wanted to forget? Without realizing what she was doing, Shelley pulled out a square
pan from the cabinet. Then, thinking that this morning
had been a particularly distressing one, she returned the
pan in exchange for one twice its size.

"What do you want me to do?" she asked with a
definite lack of enthusiasm, figuring she might as well
give in and allow Cord to stay. At least agreeing made
her feel better, as if it were truly her desire, though she
knew even if she didn't they'd damn well go ahead with
their plan anyway. This way, she was partially in control...wasn't she?

The very room itself seemed to sigh softly in relief.
She could sense the tension ease—in everyone but herself. She began to gather the ingredients for a double
batch of brownies. A good overdose of chocolate would
be a soothing balm to her ragged nerves. Besides, cooking always worked as a tranquilizer for her. Anytime
she was upset she'd head for the kitchen—day or night.
It made no difference to her whether she cooked a gourmet meal at three o'clock in the morning or six o'clock
in the evening. A grim smile curved her lips. Her cooking habit, plus her sweet tooth, had driven Anthony, a
health nut, crazy. Of course, his constant infidelities

drove her to new culinary heights. As his willpower dwindled in the wake of tantalizing aromas, she gained a small sense of satisfaction and revenge as he began to put on weight.

"Shelley, who else lives on the farm?" Nick asked.

She didn't like his tone of voice and bristled, cracking the eggs on the edge of the sink with an added force before she broke them into the ingredients already in the bowl. "Lee Tho and his wife, Vo. He's foreman and has the house situated back near the grove. Then the little brick house a couple of miles down the road—the one at the opposite end of the farm—is where Robbie and his mom live."

"They'll have to go. All of them."

The way Nick barked the orders and his lack of concern for the two families made her grit her teeth. She whirled around, the big mixing bowl tucked securely under one arm and close to her body, her long wooden spoon held like a drawn sword. "Over my dead body!"

She pointed the dripping weapon, her gaze unflinching, refusing to back down or look away from Nick. "My uncle made provisions for both families in his will. As long as I own this property they have homes. The Thos have been pushed around and threatened ever since they arrived here from Vietnam. Uncle John gave them a job eight years ago after he found them beaten up and left at the side of the road. They're loyal, hard workers and only want to live in peace. Besides, they can't move to town. They're still not fully accepted there and are forced to stay mostly to themselves. As for Robbie and his mother—they're nice people just having a hard time making it in life."

Nick shrugged, knowing defeat, but he didn't like it and the thin slash of his mouth reflected his thoughts.

"It could get dangerous. Think that over and maybe you'll reconsider."

"No, I won't. I'll tell you what," she shot back. "If it gets rough, then you'll just have to redouble your efforts, won't you? Or you can leave and call off this ridiculous plan. It doesn't matter to me one way or the other." She nodded, proud of her ultimatum, and looked at Cord to see if he was duly impressed. Instead of admiration, she saw rapture on his face, and she had to bite her lip to keep from laughing. She recognized the glazed expression as that of a fellow chocolate junkie. As she'd talked to Nick, Cord had caught the thick brownie batter that dripped from the spoon. She tried to glare at him. "Don't you have anything to say about all of this?"

"No, ma'am. Only that if you'll hurry up and put that in the oven I might be able to stay up long enough to enjoy some. I'm about to fall flat on my face, but the idea of warm brownies and a glass of cold milk are as good an eye opener as I've ever come across."

He grinned, a teasing turn of his lips that fascinated her. It actually seemed to accentuate his sensuality. But as he rose and came to stand beside her, she noticed something else. Under his tan skin lurked a gray pallor. Close up she could discern a faint bruised look under his eyes. Always a sucker for a sick animal or person, she gazed at him, concern lightening the grimness around her mouth. "Have you been sick?"

"It's a long story," Cord answered abruptly as the scraping of chairs being shoved back from the table broke the spell her eyes were working on him. The other men, except for Nick, were making their farewells and heading for the door, discussing last-minute orders. As Cord watched, Shelley's boss hurried to her side. Cord found it amusing that a brief feeling of jealousy rushed over him as the courtly old man kissed her cheek and warmly embraced the enticing body that he couldn't wait to get his hands on.

"Shelley, this will be the last time I can contact you until everything is straightened out. They've even given me orders not to tell anyone at work where you are." Lloyd coughed softly, then went on. "My dear, don't blame yourself for this, and after it's over please think about coming back to Martin. No, don't say anything now. Just think about it." He kissed her once more on the cheek and turned away, following the others out of the house.

She jumped when Cord spoke beside her, immediately stepping away from his warmth.

"If you'll pop that batter in the oven, show me to my room and help me make up the bed, by the time we get through, those brownies should be just about done."

Shelley agreed and a few moments later, leaving an astutely observant Nicholas to finish his coffee alone, she led Cord out of the kitchen and up the stairs to the guest room. When she reached the closet and pulled out fresh linens, she could feel his gaze on her and she fumbled with the awkward bundle. This was absurd! She spun around and found herself staring at Cord's pale blue shirtfront.

"I think we should get this out of the way first off."

Shelley's head jerked up at the meaning in the deep baritone voice. But before she could move out of Cord's reach, his hands clasped her upper arms, slowly pulling her toward him till the bed linens were the only barrier between them. She watched in a kind of fascinated horror as his head dipped and his mouth moved downward. "No!" she whispered.

"Oh, yes," he said softly. "I'm not Anthony."

"Don't...please."

Cord shook his head. "Sorry."

He didn't sound in the least sorry. Suddenly his mouth was on hers and for a brief panicky second, before she closed her eyes, she could only see Anthony in his face. Her muscles stiffened in revulsion. Then, suddenly, there was no resemblance to Anthony in his touch. Cord's kiss was firm, demanding, not in the least soft. His tongue plundered with a directness that left no doubt whatsoever as to what he wanted. There were no polite games for this man; he took what he wanted without a thought of right or wrong. Explanations or apologies, if he deemed them necessary, would come later.

Shelley yanked herself out of his slackening hold, her breath coming fast and shallow. Before she could find her voice and tell him just what she thought of him, he smiled, then chuckled at her angry red cheeks. For someone who seldom lost her temper, she wanted to scream. Unladylike words tripped on the tip of her tongue, and she bit her lip hard to keep them back.

"Go on, say it," Cord challenged. "But now you'll think twice before you confuse me with that weak-kneed brother of mine."

Insufferable man. "Don't you ever..." she growled. But he was right, she hadn't thought of Anthony while his mouth was on hers. Aware of her anger and how close she was to losing control, she threw the sheets at him. "Make your own bed!" She spun around, marched out and slammed the door on his light laughter. Once away from his disturbing presence, she stopped and closed her eyes, still feeling the tingle of his lips. Running a hand through her short pageboy, she sighed heavily. Just what she needed, more trouble—this particular kind spelled *Cord Lowell*.

CHAPTER THREE

THERE'S NO OTHER AROMA in the world more mouth watering than that of freshly baked brownies. At least that's what nine-year-old Robbie Taylor thought. He stopped in the middle of his game—kick the rock till your toe hurt—and sniffed the air. Something or someone had upset his friend, Shelley.

He frowned, a fierce crinkle of his brow, but his hazel eyes almost teared with hunger and excitement. Shouting a quick farewell to Lee, he took off at a run, wondering what had happened. Whorls of dust rose and followed his every step as he rounded the corner of the house. Suddenly, he rammed his heels into the hard-packed earth, struggling to remember if he'd done anything wrong lately. He patted his back pocket. Fred, his pet garter snake, was still there in its little jar. Course, it wasn't his fault if last week Fred was coaxed through Shelley's back door. After all, he was right there to take him away…and to eat the chocolate cake later.

Robbie grinned, a tiny mischievous lift of his lips, then sobered immediately. No, he'd been pretty good this week. So whatever was wrong wasn't his doing. He pulled his jeans up at the waist, turned the bill of his baseball cap to the back of his head, marched up the stone steps and opened the kitchen door only to stare in disbelief at the two men, one of them eating *his* brownies. Robbie sniffed loudly.

THE NOISE AT THE BACK DOOR made Shelley turn around. For the first time that day a genuine smile touched her mouth as she noticed the young boy's nose sniffing the air like a bloodhound on the scent of his quarry. "You hungry, Robbie?"

"Yes ma'am." Bright eyes danced warily from man to man as he entered the kitchen and immediately placed his stick-thin body protectively beside Shelley, his very stance transmitting a message to the strangers that his friend wasn't alone. His small, dirty hands balled into fists. If need be he'd be more than happy to take the brownies away from the dark-haired man.

Shelley struggled to keep a straight face as she took in Robbie's aggressive demeanor. There was a sharp sting behind her eyes as she thought of the nights she'd lain awake wishing for a baby, or the times she'd tried to talk Anthony into starting a family. "Wash your hands," she ordered, her voice gruffer than she'd intended.

When Robbie hesitated, his eyes searching hers, she smiled, turned away and began to pour him a glass of milk. "Robbie, this is Nick. He'll be staying here for a while." She moved her head in the man's direction, watching with great interest as the young boy seemed to size up the Naval Intelligence Officer. Then, as if finding something he didn't particularly like, Robbie scowled and dismissed Nick with a turned-up nose and a sniff, and turned to the sink and soap dish.

Some perverse sense of revenge made her glance at Nick, her expression a childish grimace saying, *Hah! I'm not the only one who doesn't like you.* But the sight of Nick's wide smile, the first she'd seen, jarred her out of her rude behavior. Something nagged at the back of her mind, something that didn't fit. It was as though she'd met Nick Harper somewhere before.

"Shelley, my brownies," the boy pleaded.

"Sorry. Sit down, Robbie." She set a plate piled high with brownies before the wide-eyed youngster, then realizing her mistake, took the plate away and replaced it with a smaller one.

Robbie sighed dejectedly, carefully counted the three warm brownies on his plate and picked one up, taking a huge bite.

"The other gentleman is... This—" she broke off, meeting Cord's gaze, and glared. "He's my..."

"Husband," Cord finished, and grinned, offering his hand across the table to the boy. "Nice to meet you, Robbie."

Robbie looked at the big hand, then suddenly dropped his food, wiped his fingers on his dusty jeans leg and shook hands. "'Lo," he said in a small voice, not sure how to take the intrusion of another man in his friend's life. After all, *he* was the man around here. "Do you have any kids?" His bright hazel eyes were sparkling with new interest and his expression was a little wistful.

Cord shifted his gaze from Robbie to Shelley, then back again, wanting to laugh but holding back at the quick flash of hurt he'd glimpsed in the soft jade-green eyes. "No, son, we don't." He wondered at the sadness there and promised himself it was another question among many he would have to find the answer for.

Nick stood, breaking the silence that had suddenly sprung up. "I need to have a look around." He replaced the chair next to the table and asked Robbie, "Would you like to give me a guided tour?"

For some unknown reason, Shelley held her breath,

and when Robbie looked down at his empty plate and shot her a pleading glance from the corner of his eye, she spoke up. "He's not finished." She quickly transferred two more brownies to his plate, caught Cord's mock displeasure and gave him two, also.

Nick hesitated, then shrugged and left the kitchen.

Shelley watched his retreat, wondering spitefully if dogs ran from him, also, then was instantly ashamed. She peeked at Cord, found him staring at her, and by the knowing twist of his lips she realized that he'd guessed the path of her thoughts.

"Should I have gone, Shelley?" Robbie asked, sending worried glances in the direction of the back door.

"What? No, Robbie, not if you didn't want to." She snatched a brownie from each of their plates, to the vocal protests of both, and frowned. "You've had enough—drink your milk."

Cord and Robbie eyed each other, smiled slowly then picked up their glasses and drained them before setting them down with satisfied thumps.

Anthony couldn't abide children... Shelley put a lock on her thoughts. She was confused enough trying to rationalize the fact that he was dead, yet there he sat smiling and genuinely enjoying the company of a nine-year-old boy. And Robbie appeared to feel the same. How was she supposed to remember that Cord wasn't Anthony when he was his identical twin? Shelley raked her fingers through her hair. Somehow she had to separate the two men in her mind. The best way, she thought, was to simply ignore Cord Lowell and not look at him.

"Shelley, Shelley!"

Robbie's worried tone and the light tap on her bare

arm brought her out of her dark thoughts. "Yes, Robbie."

"Did you run this morning?"

Shelley picked up a brownie from her plate and took an oversize bite, her teeth snapping together as she tried to pretend she hadn't heard the question.

Robbie snickered, met Cord's curious eyes and coughed behind his small hand, wiping away his milk mustache in the process. But the knowledge of what happened every morning won over and he began to giggle. "Did he get you?"

"No. But it was close this time."

She could feel Cord's full attention on her and refused to look at him. How could she explain the humiliating routine she experienced every morning? A man would never understand her terror of a spiteful old gander. Hell, Robbie was only nine, and even he thought her a foolish female. She decided grimly it was none of Cord's business anyway, and her lips compressed tightly together.

"Napoleon—" Robbie began, but Shelley cut him off.

"Do you want another brownie, Robbie?" It worked. The little boy, more concerned with his sweet tooth, lost his train of thought. "Maybe you'd like to take some with you for later?"

Robbie nodded, his mouth too full to speak. He accepted the two brownies wrapped in a paper napkin with one hand, stuffed the remaining one from his plate in his mouth and rose hurriedly to his feet, anxious to escape before Shelley changed her mind. He backed out of the kitchen, then stopped, yanked off his baseball cap, swallowed a few times and blew away the thick sun-streaked hair that flopped onto his forehead. Dropping his prize in his cap, he folded the fabric together, then wedged the long rolled bill into his one unoccupied back pocket. "Thanks, Shelley." He took a few more steps. "Oh! Bye. You're not going nowhere? I—I mean you'll be here from now on?"

"Yes, he'll be here, and it's not going *any*where," Shelley corrected.

"Yeah." Robbie grinned, continuing his backward steps till he bumped into a solid, immovable object. Turning, he glanced up at Nick and mumbled "Sorry" under his breath.

Shelley, her attention on the retreating boy, hadn't noticed that Nick had come in the back door. She looked at him, dismissing his entrance without knocking as another bothersome quirk she'd have to deal with.

"I've come to get my things." He hooked a thumb in the direction of the front of the house. "I left my suitcase in the hallway earlier." He started to move off, then stopped. "By the way, Lee and his wife are going to help me clean the hired man's cabin and I'll take my meals with them."

Shelley scowled as she watched him walk out of the kitchen as silently as he'd come in. She'd thought he would be staying in the house. Now she realized that she and Cord would be totally alone together. A choking sound passed her lips as she swung around and found herself face-to-face with Cord.

"Easy," he warned in a whisper, grasping her arms firmly and shooting a glance toward Robbie.

She let him touch her only because she couldn't make a scene in front of the boy, but she refused to look at him and turned her body as far sideways as his hold would allow while they waited for Nick's return. When he came into the room she frantically tried to find the words to keep him there, but it was as if Cord's nearness had robbed her of speech. Dizzily, she watched Nick, luggage in hand, leave with Robbie right behind him. She noticed that the youngster, though still leery, had steeled himself to ask Nick if he had any children.

The back door closed and Nick's answer was lost. The kitchen seemed ominously quiet to Shelley's ears, yet she hesitated to move or speak with Cord so close. Even though she refused to look at him, the differences to Anthony were already beginning to register. Standing so near, she knew he was taller than Anthony by only a fraction, but even as tall as she was, he towered over her in a way her husband never had. And, though Cord's clothes seemed to be a little loose, as if he had recently lost weight, she knew he was heavier than Anthony, his build stronger, more muscular.

A whisper of breath stirred the hair around her ear. She steadied herself as a light shiver streaked across her skin, and she tried to inch away. Cord's deep voice growled softly, and the tone stopped her cold.

"You're doing it again—comparing me with your husband—aren't you? I thought we cleared the air in the bedroom about who I am. If you like, I'll repeat myself. I'm not Anthony."

"I wasn't! Not really," Shelley lied, and began to pull away.

Cord's hands tightened on her arms, then loosened. He twirled her around. "Yes, you were." He smiled tiredly, but his eyes reflected his stormy mood. This damn woman was getting under his skin like a thorn. It angered him that she wouldn't look at him. Hell! He knew what she saw, the knowledge that she didn't see Cord Lowell irked him. "Listen carefully, Shelley. Look at me, damn it!" He was fast losing his temper and that irritated him even more. "Take a good long look. I'm not Anthony! Oh, I know we look alike, but that's as far as it goes. I repeat, I am not Anthony!" Damn, those jade-green eyes were getting to him. He dropped his hands, letting her go. His mouth twisted scornfully when she stepped quickly away and turned her back on him. "Ah, hell," he grumbled, and sat down heavily in the nearest chair. "I haven't the strength to argue or try to convince you otherwise." Cradling his head in his hands, Cord wondered once again what he'd gotten himself into. He was sitting in some dried-up Texas hick town, trying to catch spies and possibly being stalked by Russians. The absurdity of the situation made him laugh, a disgusted sound that had nothing to do with humor.

Shelley pulled out a chair across from Cord and watched him closely. Maybe the government had saddled her with a crazy man. "Are you all right?"

"No, I'm not. I'm sick, bone tired and there's the great possibility that I've lost what little sanity I had left."

"Is there anything I can do?" Always a sucker for a sob story, she forgot that this man was more than likely as dangerous as Nick. Cord lifted his face from his hands, and the glimmer in his dark blue eyes made Shelley nervous. Anthony had never looked at her that way.

"Lady…" Cord started, his voice tinged with exasperation and sexual frustration, but he gave up. He inhaled deeply and almost laughed out loud because he was even too damn tired to tell her what he'd like to do, much less do it.

The meaning in his gaze and tone of voice set off warning bells in her head. The only thing she could think of to do was talk. "How did you get mixed up in this crazy scheme?"

Cord rubbed his face and yawned hugely. "Guess I should be grateful, but somehow I seem to have jumped from the frying pan into the fire."

"Have you known Nick Harper very long?"

"About a week too long." She glared at him and he moved his shoulders in defeat, knowing he was going to have to appease her curiosity before he was allowed the luxury of some much-needed sleep. "After navy intelligence found my file among Anthony's belongings, they tried to locate me." He chuckled. "I understand they had their problems, though."

Cord scrubbed at his face roughly with both hands, fighting to stay awake and keep a clear head. "You see, I met Nick about a week ago in the middle of a jungle. He and two mercenaries air-dropped in and pulled me out of Nicaragua. Don't ask how he found me. Only God, Nick and the navy know that. I'll tell you this. I thought I was a dead man till they showed up."

"What in the world were you doing in Nicaragua?" she asked, a bright gleam of interest shining in her eyes.

Cord glanced at Shelley, then looked away and sighed heavily. He raised his fingers to his pounding temples and began a slow circular massage. Then he dropped his hands, heaved another weary sigh and pulled a brown bottle out of his pants pocket. Shaking out two yellow tablets, he washed them down with cold coffee. "About two months ago one of my reporters assigned to Central America disappeared. He was doing an in-depth exposé on the Sandinista government. The last we heard from him he had made contact with a contra leader and was on his way to a rebel camp to give them an opportunity to present their side of the story. It was his opinion that the United States had been fence-sitting too long and that one way or another the truth should be heard. He wouldn't elaborate any further, but he did say he had a blockbuster story that would rock Washington and the Kremlin… Those were his last words to me. After that phone call he dropped from sight.''

"So *you* went to find him?''

"Damn right! John had a family—a wife and two children. I'm a bachelor.'' He glared at her, then smiled sheepishly. ''To tell the truth, I'd been overworking for the past four years and the doctor advised me to take a vacation.'' Cord paused and stared off into space for a long moment. ''What a hell of a vacation. I no sooner stepped off the airplane when some Sandinista government official and his men were all over me. I was interrogated for days.'' He stopped, raked his fingers through his hair and avoided Shelley's eyes. The description of those first few days stuck in his throat. ''Some high-stepping Marxist general thought I was the epitome of American capitalism and planned to make an example of me. They were transferring me from one headquarter to another when we were ambushed by contras. I was never so glad to see a bunch of rebels in my life. It seems John, through his spies, heard what was happening to me and talked his friends into pulling a coup and rescue. I spent the next weeks moving, day and night, from rebel camp to rebel camp.''

Cord stopped and shuddered as he remembered fragments of his trek through the dense Nicaraguan countryside. ''Then one evening just as we were approaching another camp—the one where John was—the night suddenly exploded into a fireball. The Sandinistas had dispatched their version of the Green Berets, an elite battalion of anti-guerrilla fighters.''

Shelley remained quiet, letting Cord relive the horror of that night. She knew by some strange instinct that this man hadn't been able to talk about his ordeal to anyone, and by opening up now it would help lay some of his nightmares to rest. The neutral tone of his voice was belied by the paleness of his skin. A wave of fierce tenderness swept over her, and even in her confusion over her predicament she wanted desperately to reach out and take him in her arms. ''What happened that night, Cord?'' He grimaced and she felt her heart sink with pity. He didn't need to tell her; she knew by the pain in his eyes that his colleague, John, would never make it home.

Cord propped his elbows on the table, rested his forehead on the heels of his hands and closed his eyes. ''Fire was everywhere, ammunition depots exploding, men running and screaming, their clothing a living flame. Bullets were flying in every direction and two of the contras with me shoved me to the ground. They were dead before we hit the earth. I was pinned down, too weak to push them off, when I saw John running in my direction. I tried to warn him, but my scream was just one in a hundred that night. They got John. I saw him get hit and fall. Then there was this blond man leaning over me, his face blackened with streaks of camouflage paint. I thought I was done for, but he began dragging me from under those men and into the jungle. It was Nick Harper and his mercenaries. It turned out they'd been tracking us for days. There wasn't a thing we could do but save our own skins. The next few days we used all our energies just keeping out of the way of the Sandinistas and reaching the rendezvous spot where

Nick, his two friends and I were airlifted out of the country and back to the States—Washington, D.C., to be precise.''

Cord dropped his hands from his face and stared at them as they lay limply on the table. "Nick checked me into a hospital where the doctor pumped me full of penicillin and antibiotics, then we were packed on another plane headed for Houston where we met the admiral, Roger Higgins and your boss and drove here. All the while they bombarded me with the plan they'd hatched to catch your spies." He rotated his head and groaned. "God, but I'm tired. Do you think that will hold your curiosity in check till after I get some sleep?"

"Yes, of course." Shelley jumped to her feet, suddenly flustered and angry with herself. She had no business prying into Cord's life. Hearing his tale only made him more real, more a threat to her own peace of mind. "Listen, Cord," she began as she followed him out of the room. "Listen, you can't stay here. It's not right."

"Tough! Right now I'd strangle you for some peace and quiet and a bed." He stopped and turned so abruptly that he had to reach out and catch her before she ran into him. "Besides, what's wrong with my staying here?"

"It just won't do, that's all. I—I, damn it. I'm sorry, but I don't want you here."

Cord inhaled deeply and let his eyes run slowly up and down her delicious body. "Don't trust yourself to keep your hands off me, huh?" He let go of her arms and walked away, leaving Shelley sputtering while he climbed the stairs, his steps as slow and carefully placed as an old man's.

The nerve. Hands off, indeed! She wasn't some sex-starved divorcée. "Now you listen here," she shouted from the bottom of the stairs, then charged up them when he refused to stop. "Wait a minute!" Shelley pulled up short as she reached the bedroom doorway, her lips forming a perfect O as she watched Cord begin to strip. Without a thought as to how silly she looked, she slapped her hand over her eyes and continued her argument. "You don't seem to understand the problems you'll cause. I'll have to introduce you as my husband and he's...dead. Then when you leave, you'll have to die all over again. I mean—"

"Do I make you nervous, Shelley?"

She jumped as his warm breath fanned her cheek and squeezed her eyes tighter behind her shielding hand. "No. Why should you?" she challenged, then wished she hadn't and quickly changed the subject. "I just don't think this insane plan is going to work. I want to forget Anthony," she wailed, fast losing control, "and I can't with you here." She waited for an answer, but when none came she opened one eye and peeked between her fingers. *That man* was neatly tucked between the sheets, apparently sound asleep with a pleased grin on his lips.

Shelley dropped her hand and glared. "This is not the end," she growled. Turning to leave, she paused, shrugged, then picked up an old patchwork quilt and spread it over Cord's lower body. "You can't sleep forever. And government plans or no government plans, you are not staying under the same roof with me." She didn't dare question her decision. Cord might look like Anthony, but she knew they were worlds apart. A light snoring brought her wandering thoughts back to the present and she stomped out of the room, down the stairs and into the kitchen. "I will not lose my cool," she said to the empty room, then picked up the last remaining brownie and stuffed it into her mouth, thinking another double batch was called for in a situation like this.

CHAPTER FOUR

THE BACK DOOR SLAMMING SHUT sounded like a gun-shot blast. Shelley twirled around, her heart in her throat as a length of string quivered through her trembling fingers and landed on the floor. Her nerves were frazzled. "Robbie!" she reproved softly, glancing at the ceiling toward the slumbering Rip Van Winkle upstairs. A tiny frown puckered her brow as she watched the red-faced boy drop like a stone into the nearest chair, cross his arms over his chest and glare at his worn tennis shoes. She waited.

"Shelley, are kids supposed to like grown-ups? Is there some law or something?" He pulled the front of his T-shirt up and out, stretching it to its limits, then wiped his sweaty face. I know I have to be re—respec—respec..." he struggled with the seldom-used word, grimaced and gave up. "I have to be nice." He tore his gaze from the tips of his shoes and looked at Shelley. "But do I have to like him?"

"Who?" Shelley bit her lip to keep from smiling at the angry boy. For three days now he's struggled between awe of Nick and his dislike of being supervised by a man he hadn't even decided if he wanted around.

"Nick. That's whose."

"Who," she corrected.

"Yeah, Nick." Robbie nodded, his silky blond hair bouncing over his damp forehead.

Shelley closed her eyes and sighed loudly. "What's he done this time?" There had been a hundred little complaints and she wondered who was worse, Nick or Robbie.

Robbie's chin lowered to his chest and he mumbled, "Said I had to wear a hat if I was to work in the sun."

"But you always wear some sort of hat in the fields, don't you?"

"Yeah." He kept his eyelids lowered and his jaw stiffly clenched.

"Robbie, are you upset that Nick has become such good friends with Lee and Vo?"

"No," he said sulkily, his chin dropping a little lower onto his chest as the tip of one shoe began to draw circular patterns on the hardwood floor. "They're just laughing all the time, and I don't understand what's going on 'cause they don't talk English."

"Nick, laughing?"

Robbie gave a quick slanted look at Shelley and smiled a little shamefacedly. "Yeah. I guess I'm wrong. After all, they're grown-ups." His expression spoke volumes. Robbie glanced at the ceiling. "Is Cord going to ever wake up or is he real sick?"

The quick capitulation and change of subject left her a little dazed. "Are you going to apologize to Nick?" She was determined to regain control of the situation. "Your mother wouldn't like you being rude, Robbie."

"I will." He gave her a direct look and smiled his most charming smile. "I will, I promise. Is Cord real sick?"

Shelley chuckled. It seemed Robbie was equally determined to have his answer. "I don't know." She watched a concerned frown pleat the smooth brow and hurried on. "I don't think he's as sick as he is exhausted.'' Robbie opened his mouth and she quickly stopped the flow of endless questions she saw coming. ''Why don't you go watch some television till it cools off a little and you have to go back outside to finish your work?''

''Can I have a Coke?'' He was at the refrigerator before she could answer, his fingers wrapped around a cold bottleneck. With a flick of the opener he had drained half the contents, all the while taking in every move she made. Robbie lowered the bottle from his lips. ''Why are you tying steaks together with my kite string for?''

''They're not exactly steaks.'' She turned her attention back to the huge hunk of beef she'd been struggling with. ''It's a standing rib roast.'' As quick as a bee her hand popped his as it inched its way toward the cookie jar.

''Oh, Shelley. Come on, just a few.'' He gave her his pitiful ''I'm a starving growing boy'' look.

As intended, her heart melted and she glanced away so as not to see the mound his small hand managed to clasp. A smile tugged at her mouth as she listened to the squeak of his rubber soled shoes making a fast getaway from the kitchen. She wished Robbie was hers. But that wasn't fair to Sara and she immediately took back the wish, afraid something awful might happen if she didn't. Her smile slowly died. If only... Shelley shook her head sadly. There was no sense going over that ground again. Those dreams brought nothing but heartache. As if pulled like a magnet, her gaze lifted upward and she wondered what the man sleeping upstairs would think if she asked him to give her a child. A cold shiver streaked across her skin as she realized with horror what she'd been considering.

She leaned forward, rested her head on the edge of the cabinet and closed her eyes. *I must be going out of my mind. That's what this whole experience with Anthony has done to me. It's made me a little crazy.* The man upstairs might look like her ex-husband, but he wasn't, and she wasn't fool enough to confuse the two. There was a strong feeling in her gut that Cord Lowell simply took what he wanted. He didn't need all the charm and smooth words Anthony had used. She shivered again.

THE SHARP SOUND of a door being slammed somewhere woke him. Cord lay still, sweat beading his forehead as he tried to orient himself. For one awful moment he had thought he was back in that hellhole of a jungle with the world exploding around him and dead bodies on top of him. For a split second he could almost smell the rot of death. He inhaled deeply, then let the air out slowly to clear his head. Now there was only the scent of clean sheets smelling of sunshine.

He opened his eyes, gazed around the room and scowled. Where was he? Then he remembered and a smile tipped one corner of his mouth. Shelley. She came to him as vividly as though she was standing across the room. All legs and firm rounded breasts. A woman to whet the appetite of any man. Then he remembered the rest of it—the whole mess he was in—and groaned. God, how had he allowed himself to be talked into such a crazy scheme? He rolled over, and his gaze came to rest on the now-empty bottle of pills. Of course! He'd been sick with some tropical fever when Nicholas had presented his plan.

Cord mumbled a few curse words. Hell! He'd been so ill and so grateful to be out of the jungle he would

have agreed to anything. But now, in the light of day
and with his fever gone, the full impact of what he'd
gone along with hit him hard. He quickly sat up, swung
his legs off the bed, then grabbed his head in both hands
as the room began to spin in colorful circles. His body
went limp and he fell backward onto the sheets.

Physical weakness was something he'd never experienced, and it's sudden appearance made him angry.
But his anger only drained him further and he closed
his eyes and sighed, letting the cool air caress his body
and calm his ragged nerves.

But there was no peace behind his eyelids. She was
there with her soft jade eyes and the short cap of dark
hair. Cord chuckled out loud, trying to rationalize his
thoughts. Hell, he was horny. How long had it been
since he'd had a woman? He frowned. There was absolutely nothing to worry about, he reassured himself.
The attraction was only physical. He only wanted to
know her enough to get her into his bed. Well, he
amended…to be fair…her house, her bed. He didn't
want to know her past, her present or her future. He
didn't have the time or want to exert the emotional effort to get involved. He'd done that once before and
look where that had gotten him.

No, Shelley would be fair game for the next couple
of days or weeks. However long it took, he'd get this
business over with and get back to his life once again.
Cord's thoughts went blank for a second and he shook
his head. He'd find out just enough about her to learn
about his brother. Another string of curse words left his
lips. His brother! And a twin to boot! Maybe that's why
he found her so interesting and desirable. Wasn't there
something about twins having the same tastes? The

same wants and needs? Had they shared the same feelings, the same passions?

Slowly he eased back into a sitting position on the edge of the bed. What he needed now was a shower, a shave and some food—lots of food.

From the knocking sound caused by the pressure of water working upward through the old pipes she knew *he* was up and moving, showering, and would soon be downstairs. *Cord,* she told herself. *You must call him Cord, Shelley. Be polite, be distantly sympathetic, but don't allow him to get too close. Feed him. Listen if he wishes to talk, but don't tell him anything of yourself, old girl. You trusted Anthony and look where it got you. This man with Anthony's face is a far worse threat than Anthony could ever have been. He's the type,* she told herself sternly, *who would want to know you right down to your soul, then strip it bare.* She would be left with nothing to hide behind, and God knew she only wanted to hide.

A few minutes later a noise behind her caught her attention and she swung around. The first sight of him hurt. With that unguarded initial glimpse her brain told her it was Anthony come back, but her heart told a different story with each frantic beat. She felt her muscles tighten and her mouth was dry, but she could only stand there and stare.

Cord broke the strange silence that seemed to hold them spellbound. "How long have I been out?"

He was pale and weak. She gave herself a mental shake and was quickly at his side, taking his arm and leading him to the nearest chair at the long oak table. "Three days." His jeans were a little loose and hung low on his hips, but the white knit shirt fit with disturbing snugness across his broad shoulders. His chestnut hair was still damp from the shower, and the navy blue eyes seemed darker with the residue of his illness.

"Three days! No wonder my mouth feels as if a herd of buffalo have been grazing there. Could I have something to drink?"

She quickly turned her back on him, disgusted for the lapse in her promise to herself. "Distance, Shelley," she growled softly.

"What?"

"Nothing. Would you like some iced tea? Are you hungry?" She reached in the refrigerator and began pulling out the container of homemade vegetable soup. His eyes followed her everywhere. She could feel them on her, and when he didn't answer her questions she was forced to look around. Their eyes clashed and she knew he realized she was uncomfortable with him watching her. "Well?"

"I'm so hungry I could eat a horse." He saw her relax and wondered why he found it so odd that this woman seemed at home in the kitchen. He remembered being told that she'd spent a good portion of her life going to college to get her degree in business, then working for Martin Aviation in an executive position. He knew from experience that such professional women usually didn't have the time, talent nor the inclination to become comfortable with what was nowadays often considered menial women's work. He frowned and reminded himself that he didn't want to know too much about her past.

"You don't by any chance have a horse cooked, do you?" She looked over her shoulder and smiled at him. For some reason he had trouble breathing. He picked up the glass of iced tea she'd set before him and took a huge gulp.

"We don't have any horses here." He raised an inquiring eyebrow but she ignored the gesture. "How would a big bowl of soup and some warm French bread do for a start?"

Cord eyed the mound of raw, red beef tied up and ready to be slipped in the oven and nodded. "Is that for dinner? Because if it is, I hope you've fixed something else for yourself."

Shelley grinned at the teasing look he sent her, then immediately sobered. This wasn't going to do at all. With quick efficient movements she busied herself with heating his soup and slicing the still-warm French bread she'd made earlier. The silence that fell between them was strained, tight with a tension she couldn't put her finger on. And the knowledge that his eyes followed her every move made her as nervous as a canary with a cat on its tail.

While she waited for the bell on the microwave to signal that his soup was hot, she turned her back on him and picked up a knife and a small round potato and began scoring deep cuts down its length. Ignoring him was one thing, she told herself, but forgetting his presence was another. Lost in thought, she finished the work on the potato, dropped it in a bowl of ice and water, then picked up another and began the delicate job once more.

He watched her, feeling a tingling sensation along his nerves. The skimpy shorts left most of her legs exposed for a full inspection, and they were lovely, long and tan. His gaze narrowed a fraction as her body moved with each forward stroke of her arm. It was a sensuous move, just a barely discernible thrust of her hips and a tightening of her buttocks, but it was enough to spark his desire. "Why are you soaking those potatoes in ice water?"

His question almost made her slice the end of her finger. There was nothing of Anthony in that voice. It was deep, husky, with a sexy raspiness that sent a deep feeling of dread through her. Oh, yes, she could close her eyes and listen to him talk for ages.

Shelley shook her head in total disgust. Her sexuality was emerging after more than a month of being in a deep freeze. She'd tried to forget what it was like to be held in a warm embrace, but her mind wouldn't let go of the memories. *Damn you to hell, Anthony.* She squeezed her eyes shut. Would she ever be able to deal with what he'd done to her self-esteem? She forced her eyes open and cleared her throat, applying the knife to another potato. "They need to be chilled so that when I roll them in a combination of melted butter and herbs the mixture will harden and stay in the creases. Then I put them around the half-cooked roast and the butter melts slowly and seeps into the potatoes." She heard a low moan, spun around and couldn't help laughing at his expression of rapt anticipation.

While Cord had her undivided attention he asked, "By the way, what do you raise on the farm? Cattle?"

He was just full of questions. "No."

"No?"

She shook her head, then bit her lip, knowing the answer was going to be a real eye-opener.

"Corn?" When she didn't answer and only continued to look at him with a half smile as he went on. "Wheat, oats, rice? This is going to be a guessing game, right? Okay, let's see what I've left out. Fruit? Peaches—must be peaches."

"No," she gurgled, half choking on a silly giggle.

God, she thought, she hadn't felt like laughing in months.

"Apples, oranges, plums? I know—I know! Grapefruit?"

She struggled hard to hold in her laughter, but something deep inside her snapped and the laugh rushed out. She threw back her head and let it come.

Cord was enchanted. The breath-catching combination of half giggle and half belly laugh was contagious, and he automatically joined in, realizing it had been a long time, too long, since he'd laughed so freely and openly.

Shelley eventually got control of herself, her lips curving into a smug smile as she answered his question. "This farm is a pecan plantation."

His eyes widened, then narrowed with laughter. The long lines accenting his mouth deepened till a rich chuckle escaped his lips. "Well, I'll be damned. A pecan plantation. How many trees?"

"About ten thousand."

Cord whistled loud and long, impressed. No small operation that. "But pecans are seasonal, aren't they? What has Nick been doing, then?"

"This is a very unique farming community, Cord, since we're so close to Houston. I'd guess an outsider would call it a gourmet market. We produce specialty crops that draw the restaurant and grocery brokers nationwide. Lee and my uncle were partners in some specialty crops. My uncle furnished the land and Lee plants and tends it. His strawberries have become a legend. Big, ruby red and very sweet. He also raises asparagus. Most of the other farms raise different crops so that there's a wide range for the brokers to choose from and so the neighbors are not competing with each other.

Unfortunately that hasn't always worked out, and lately there's been some trouble. Anyway…the specialty crops are big business for this community, and though a couple of farms are floundering from mismanagement, the rest are flourishing.''

The bell on the microwave sounded, and she reluctantly tore her gaze away from his. *This has to stop,* she warned herself. She was getting entirely too chummy with him. Gathering his food, she set it down before him with an irritated thump. When Robbie bounced into the kitchen, it was almost a relief.

"Hey, I smell food.'' He did a quick double take of the man sitting at the table and charged over. "How you feeling? Boy, you sure slept a long time.'' He leaned forward, sniffed at the steaming bowl of fragrant soup that was rapidly disappearing, then turned up his nose. "I'm starving to death, Shelley. Can I have a peanut butter and jelly sandwich?'' When Shelley nodded he returned his attention to his newfound friend. "Shelley rented all the Star Wars movies. Why don't you bring your lunch into the den? It's okay,'' he hurriedly reassured the frowning Cord. "She'll let us eat in there as long as we're careful. Course if you spill anything she'll make you clean it up yourself.'' He took a deep breath, his face serious, but there was a teasing twinkle in his hazel eyes. "She stands over you real threatening like with this monstrous leather belt hanging around her neck.'' He accepted the plate and glass of milk Shelley handed him and backed away, laughing with each step. "Will you come watch, Cord?''

Cord grinned at the boy's eagerness and nodded. "Sure. Why don't you go on. I'll be there in a few minutes.'' When Robbie's wide mouth turned down dramatically at the corners, he quickly went on. "I need

to ask Shelley a question or two, then I'll join you."
Still, the boy hesitated at the door. "Go on, Robbie, I
promise." He smiled at the retreating back.

"That was good of you," Shelley said. "I'm afraid
he gets lonely for male company."

Cord scowled at the empty bowl before him. "Hell,
I'm sick of that bed upstairs, but too damn weak to do
much else but lay around for the next day or so. Hasn't
Nick been with the kid? I thought he liked Robbie?"

Shelley snorted. "I think your friend needs to learn
that he can't order Robbie around the way he probably
does his men. Robbie's taken a marked dislike to the
man's helpful suggestions and revolted a couple of
times. Surprisingly, they seem to be very much alike."
She glanced toward the den, then shook her head at the
absurdity of her remark. But it was true, and the thought
troubled her because she couldn't put her finger on the
reasons. "They've been playing tattletale on each other,
and I've been the recipient of their complaints."

"Nick?"

She chuckled, but the sound held little amusement.
"Yes, indeed. And even stranger still, you should see
the change jeans and a work shirt makes in the man.
You'd think he was born to farm work the way he goes
at it, too." Without thinking she pulled out a chair
across from Cord and sat down.

"I take it you and Nick have been getting along a
little better than you first did?"

"You must be crazy! I left early yesterday morning
to go to the store, and when I got back he was waiting
for me. You would have thought I'd committed a breach
in national security the way he yelled at me for leaving
the farm without him. The man's a cold fish." She shiv-

ered at the memory. "Needless to say he has yet to make a favorable impression on me or Robbie."

"Where's Robbie's father?"

Shelley reached around and picked up her glass of iced tea from the counter before answering. She looked at him a second, wondering if she should lie, then decided against it. Sara, Robbie's mother, never lied about it, so why should she? "Robbie doesn't have a father."

There was a long pause, then Cord nodded. "I see. And his mom works so you take care of him?"

"Not really. Robbie—" She was cut off as the back door opened and Nicholas Harper strolled in.

"Is Robbie here?" Nick jerked to a halt at seeing Cord. "You're looking human again."

"Thanks." Shelley was right, Cord thought. Nick didn't even resemble his old self. He'd seen him in his naval uniform, in an expensive three-piece suit, even in jungle fatigues, but this man before him in worn jeans, scuffed cowboy boots and a faded blue work shirt was a total stranger. Even his stance was different, less stiff-backed military and more relaxed.

"Where's Robbie?" Nick repeated.

Shelley sighed and lowered her forehead into her hands. "Nick, leave the boy alone. It's too hot for him to be working outside. Besides, he's mad at you, and any orders you hand out are likely to be met with outright mutiny."

"I know."

"If you would remember he's not one of your subordinates you might get along a little better. Damn it, he's only nine years old."

"You're right."

Her head jerked up and she stared at him, shocked to hear his admission, yet it was the spark of emotion in the usually lifeless green eyes that left her speechless. He actually liked Robbie and obviously wanted the child to return his feelings.

"I want to apologize to the kid. Where is he?"

Cord placed his hands on the table and pushed himself to his feet. "How would you like to join Robbie and me in a marathon of Star Wars movies?"

The tightly held mouth stretched into a grin. "Don't mind if I do. It's too damn hot to go back outside. Thanks." He turned his attention to Shelley. "Sorry I chewed you out yesterday, but please don't leave the farm without at least telling me."

His eyes shifted from hers and she followed the path of his gaze to the standing rib roast ready to be put into the oven.

"If you have to leave the farm, I'd prefer that either Cord or I go with you." He cleared his throat and looked back at her. "Lee and his wife are vegetarians." His hungry gaze glided over to the huge mound of beef again. "I'm not."

Sucker! she reprimanded herself as the invitation to join them for dinner left her lips. Then she immediately regretted her gesture with his next words.

"Have you had time to go through any of your belongings you had shipped out here?"

Shelley shoved her chair back and quickly stood up. "No, I haven't." All three knew it was a lie. She just couldn't face digging through the past yet.

"Shelley…" Nick began, then stopped.

"I know, I know. I'll get on it."

Cord followed Nick from the kitchen without a word. Not a thank-you for the lunch or an offer of help to clean up. Not even a backward look of compassion for

her predicament. He left her feeling strangely empty—
and with his dirty dishes to wash!

Once the kitchen was clean and the roast in the oven,
Shelley straightened her shoulders and neatly hung up
the dish towel to dry. It was time to tackle her uncle's
study and the stacks of boxes that held evidence of her
life with Anthony. But as she left the room her steps
lagged. When she passed the den and stopped to listen
to the male laughter, her resolve fled completely. Taking the stairs two at a time, she shoved open her bedroom door, flew across the room and landed disgustedly
on the double bed. She rolled over, covering her eyes
with her forearm. She just couldn't face going through
those boxes, not yet. Not until she could come to terms
with what Anthony had done to her. She clenched her
teeth to stem the moan of humiliation that tried to escape. How could one woman be so damn blind?

"Need a shoulder to cry on?" Cord asked from the
doorway. He leaned against the frame, his skin pale as
beads of moisture dotted his brow. "Mind if I sit down
before I fall down?"

"Go away." She rolled over, turned her head away
and spoke into the bedspread. "I don't need your help."

"It's obvious you need someone's. You're not doing
a very good job by yourself." He frowned as he lowered himself into the nearest wing chair and let the silence soothe away his irritation at the effort it took just
to climb the stairs. He leaned his head back and sighed,
his eyes taking in everything—the antiques that filled
the room and the cheerful floral curtains and matching
bedspread in peach and green. Without conscious
thought, his gaze wandered to the woman lying across
the bed. His frown deepened. *Why in hell,* he asked
himself, *did I come up here?* He'd seen her walk past

the den, and he'd also seen the expression on her face. What lengths men go to for women! He shook his head; the joke was on him. He was too damn weak to do anything even if she stripped buck-naked and performed some exotic mating dance before his very eyes.

"Go away."

"Tell me something, Shelley." He inhaled deeply and rose to his feet. "Are you feeling sorry for yourself because your husband's dead and you have to face his crimes? Are you sniveling because you were a fool and married a man who only wanted to use you?"

She flopped over and jerked into a sitting position. "Because I was a stupid fool," she yelled. "I found out my husband was seeing other women, and I stayed with him thinking we could work it out." She didn't know what she was saying, but as hard as she tried to stop, the words just kept coming. "I think if it had only been the women I could have come to terms with a divorce. But, my God, to be used strictly because I had access to top secret designs…" Tears streamed down her face. For the first time she really began coming to terms with what had happened. And as the emotional wall she'd built around herself began to crack, she lashed out in panic. "Get out. Get out of here this minute! Don't you see I can't stand the sight of you! You're Anthony. Every time I look at you I see him and I hate you."

Cord was at her side before she could draw a breath, grasping her arms and pulling her to her feet.

"You don't hate me, lady, you want me. And not the way you wanted that weakling husband of yours." He gave a triumphant laugh. "You want *me* to make love to you."

Shelley shook her head frantically.

"Liar! That's what's been eating you up this afternoon and why you can't look at me. You hate yourself for those feelings and you're feeding on your own guilt."

"That's not true," she spat. "I'm guilty of nothing."

He pulled her closer, their mouths almost touching. "Your husband isn't even cold in his grave and you want another man. He used you and made a fool of you and you never wanted to feel again, but I make you feel, don't I, Shelley?"

"Stop it." She struggled in his hold, trying to get away. "Please stop this."

"You're not going to take your frustrations and hate for Anthony out on me just because I look like him."

His mouth touched hers then, and she steadied herself for the harsh assault. Instead her knees went weak with the tenderness of the kiss. She wanted to scream, to beg him to stop. She'd never expected the overwhelming onslaught of emotions to wash over her, and she grabbed for him, only to have him break their embrace. Breathless, her eyes pools of bewilderment, she struggled for air, but great heaving sobs racked each breath.

Cord watched her for a moment, then gathered the trembling, heaving body next to his, letting her soak his shirt. "Go on, honey, get it all out of your system."

She didn't know how long he held her, standing, rocking her, rubbing her back and speaking softly to her. After a long time she began to hear what he was whispering and eased away to look at him. "You said all that on purpose, didn't you. You deliberately tried to make me lose control. Why? Why would you want to do this to me?"

Cord let her escape from his arms and grabbed the bedpost for support. He was as drained and exhausted as she looked. "In my business I've seen a lot. Shock, for example. Shell shock, shock from death, war, emotional and physical. It can be devastating if it's not treated. I'd be willing to bet, though you've shed a few tears, you've never truly faced what has happened to you, have you?"

She didn't answer immediately, but just stared at him in growing horror. "You were playing games with me."

Tiredly, he turned his back on her and began to leave the room. "One thing you'll have to learn about me, Shelley Morgan—I never play games. What I did, I did to help you. Think on it awhile." He closed her bedroom door softly behind him and made his way down the hall to his own bed, berating himself for being a fool. What right did he have to interfere? She could damn well work out her own problems. What did he care that she'd cried her heart out? He worked his jaw, releasing the knotted muscles that ached from clenching his teeth while he'd held her in his arms. Women! They were nothing but trouble.

CHAPTER FIVE

THE FAINT, STEADY SQUEAK in the ceiling fan finally won the war with his nerves and dragged him up from a deep sleep. He opened his eyes a fraction, then quickly closed them again with a moan. A bright dawn streamed through the window. His lips moved in a low string of profanities at his neglect in pulling the curtains shut last night. Even as he rolled over and covered his head with a pillow, fighting to ignore the coming day, the irritating noise from the fan refused to let him sink back into oblivion. He was going to have to get up.

Cord rolled over on his back, yawned and stretched, realizing as he did that for the first time in weeks he felt like a human being. He relaxed, enjoying the comfort of the big bed and listened to the Victorian house as it, too, came to life with the new day. Yet, with the creaks and pops of aged wood as the heat outside fought with the air-conditioned coolness inside, he knew only the house itself stirred. Shelley must still be asleep, and rightly so.

Guilt tightened his mouth. He'd been rough on her, he admitted, much harder than he should have been. After all, what business was it of his if she ended up having a breakdown? But, damn it, she had to begin to face her feelings so she could get on with the business of living. He knew what a devastating effect emotional trauma could have on a person. He'd seen enough to last him a lifetime, to say nothing of experiencing his share.

Cord shook his head and frowned, quickly pushing away the intrusion of his problems and past. He sat up, swung his long legs over the edge of the bed and rubbed his stubbled chin. Coffee was what he needed to chase away the effects of a night spent wrestling with a nagging conscience, not to mention his fading illness. He rose, amending his thoughts. A shower, a shave, then the coffee.

Fifteen minutes later, dressed in faded jeans and a short-sleeve pale-blue knit shirt, Cord leaned against the open door of the screened-in back porch watching a partially clouded sky turning shades of pink as it slipped away from the night. He lifted a mug to his lips, drank deeply of the strong dark liquid, then scowled, a little puzzled at the obviously freshly made coffee and the empty house at this time of the morning. A tiny puff of air fanned his face and he inhaled deeply, realizing that in only a matter of minutes the faint dampness on the breeze would soon be absorbed by the relentless sun. God, did it never rain? Did the air never take on a moistness that nurtured land and man?

Where the hell was everyone? He'd always thought farm people were up while the rest of the world still dreamed away in blissful ignorance. The only sound of life was that of birds. Taking another sip of coffee, he let his gaze wander over the farm. The place was impressive. Huge red brick buildings sat in a massive heap off to the left. *They must hold machinery,* he thought. *They are entirely too big to be barns.* Scanning beyond the fields of neat green rows to the north, he was somewhat surprised to see what looked like a jungle of tall pines and thick vegetation. It was a little parched and

brown round the edges, but still daunting enough in
appearance to remind him of the Central American jungle he'd recently been rescued from.

Cord turned slightly, his ears attuned to a muffled
sound. Curious, and wanting company, he pushed away
from the doorframe and stepped down onto the ground.
Dry grass crackled under his rubber-soled shoes as he
walked to the side of the house. He grimaced in sympathy for the parched earth and the unforgiving Texas
heat that refused to give up its assault on the land. Stepping out of the shadow of the house, the sun cut sharply
across his eyes and he shaded them as he gazed off
toward the impressive line of pecan trees. Ten thousand
trees, Shelley had told him. He whistled at the sheer
magnitude of the work involved come harvest time.
Trying to picture the feat, even without the knowledge
of the modern procedures, was impossible.

Still scanning the endless lines of trees he absently
brought the coffee to his mouth, but the cup's rim never
touched his lips. A bloodcurdling scream rent the air,
making him drop the mug. He spun toward the front
road and froze at the sight that met his eyes. Shelley,
dressed in jogging clothes, was running toward him as
if the devil himself were at her heels. He squinted into
the sun, doubting what he was seeing. From where he
stood it looked as though there were big white feathered
wings spreading from her legs. Then, as he continued
to watch, she screamed again. This time he understood
what she was saying—she was yelling at the top of her
lungs for Lee. Cord took a step then, stopped once more
as Shelley began a crazy running-hopping movement.
The change in her stride allowed him full view of the
devil chasing her: a big white gander with wings flapping, webbed feet working like pistons, barely touching

the ground. His long neck was stretched out as his bill snapped repeatedly at her heels.

Cord began to laugh. At first it emerged as a deep chuckle, but it quickly erupted into a full-blown roar as the scene exploded with people and voices raised to a panic pitch. Lee, Robbie and Nick all careered around the corner of Lee's house. The Vietnamese wielded a long wooden staff in the air like a sword. Robbie, flushed and laughing, had yanked off his baseball cap and was frantically waving it. And Nick, following close, was running half bent over as he grappled with something at his ankle.

As Cord watched, the scene changed and played out in a more dramatic vein. The old gander, realizing his fun was over, came to a flapping halt. Shelley, hot and sweaty, ran directly into Cord's arms and collapsed. Robbie, the only one watching Nick, screamed as he caught sight of the small gun Nick had finally managed to pull from his ankle holster. The child dived for the goose, wrapped his arms protectively around the thick white neck and stared with a mixture of round-eyed horror and fascination at the menacing man now crouching in a firing position.

"It's only Napoleon!" Robbie shouted, lovingly pulling the passive gander closer. "He's our watchdog, that's all."

Nick spun around, breathing hard and cursing himself.

Lee walked over to the naval intelligence officer and patted his shoulder comfortingly.

Fascinated, Cord, like Robbie, pulled his catch closer. Yet, unlike the preening gander, Shelley was a trembling wreck. It took him a minute to understand her breathless words, but when he did he was forced to bite back another fit of laughter.

"I swear I'm going to kill that monster," she said shivering. "Disgusting, filthy animal. Evil. Mean to the bone."

"Oh, I don't know, Shelley," Cord said. "He looks pretty tame to me."

She wrenched herself from Cord's arms and glared. "Are you out of your mind?"

He cocked his head toward the gander and Robbie. "How can you possibly call him evil? Just look."

Twirling around, her glare immediately changed to a murderous stare. Still in Robbie's arms, Napoleon was affectionately running his bill through the boy's thick hair and standing calmly under the caressing hands. "Devil," she mumbled under her breath, then unable to control herself she raised her clenched fist and yelled. "I'll get you one day!"

In answer Napoleon freed himself from Robbie's arms, swished his pointed tail feathers, turned his back on the whole scene and marched off.

"Miss Sherrey."

She whipped back around. "Yes, Lee."

"How many times I ask you come Ree when you want lun? Naporeon, fine guard, fine husband and father. Watches over strawbelly fields in the earry hours to eat pesky bugs and worms. Make Ree much money. Make Sherrey money."

She could tell he was having trouble keeping from laughing by the way his black eyes in their epicanthic folds tightened and pulled almost shut. She could see Cord's chest shaking, hear Robbie snickering and caught the smile on Nick's usually grim lips. "I guess you all think this is a real joke? Well, we'll see just how hard you laugh when that *thing* turns on you.'' She twirled and headed toward the house.

''Wait, Shelley.''

She came to an abrupt halt at the back door, swung around, gave Cord a withering look and spoke before he could. ''And don't you ever pull what you did on me last night.''

''What?'' he demanded in all innocence. ''Oh, *that*. Well, it was the only thing I could think of to get a rise out of you. Believe me, you needed to let go or you would have burst.''

''And just who are you to care about me? Who assigned you as my keeper?'' She didn't wait for an answer but whipped back around and stomped into the house.

Cord shrugged and followed, realizing that her question was a good one.

BY THE TIME Shelley had bathed, blow-dried her hair, applied makeup, dressed in white jeans and a red, white and blue cotton crop-top, she had managed to cool down. In fact, she actually felt a little shamefaced at her snappishness toward Cord. Her hateful words of last night came back and she grimaced. Granted, she'd been provoked, but nevertheless she was ashamed of what she'd said. What in the world was happening to her? She was going to have to make a concerted effort to be civil.

Shelley stepped through the kitchen doorway and came to a stop. Cord, with his back to her, was busy at the stove, his attention consumed with what he was doing. Or was it, she asked herself. She noticed the slight tightening of his shoulders as she quietly walked over to him. Was he as perceptive to her presence as she was to his? She studied him for a second before speaking, noting the broad back that tapered to narrow hips and long legs. He certainly wasn't built along the same slim lines as her ex-husband, that was for sure. There was muscle and power there, and a steadiness of spirit that a woman, if she wanted to, could lean on.

"What's with you and Napoleon?"

His question jerked her out of her musing, and she stepped around him to see what he was making. She watched him carefully fork cooked round slices of Canadian bacon onto paper towels before she answered. "Napoleon took an instant dislike to me the second I stepped foot on the farm. The feeling is mutual, believe me." When Cord reached for one of the six eggs lined up on the counter, she stopped him. "Surely you're not going to fry those eggs in all that grease, are you?"

He turned his head slightly and looked at her for the first time since she had entered the kitchen. His navy blue eyes, on closer scrutiny, were actually darker than Anthony's; his mouth firmer, his jaw squarer, more honest and determined. Standing so close, she realized suddenly that if Anthony were still alive and these two were standing side by side, her ex-husband, with all his elegant good looks, would appear a little effeminate compared to Cord.

"What's wrong with fried eggs?"

She made a face at him and he chuckled, a deep rich sound that brought a flush to her cheeks. "Would you like an omelet if I made it?"

"Absolutely." He grinned, his eyes sparkling. "I'm always willing to turn over the cooking to a more able body." He let his gaze drop slowly, taking in the snug-fitting white jeans and the short striped top that hugged her unfettered breast with a tantalizing closeness. *Oh, to be so near…*

Shelley tried to ignore the look, plucked the fork from his fingers and began pouring the grease from the skillet before it burned. As she moved, her arm brushed his and the touch was like an electric shock. A surprised murmur escaped her lips. She pulled back and tilted her head to see if he'd noticed her strange behavior.

But Cord had quickly turned away in an effort to hide his own reaction to her soft skin skimming his arm. He gritted his teeth. Did she think his illness had obliterated his sexuality for the duration of his stay? From the singing heat racing through his veins he could assure her she was way off base. He swung around, harsh words of warning on his lips, but he stopped himself before they could be spoken. Horny. He was just plain horny, and construing her every move and look as a seductive provocation. He had to get his mind off sex…and this woman in particular. "Do you jog every morning?" He picked up his mug and refilled it. "And does your feathered friend usually tag along?"

With one hand Shelley cracked each egg in a bowl. "I only jog about four or five times a week, and that feathered *monster* lays in wait for me."

Cord chuckled again, then sobered when she threw him a scorching look. "What was all that Lee was talking about—husband and bugs? Hell, the man was trying to keep from laughing so hard I could barely make out what he was saying."

Shelley yanked open the refrigerator door and while she pulled out mushrooms, green pepper, fresh onions and a pimento, she told him. "Napoleon has a harem he rules over, and every morning as Lee trained him to, he marches his regiment to the strawberry patch to eat all the bugs and worms from the plants. I guess you could say he's Lee's living pesticide.''

Cord leaned against the counter and watched Shelley chop and slice the ingredients for the omelet. ''You're very good at that.'' Her head jerked up, her eyes questioning. He nodded at her hands as they made expert work of their chore.

''I've had plenty of practice.''

Now it was his turn to raise an inquiring eyebrow. He was surprised at her friendliness and didn't dare ask the reason for the change.

''I was kitchen help in my father's restaurant for years before being allowed to boil water, and even that was under his supervision.''

Cord set his coffee mug down on the counter with a thump, then straightened. ''Where is your family from?''

''Carmel, California. Why?''

''You're not one of *the* Morgans—of the famous Morgan's French Restaurants in Carmel and Beverly Hills?''

He was excited, and it amused her to see the connection had left him a little awed. ''One and the same. My father's the owner and chef of Morgan's in Carmel. My older brother and sister have the Beverly Hills one. Have you eaten there?''

''You must be joking! Of course I have. So has everyone in love with French cuisine and superior service. I haven't been there in more than a year, more's the pity,'' he murmured. Cord shook his head in amazement. ''Well, I'll be damned. No wonder dinner last night tasted as if a master chef had prepared it. You're a cordon bleu chef yourself, aren't you? You studied in France?''

"Yes, and under my father's tutelage."

"My God!"

"No, not him. Though if you'd ever had my father for a teacher you would wonder."

She waved her hand at Cord, but instead of moving as she'd indicated, he stood where he was and demanded, "What the hell are you doing working as assistant to the president of an aviation company in Seattle, Washington?"

Shelley held the knife she'd been using in front of her and studied the tip as if she were contemplating a carving job on Cord. "Move it, will you? I need to get the whisk from the drawer, and you're blocking my way."

"Answer my question." But he moved after taking a second look at the glint in her eyes and the firm grip on her weapon.

She rummaged around in the drawer till she found what she was after, then picked up the bowl and began to whip the eggs. "My father... no, my entire family— mother, brother and sister—are creative, highly strung people. They yell and shout and wave their hands and arms. They're artists. I'm quiet, practical and unimaginative. I can follow a recipe, copy pastry designs, but I was never smart or talented enough to create my own concoctions. If you've been to Morgan's you know that Medallions of Veal Jarre is one of my father's specialties. The Breast of Chicken Savannah—just one of many dishes my mother's famous for. Now my brother and sister are contributing to the long culinary list and making names for themselves...."

She trailed off with a shrug. "Anyway, years ago we had a falling out. My dear family are geniuses in the kitchen but have absolutely no head for business. I was only in high school then, but I could see that the restaurant was headed for trouble. After much yelling and an uncountable number of scenes, I talked them into allowing me to go to college instead of into the family business. Oh, eventually I planned to rejoin the fold, but in the management end of things.'' She stopped talking to test the frothiness of the eggs, then began adding the chopped vegetables.

"I nearly killed myself getting through school as quickly as I could—year-round, winter and summer. Then just before I was to graduate, my sister married a man with a degree in business from Harvard and Peter started managing the business.'' She watched Cord's expression of avid interest change and forestalled his question. "No, I was not hurt. A little jealous at first, but I realized it was for the best. I needed to get away from my family and make it on my own. I would never have been happy working in their shadow.'' She chuckled softly. "If you must know the truth, I'm relieved that I don't have to work for any of them. I enjoy cooking, but when *I* want to and not as a job.''

She smiled with genuine pleasure, and he couldn't take his eyes off her lovely mouth. "I think Morgan's lost a great asset.''

"Why, I thank you, sir. They might have lost an asset, but I've kept my sanity. They're all quite crazy, you know. Wild, exuberant people who take command of a room just by walking into it. I was always the calm, cool and collected one. The one who never raised her voice or lost her temper.'' She chuckled and glanced up at him. "I think my *unnatural* behavior drove them a little nuts, too.''

Cord laughed, a sound of gently mocking disbelief.

"I guess last night's outburst and this morning's was someone else?"

A tiny frown crinkled her brow. "That's right."

"How did my brother get along with your family?" He could have kicked himself. Wasn't it going to be his policy not to get emotionally involved with this woman? Her personal life had nothing to do with him, and he didn't intend to become embroiled. Then he relaxed. After all, it was only his brother he was curious about. If he had to learn about Shelley in the process, then so be it.

Shelley poured the omelet mixture into a hot buttered skillet, wanting to avoid any talk of Anthony. She glanced up again, wondering why she didn't immediately cringe at the sight of Cord. He was Anthony, yet the longer she was around him the less he looked or reminded her of her ex. "My family adored him. But you'll have to remember, everyone loved Anthony. He could and would charm anyone to achieve his purpose." After a moment she worked the spatula under part of the fluffy omelet and folded it over the other half. "But Anthony didn't like my family. He said they wore him out emotionally and physically. After the first couple of visits he always made excuses not to go again." She flipped the whole omelet over. "Personally, I think he was jealous of the closeness we had." She shrugged. "Or, maybe he just didn't know how to handle a true, loving family. I guess being moved from one foster home to another and never being adopted left its mark. Whatever the reason, his actions hurt my family and made it difficult for me to enjoy my visits even when I went without him." She stepped away from the stove, opened the overhead cabinet and stretched to grab the bag of bagels.

Cord's eyes swept the length of her, and his own body reacted to the sight of the wide expanse of tanned flesh her short top exposed. He watched her fingers work the wire twist to the plastic bag and wondered what it would feel like to have those long strong fingers stroking him. He swallowed. There was a supple, feminine softness about her that aroused him tremendously.

Feeling his gaze on her, an alarm went off in Shelley's head, a warning as familiar and unwanted as the warmth that was rapidly invading her stomach and legs. Angrily, silently, she sliced a couple of bagels in half, slapped some butter on them, then shoved them under the broiler. She knew he followed her every step, her every move. The quiet stretched between them until her nerves felt frayed. She dropped the spatula and had to rinse it off. She barely got the two plates to the table before they slipped from her shaking hands. She almost burned the bagels, and by the time they sat down to eat she'd lost her appetite completely.

"How did you meet my...Anthony?" Cord asked, still uncomfortable with the term *brother*.

The deep husky voice and its question brought her out of her reverie. "What?"

"Your husband—how did you first meet him?"

Any conversation was better than the unnerving tension that had sprung up between them. She jumped at the chance to talk and take her mind off her feelings. "My best friend, Dee Radford." She smiled with pleasure at thoughts of Dee. Short, a little plump and topheavy, yet with a seductive surliness that never failed to attract the male eye. "She came to work at Martin Aviation about six months before Anthony did. They had worked together at the same company for a couple of years. It's strange, but Dee's about the only person, certainly the only female, who couldn't be charmed by Anthony.''

Cord scowled. "Had they gone together or had an affair?''

Shelley almost choked on her bite of omelet. "Lord, no! They'd end up sniping at each other if they were in the same room together for more than ten minutes. Dee told me that they'd taken an instant dislike to each other from the beginning. But she could never tell me why she disliked him. I don't think she knew.''

Cord's scowl deepened, but before he could voice his troubled thoughts hot air washed over the back of his neck. The back door slammed shut, followed immediately by the banging of the screen door. A small, sweaty whirlwind flew into the kitchen.

"Wow!'' Robbie crouched, his skinny arm extended, one fist clenching the other in an imitation of Nick's earlier stance. "Did you see him? He almost killed Napoleon, dead.'' A series of strange noises issued from pursed lips as one of his fingers worked in a rapid succession as if firing a gun. "Man-o-man. Did you know Nick was a—'' he stopped to gobble a huge breath of air and get his words right ''—intelligence agent?'' in awe. "Did you know, Shelley?'' Hazel eyes, now green with accusation, glared at her, but he didn't give her time to answer. "A secret agent!'' His face screwed up for a second in thought.

"Oh, I don't think—'' Shelley tried.

"Like that old guy on television. What's his name? Oh yeah, James Bond. Secret agent, Nick. Wow!'' Robbie straightened his shoulders and wiped away his smile. "He explained it all to me. Said I was to keep my mouth shut.'' He followed the words with a quick motion and another weird sound as if there was a zipper attached to the corners of his lips. "Can't even tell my mom 'cause females can't keep their mouths shut when they're 'spose to. That's what Nick said."

Shelley couldn't make up her mind whether to laugh or yell with indignation at the derogatory statement about women. She fought to keep her expression neutral as Robbie literally danced around the room then out the door. When she heard the sound of wood meeting wood securely, she looked at Cord and they burst out laughing. "That *old* guy, James Bond!" She wheezed out when she could catch her breath.

"Damn, but he makes me feel ancient." Cord chuckled, then sobered as he watched the change on the face opposite him. Happiness and laughter became her. It brought a lovely pink to her cheeks, made her soft green eyes take on a sparkle and chased the sadness away.

"I guess with all the spectacular special effects nowadays, some of the older James Bond movies do seem outdated."

Cord grinned. "I guess so."

"Cord, you don't think Nick told Robbie the truth as to why he's here, do you?"

"I wouldn't think so, no." His half smile widened and made the long lines that accented his mouth deepen. "Did you see the look in the kid's eyes? He's mesmerized by the fact that Nick's an intelligence agent. I think the man's worth has gone up about ten points in Robbie's mind."

Still chuckling, trying to finish their breakfast, they braced themselves once more for the two-legged tornado when the back door banged shut, but Nick walked in instead.

"Morning, Shelley, Cord." He pulled out a chair and

sat down, sighing at the coolness of the kitchen. "Could I have a cup of coffee please?"

Shelley pushed her half-eaten food away, her recovered appetite disappearing with Nick's entrance. Every muscle tightened, anticipating his next words. She was about to be berated for not going through the packed boxes she'd shipped from Seattle. To her surprise, though, he began talking to Cord about the farm. As she retrieved a mug, filled it with coffee and set it down in front of Nick, she realized that he wasn't merely posing as a farmhand. The man knew what he was talking about.

She studied him briefly from under lowered lids. The sun had turned his hair a paler shade of blond, almost as white as Robbie's; his face and arms were as brown as a walnut. She picked up her coffee and took a sip. Somehow, the cold, lifeless eyes that had so bothered her were less deadly now. She could even see laugh lines extending from the corners. "You seem to know a lot about pecan plantations and farming in general."

Nick looked away from Cord, studied her a few seconds as if weighing his thoughts. He smiled. "I was born and raised not more than thirty miles from here. That's part of the reason the Navy wouldn't take me off this case when they found you." A mocking quirk of his lips followed his statement. He lifted the mug then returned it to the table. "This sort of duty is not generally in my line, you understand. It's a little tame. But the powers that be decided, since I knew the territory, that I would have an advantage."

"Farming agrees with you," she blurted out, then decided to go on despite his scowl. "You look ten years younger since you've been here...relaxed and a little content." *In for a penny...* she decided, and plunged on. "Do you have any family or friends around here?"

"Not anymore." He could see she wasn't going to drop the subject. It was bound to come out sooner or later, anyway. Better now while she was in a friendly mood and before he told her what he'd come to tell. "I ran away from an abusive and alcoholic father at sixteen, Shelley. I forged his signature on enlistment papers to join the navy. The only time I came back to this part of the country was ten years ago to bury my father. I wouldn't even have done that except I was given a direct order from my commanding officer." He rubbed his face wearily as the long-dead past threatened to rise from the dust of his memories. "Hell," he said with a self-mocking laugh, "I got so drunk the day of his funeral I don't remember half of what happened or what I did or said." He looked up, saw the concern and pity in her eyes, and his face became an expressionless mask.

Shelley saw the change and looked at Cord. There was understanding in his gaze, but he had hid his concern better than she had. "You're awfully hard and cynical, Nick." She rose, gathering the breakfast plates. "Maybe what you need is to get out of the navy." Looking over her shoulder, she grinned hugely. "Have you ever thought of returning to country life? I might even be willing to sell you the plantation."

Nick shuddered.

"Yes, I know, it's not exactly my choice, either. I like the city—the bright lights, people and noise. But you—" her grin grew and her teasing continued as Nick's eyebrows descended lower and lower "—you were born and bred to the farm life. It's in your blood."

"Stop!" he demanded. Nick glanced at Cord, then to Shelley. Slowly his grimace turned into a smile.

Rising to his feet, he shoved the chair under the table and straightened. "I came here for a reason." His mouth thinned as he looked at Shelley. "Have you started going through your belongings from Seattle yet?"

Shelley stiffened. "No."

"Well, I think you'd better get busy, lady. Martin Aviation was broken into yesterday and Mr. Martin's office was thoroughly searched. This morning while his wife was at the grocery store they hit his house. Again, a very professional job."

Shelley paled and Cord pushed his chair back and rose. In two strides he was beside her.

"Was anyone hurt at either place?"

"No."

"I need to call Dee. She'll know what's happening." Shelley made a move toward the telephone but Cord stopped her.

"Absolutely not."

"But, Nick, she's my best friend. She would never say anything. Dee can be trusted!"

"No calls to anyone, least of all anyone connected with Martin. And if you keep this up I'll rip out every phone in this house. Lady, this is no game."

"Do you think they found anything at the office or at the Martin's house that could lead them here?" Shelley asked anxiously.

Nick shrugged, struggling to regain his composure. He ran a hand through his hair, realizing that he was way overdue for a vacation. Where was his cool authority, his professionalism? "Maybe, maybe not. But we'll have to be extra careful. No more jaunts to town without either Cord or me along for protection. I'd rather *neither* of you showed your face in town at all. The fewer local people that know you're here, the fewer explanations will be necessary.''

"Now, look here—" Shelley began but was immediately cut off.

"No, you look here. This is dangerous business whether you think so or not. I don't want some so-called friends dropping by or your family showing up. I can't protect everyone. And God knows there're too many people around here already. Use your head, woman!''

"That's enough, Nick," Cord roared.

Nick's sharp green eyes narrowed. "You're pretty cocky for a man I pulled from certain death only days ago. You were supposed to cooperate with this plan, Cord, not hinder it.''

"And I will, damn it, but you're not talking to one of your men here. I warned you…''

They eyed each other, then Nick nodded. He glanced at Shelley. "I'm sorry. Maybe you're right. I've been in this business too long and have forgotten there are decent, respectable people in this world. I've seen too much dirt.''

Suddenly she felt sorry for Nick. He was a man struggling with some inner demon, and if he didn't come to terms with it soon it was going to eat him alive. "I can't stay on this place forever, Nick. It's okay for a visit, but to sit here day after day…" It was her turn to shudder. "I'm a city girl and I'm already stir-crazy.''

Nick looked at his watch. "Lee and I have to finish picking and packing the strawberries, then we'll be taking them into the morning market. If you have to get any supplies in town, you best come with us.'' He glanced at Cord. "You better tag along. You might find this interesting—even newsworthy."

After the door had closed behind Nick, Cord asked, "What did he mean, 'newsworthy'? What's so important about taking a load of strawberries to market?"

Shelley kept her eyes on the back door and answered absently, "Prejudice. Some of the townspeople have taken a dislike to Lee. Not only because he's Oriental, but because he raises a superior crop and demands and gets higher prices." She tore her gaze away from the door and the retreating Nick and looked at Cord. They were going to make her a prisoner in her own home, on her own land; suddenly her guard seemed more dangerous than the people who were supposed to be after her.

CHAPTER SIX

SHELLEY PULLED the chocolate cheesecake from the oven, carefully placing it on the wire rack to cool. She fussed with the pan unnecessarily for a second, touched the hot center lightly, then sighed. Cooking had always been an emotional outlet for her, and today the feeling of impending disaster was so strong she'd begun cooking before anything had happened. With a fatalistic shrug she pulled off the oven mitts, picked up her frosty glass of iced tea and headed for the back door.

The heat hit her like a slap in the face; the air so still and hot it seemed for a second as if all the oxygen had been sucked from her lungs. She took a sip of the cold tea and sat down on the top step, thankful for the small amount of shade the roof's overhang afforded. All of a sudden she remembered her clean white jeans and quickly rose, dusted off her bottom and swept the concrete step. Seated once again, she propped her elbows on her knees and stared down at the dirty step between her feet. She'd made a fatal error this morning by going braless and wearing the skimpy crop-top. A mistake she hoped she'd now corrected with a loose T-shirt covered by a turquoise cotton print blouse tied at the waist.

Now, looking back, she realized the problem. In her concerted effort to ignore Cord's existence, she'd made the mistake of forgetting the man was all male—with a male's appetite. Her lack of perspective, she knew, would only appear to be an open invitation to Cord. Thinking back and seeing herself from Cord's point of view, she was ashamed to admit her manner had seemed that of a tease.

She wasn't a jackass. It didn't take a blow between the eyes with a two-by-four to notice that look of hunger in Cord's eyes, nor did she miss the tension that tightened his body whenever she was near. She'd experienced the same reaction herself when he was close. A self-mocking grin curved her mouth. She wanted Cord, but she wasn't going to give in. That road only led to more heartbreak. A torrid summer affair wasn't on her agenda. Besides, in her unstable emotional condition she couldn't handle the ramifications surrounding Cord and his presence. What a psychiatrist would make of their attraction for each other didn't even bear contemplation.

Lifting the sweating glass, she rolled the cool wetness across her forehead. The sun beat down on the baked earth with such intensity that it was hard to believe it was still early. The fact that she was dressed, ready, and actually looking forward to the trip to town made her mouth turn down in a wry smirk. Damn it, she was bored to death with the never-changing weather, the heat that seemed to burn through her skin and the simple routine that made up each day. Reaching down, she picked up the hose and turned on the water, then cursed. Even the water was hot. She missed Seattle; the cool moist breeze that smelled of pine mist instead of scorched grass. She missed her friend Dee. Dee would make her laugh when she wanted to cry. Wrapping her thumb over half of the hose nozzle to force the flow to jet out in a hard stream, she aimed it at a fat, brown beetle that was crawling across the ground, leaving its tiny steps in the sandy soil. *Reduced to zapping helpless bugs,* she thought to herself in disgust.

When a high-pitched, childish giggle drew her attention, it was with relief that she dropped the hose into the flower box. She shaded her eyes with a wet hand, looking out toward the strawberry field, the only green spot left in the world of tawny grass and trees.

Nick and Cord, shirtless and on their knees, had paused in their work, their attention on the small boy who stood between them with a large straw basket held out with both hands. He gestured expansively, tipping over the basket that Nick and Cord were trying to deposit their strawberries in. As she watched, Robbie dropped the basket and began to run. Cord was on his feet in a split second and after him. Loud squeals punctuated by shouts and deep chuckles swelled in volume and drifted back to her. Nick had joined the chase, but Robbie was as slippery as an eel and as fast as a field mouse in eluding his friends. They ran back and forth, over and around Lee's neat rows of strawberry plants. Bedding straw was sent flying with clogs of moist dirt.

Shelley began to laugh. Soon another voice was added, but this one was angry and totally unintelligible as it was in Vietnamese. Lee stood at the edge of his field thumping his wooden staff at the three males who romped across his plants. His raised voice only succeeded in throwing Robbie's speed off, and as Shelley watched, Cord and Nick carried a begging, laughing Robbie to the creek. In a few minutes she heard a small splash, followed by two more, louder than the first.

She rose, dusted off her bottom, then opened the screen door, pausing a second to listen to another burst of laughter before going in. Nick's efforts to change his hard-line attitude toward Robbie seemed to be working.

The boy had barely left his side since yesterday, and when he did, it was only to be near Cord. As she refilled her glass with ice and more tea she wondered thoughtfully why Cord wasn't married, with a family of his own. He was so good with Robbie, he should have a son.

The sound of a door closing jarred her out of her reverie. She swung around, then wished she hadn't. Cord stood there, naked to the waist, his jeans soaked, his canvas shoes in one hand as he dripped creek water all over her polished wood floor.

"Sorry about the mess." He glanced down, then back up, meeting her stare with an amused twist to his mouth and a devilish twinkle in his eyes. "I could have avoided this by stripping, but I didn't think you would appreciate the gesture." He didn't wait for her to respond but vaulted across the kitchen and up the stairs.

Shelley hadn't moved, couldn't move, until she heard water knocking in the old pipes as it struggled to reach the shower off Cord's bedroom. God, he was gorgeous. She blinked and shook her head, seeing again the wide smooth shoulders with tan skin stretched like satin over sculptured muscles; the broad chest with its thick mat of dark hair; the jeans that were plastered to his body, leaving little to the imagination. She wished for a flaw, a little extra flesh around his middle, but his stomach was as solid and as flat as a washboard. Shelley raised a fist and thumped her chest. *Beat, heart, beat. He's just a man. Get hold of yourself!*

She whipped around and blindly began to loosen the cheesecake from the springform pan. Her hands stilled in their work. She was in deep trouble. Cord had shown her another side to his personality. That wicked sense of humor combined with his compelling sexuality was dangerous. She was growing weaker by the hour. A chill shocked her out of her musing, and she continued working the pan from the cake. Once the dessert was free she slipped it onto a serving dish and was about to place it in the refrigerator to chill when Cord's voice stopped her.

"Chocolate cheesecake." He sniffed the air with such obvious delight that it brought a tiny smile to Shelley's lips. "I've had this sweet tooth all morning."

He said it with a hopeful eagerness and a pleading look that reminded her of Robbie. "Sorry, it's not cool enough to slice." She took a quick appreciative glance at the strong, long legs, white shorts and the blue-and-white striped polo shirt before she braked her straying thoughts.

"That's not by chance the chocolate cheesecake from Morgan's, is it?"

"Yes." He licked his lips and the simple gesture caused the air in her lungs to hang painfully in her chest.

"Topped with whipped cream laced with Grand Marnier and grated dark chocolate?"

"Hmm." She shoved the cheesecake in the refrigerator before he could reach her, then slammed the door and barricaded the appliance. His nearness left her suddenly breathless as he placed both hands on the door, one on either side of her head. He was going to kiss her, she could tell by the heavy-lidded eyes so close now. She could stop him before he moved another inch, but she didn't. Instead, she stared at him and waited.

Cord leaned forward a fraction, his gaze on the parted lips just kissing distance away. He grinned. Never one to do the expected, he pulled away, not enough to let Shelley go, but enough to see the brief flash of confusion and disappointment in her eyes before she managed to control herself. Anticipation only made victory sweeter. "What would I have to do to get a slice?" he asked, his voice low, leaving no doubt what he was offering.

The heat from his closeness made her knees weak, and she wondered if he could sense their trembling. Forcing herself to concentrate on his words, she frowned. "Nothing. Will you please move?" She reached out to push him away, then snatched her hand back. She didn't want to touch him.

"Sure." He turned around and walked off, rotating his shoulders. "I believe I've changed my views of farmers, especially those whose crops have to be picked by hand." Placing both hands in the middle of his back, he stretched.

Shelley twisted her head away sharply, but not before she'd taken in the arched body, muscles strained against material and hips thrust forward. She swallowed and said a silent prayer for help.

"My knees may never be the same again. To say nothing of my hands. Do you have a couple of Band-Aids?" Holding out his hand, he showed Shelley two large blisters that had formed on his thumb and forefinger.

Without a word she reached into a cabinet and handed him the first-aid kit.

Cord gave it back. "Would you? I can't manage it by myself."

Liar! she thought, snatching the metal box back and snapping open the lid.

"You could have warned me that Lee was a slave driver and that each berry had to be carefully picked by hand, with a two-inch stem, no less. Hell, do you know he had the nerve to measure a couple of my stems, then scold me because they were half an inch too short? Ouch! And did you realize that they don't wash the strawberries? Instead, Vo dusts the dirt and sand off them with a small brush. Damn!'' He attempted to pull his hand from the death grip she had on it.

"That's why Lee gets top dollar for his produce.''

"Shelley, what are you going to do with that needle?'' He managed to snatch his hand away this time.

"Pop the blisters.''

"No thanks. The Band-Aids are just fine, thank you.''

Shelley shrugged and put the long needle back in the first-aid kit.

"Robbie sure picks quickly. Kid works about as fast as he talks. He's a fine young man. How can his mother let him run wild and unsupervised so much?''

"Robbie doesn't run wild.'' She shot him an irritated glare, pulling the Band-Aid a little tighter than necessary. "His mom works at the local bank, Cord. Because it's summer holidays, he's here three or four days a week, *supervised* by either me, Lee or Vo. He has chores and a job, which he gets paid for. On Fridays she attends college in Houston and takes him with her. She also makes it a point to spend the weekends with him. Saturdays they do anything he wants. Sundays they go to church and usually spend that day together.'' Finished applying the adhesive strips, she gave him back his hand with a flick.

"I'm sorry. I guess I was worried about him. He's such a bright, likable kid.''

Shelley agreed. Robbie was neutral territory and a safe topic of conversation. "You're good with him. You should have children of your own.'' She looked up from retrieving the Band-Aid wrappers that had fallen to the floor and wondered what she'd said to bring on his complete change of expression. "Do you have children?"

"No children—divorced. Thanks for the doctoring. When does Lee usually go to market? I want to get my camera loaded and ready. This might make a good story."

Shelley turned to drop the bits of paper in the trash and glanced over her shoulder. A tiny frown formed twin lines between her eyes. She looked at the kitchen clock. "He likes to be there before nine. We'll probably leave in about fifteen minutes." What had she said? Cord had withdrawn from her as surely as if he'd turned and walked out of the room.

A long silence spread between them before Cord spoke again. "Nick filled me in a little on what's been happening in town. I find it hard to believe anything like this could still be going on this long after the Vietnam War."

"The war has nothing to do with it, Cord."

"Of course it does."

"No, the people causing the trouble are too young. The closest they've ever gotten to the war is reruns of documentaries and news shows."

"Then why the prejudice?"

"Times have been very tough for farmers."

"Are you defending them?"

"Heavens no! The group of men who oppose Lee and Vo are layabouts who have skimped on taking care of their crops but still feel they should get at least as much as Lee does for his produce."

"What happened last time in town? Did you go?"

"Yes, but I was at the bank and not with Lee. They only pelted his truck with rotten tomatoes."

"Then it could get worse?"

"Oh, I don't think the local sheriff will let it go much further. He's turned a blind eye so far because this is an election year and these people are his neighbors and friends."

Cord was quiet for a moment, staring out the kitchen window at the brown, thirsty land beyond. "The weather won't help. Passions run high and tempers are fast to flare in extreme heat, especially if there's been a long spell with no relief. Maybe Robbie should stay here with Vo."

Shelley threw back her head and laughed. "Keep Robbie out of the action? Just you try it." The back screen door slammed shut and before the door to the kitchen was thrown open, she said, "Speak of the devil."

They weren't expecting the supersleuth in a yellow plastic raincoat with a red-and-green print scarf cinching the waist in, or the lady's fedora cocked rakishly over one eye. Shelley wondered how much paper Robbie had stuffed in his mother's hat to make it fit. "Robbie." She coughed, cleared her throat and took a shallow breath to keep from laughing. "Robbie, you can't wear that to town."

"Why not?" The young spy steadied the hat that tended to rock a little on his head.

"It's 103 in the shade, for Pete's sake. You'll suffer a heat stroke."

"But, Shelley, Nick said I was to be his right-hand man."

"Fine, but I don't think he meant you to get sick."

"But, Shelley..."

"No. Take it off."

He turned to Cord for help, but Cord bit his lip and

shook his head in answer to the pleading look. Robbie's shoulders slumped as he began to untie the scarf-belt. "I don't see what all the fuss is about," he mumbled. "The truck is air-conditioned. Can I put it on again when we get back?"

"If you stay indoors to play."

"Aw, Shelley, that's no fun."

Once she got a good look at what was underneath the coat, the laughter that almost choked her came out as a strangled sound. Robbie had ingeniously made a shoulder holster for his plastic water pistol with a pair of his mother's panty hose.

"Do I got to leave this here?" He touched his prize weapon lovingly, his hazel eyes sparkling with hope.

"It better stay behind with the clothes," Cord said, knowing Shelley would never be able to open her mouth without severely injuring the boy's pride.

"What's wrong with Shelley? She's all red in the face."

"I'm—I'm fine." She had to get out of the room before she broke up. She grabbed her purse, leaving the two males to quietly discuss the peculiarities of women as they struggled with the knots in the panty hose holster.

The inside of her Volvo felt like an oven; as fast as she jumped in she jumped off the scalding leather seat before it could blister her. "Hot damn!" she yelled, shifting her weight from one foot to the other, pulling at her cotton shirt and the back of her jeans. They felt as if someone had ironed them to her skin. Shelley walked around and opened the passenger door, hoping the cross ventilation would cool the interior.

Finally seated again—hot, sweaty and irritable—she jammed the key in the ignition, pumped the gas pedal, then turned the key. Nothing happened. Trying again, she gave the pedal another couple of hard, rapid pumps. Nothing. Then out of the corner of her eye, movement caught her attention and she turned her head slowly. What she saw made her twist completely around to get a good look. Three men and one boy stood a few feet away, staring.

It wasn't the fact that they were just silently watching that bothered her, it was the expressions on the adults' faces. She shoved open the door and jumped out. "Okay, which one of you messed with my car?" She could have screamed. They didn't even bother to fake innocence or surprise, or even lie—they just stood there. "Well?"

Robbie gave a nervous giggle, but immediately shut up and slipped behind Cord when she cut her eyes toward him.

"I thought it best," Nick said. "Cord or I can drive you anywhere you have to go. You don't need your car. Believe me, Shelley, I've done this for your own good."

"You did, did you?" She was so angry she couldn't think of anything else to say. The men relaxed a little. "*Et tu*, Lee?"

The Vietnamese leaned on his staff, his face solemn, but his black eyes were sparkling slits of laughter. "Velly solly."

"You don't sound it. If any of you think I'm staying here, you better think again." Crossing her arms over her chest, she waited for the argument to break out.

"You come." Lee waved to the loaded produce truck. "We go rike one happy famiry." He spun around, walked to the truck and climbed in behind the wheel.

"Justice *is* mine…" Shelley mumbled, then sprinted

toward the truck, her grin widening with each step.
"You driving, Lee?"

"You betcha, Miss Sherrey."

"Good."

She didn't know how it happened. Somehow when
everyone finally quit arguing about who was going to
sit where and was seated in the cab, she ended up on
Cord's lap. But it was worth it. She wrapped her arms
around his neck and held on for dear life. Oh, yes, it
was worth it all right, just to see Nick and Cord pale a
little more with each mile. Only once had she been ig-
norant enough to ride with Lee, and afterward she'd
sworn never again. Cord's body was as stiff as a corpse
as Lee wound the truck around the curves and sharp
turns in the road at a rapid and somewhat erratic speed.
She grinned when she heard Nick's sharp intake of
breath, Robbie's excited squeal and Cord's whispered
words that sounded surprisingly like a plea for help
from someone with high authority. *Dear me,* she
thought, and buried her face in the curve of his neck.
How swift the mighty fall! Her shoulders began to
shake.

"You think this is funny?" Cord's last word came
out as a low strangled cry when the truck hit a deep
pothole and veered off the road, heading straight for a
speed-limit sign. Lee hit the brakes and twisted the truck
back onto the pavement.

"Go, Lee, go!" Robbie encouraged his friend. They
hit another pothole dead center and everyone was sent
toward the ceiling of the truck. Robbie whooped. "All
right!"

"Hush, Robbie," Nick scolded, his stern voice husky
with feeling. "You'll make Lee lose his concentration."

The wild ride finally ended when they entered the

city limits and Lee slowed to a crawl. Old, restored two-story brick buildings lined both sides of Main Street. Their gaily painted signs hung over the doorways, motionless in the still air. Farther down the street the only modern structure, the bank, sat nestled between Hailey's Emporium and Rex's Drugstore. The original bank had a colorful history, one her uncle had always delighted in telling since his great-grandfather had been the local lawman seventy years ago. He'd caught bank robbers in the middle of their second holdup attempt and had trapped them inside the bank. With a reputation for violence and a penchant for bloodbath killings, the robbers were determined to hold the taxpayers' funds and a female teller hostage. After the sheriff, frustrated and just as ruthless as the men holed up inside, had finally managed to get the young woman out, he'd given the bandits three minutes to surrender. When they'd refused he'd set the bank on fire, flushing the men out of their hiding place. They were arrested, but the bank was lost and only a few treasures salvaged: the old plate-glass window, with its original gilt lettering that Shelley loved, and the wrought-iron tellers' cages.

She shifted her weight on Cord's lap, snapping his attention back from his inspection of the old-fashioned buildings and the quaint street. "Welcome to Pecanville, population 3002." She gave a little wiggle and leaned forward, smiling inwardly as she felt Cord suck a deep breath through his nose. This morning's episode in front of the refrigerator was forever imprinted on her brain, and she figured two could play his teasing game. "Lee, you can let me off at the bank. I'll meet you at the market in an hour." The truck came to an abrupt stop, making everyone grab for a steadying handhold. She twisted around, opened the door and began to climb out. "Come on, Robbie. You can visit with your mother while I take care of some business."

Long after she was out of the truck, watching it take the nearest corner and drive out of sight, she stood perfectly still, waiting for the feeling of Cord's body against hers to fade.

Robbie tugged at Shelley's hand impatiently. "Why are we standing here?"

She shook her head, looked down at the boy's puzzled face and grinned. "Why, indeed?"

"I asked you."

"One day a girl will come into your life and you'll stare off into space, too."

"Girls! Not me." He shuddered and made a gruesome face as if just dosed with a nasty medicine, then took her hand and hauled her through the bank door.

CHAPTER SEVEN

THIRTY MINUTES LATER the bank doors were thrown open and Shelley and Robbie were running down the sidewalk, blind to the few curious onlookers. The sun hammered down on her, the relentless heat working like an invisible hand to slow her every step. Sweat trickled down her back. She shivered with dread. Finally, after four long blocks, she reached the corner and turned, pausing only to give a quick glance over her shoulder to reassure herself Robbie was right behind her. The farmers' market was only a few blocks away, and from where she was now she could make out the trucks and cars crowding the square, open-air, tin-roofed building.

Out of breath, Shelley slowed to a fast walk. But when raised voices and the sounds of a mob reached out and filled her heart with fear, she sprinted up the wide concrete steps of the building that housed stall after stall of beautifully arranged produce. The air was pungent with the rich fragrances of vegetables and fruits, sun and soil...and the excitement of a fight.

The far end of the market was crowded with people. Some stood watching with disapproving expressions, yet did nothing to interfere. Then there were those who were yelling, egging on whatever was happening in the center of the crowd.

Shelley elbowed her way through the spectators with Robbie at her heels. The people parted to let her through, and when she came to the edge of the circle she stopped, her mouth a grim line. Cord, Nick and Lee were shoulder to shoulder, a triangle, moving as two men circled them like hunters with captured prey. The air crackled with violence and hate, and Shelley held out her hand to stop Robbie from rushing in to help his friends. The child pulled at her arm, pointing at two other men lying on the sawdust floor, bleeding and out cold.

"Come on, chink," one of the troublemakers yelled, his face as red as his hair and his light eyes fierce with hatred.

As Shelley watched, frozen by the crowd's excitement and anticipation, the young farmer made a move toward Lee. Shelley sucked in a breath, then let it out slowly. She now realized why Lee was never without his wooden staff. Small and frail, the elderly man would have been like a dry twig in the other man's hands. But Lee's tormentor wasn't able to get within reach as the long, thick piece of wood blurred, whirled, then stopped only long enough to tap the farmer's shoulder. But by the way the man staggered back, clutching his arm, Shelley knew it wasn't a gentle nudge.

The triangle of men rotated, putting Nick in front of the injured bull of a man. Cord lifted his camera, snapped, then dropped it, letting it dangle at the end of the strap as the bull's friend made a sharp move. Shelley's heart sank to her toes, and she flinched as the man's fist connected with Cord's chin.

Cord staggered, regained his footing, shook his head and at the same time drew back and let go with a right punch that sent his assailant sprawling backward into the crowd and sliding to the floor. Suddenly Nick lashed out, his leg high and pumping like a piston as the heel of his foot jabbed the red-haired man in the chest several times. But the kicks were short and only stunned the bull a second.

"You're a smart gook to hide behind your friends," he taunted Lee. "But it won't always be that way. Get out of town, chink. We don't want your type here."

"Shelley, Shelley…Shelley!" Robbie grabbed her hand, jerking it to gain her attention. "That's him. That's the one Mom told us about."

She glanced down, Robbie's words finally sinking in. "Glen Ferris?"

"Yeah, that's him."

A peculiar hush seemed to hang over the market and, moving as one, the crowd retreated. Shelley stood firmly, snatched Robbie's arm and pulled him behind her. She cleared her throat and yelled at the top of her voice. "Tinkle Ferris, you stop that right now!"

A stunned, fearful quiet washed through the big, open-air building. There seemed to be a simultaneous swallow in the crowd, followed by a nervous gulp. Then came a single rusty chuckle, then another and another until finally everyone was laughing. Everyone but Glen "Tinkle" Ferris. He stared at Shelley, took a step toward her, stopped, collected himself, then whirled and stalked off. She felt a chill chase over her skin at his murderous glare, knowing she'd made him look a fool and that he wasn't likely to forgive…or forget.

With the excitement over, the crowd began to break up and slowly move away in small groups. Shelley marched past the three surprised men still standing shoulder to shoulder, gave them a disgusted look and walked over to Lee's stall. Only one crate of strawberries was left and it was tipped over on its side. Some of the red fruit was scattered like dark rubies on the sawdust floor.

"Hey, Shelley. Let go, will ya?"

"Oh, I'm sorry, Robbie." She released his hand and watched as he ran to the men who were just beginning to move in her direction. *Men!* she said to herself, and turned her head, trying to ignore the unspoken question in their eyes. She bent down and began picking up the undamaged strawberries. "Did the food brokers buy all but these, Lee?"

"Yes, Miss Sherrey." He squatted down beside her, his hands gently plucking up the fruit. "Buyers alleady come before Mr. Fellis can make trouble." He glanced at her and asked, "How you make him go?"

"Not now, Lee." She darted a killing glance at Cord and Nick, speaking loudly enough for them to hear. "Ferris's liable to decide I didn't embarrass him as badly as he thought and come back with his friends to finish the job. They looked like they were beginning to make headway when I got here." Her gaze shifted between Cord and Nick. "I'm sure you two would just love that." Lord, she hated violence. "Of all the stupid, macho... Why didn't one of you go call the sheriff? Oh, never mind." She took a quick deep breath and tried to calm herself before she opened her mouth again. But her next words stuck in her throat when she noticed two old ladies approaching. The sisters Randall—the highly respected town gossips—came to a stop before Lee's stall with eyes bright, blue-gray finger-waved hair, matching cotton-print dresses, support hose and sensible leather shoes. Shelley sighed. They'd never get away now.

"Mr. Tho," Miss Milly Randall said loudly enough to catch the attention of the milling crowd. "Sister and

I would like to buy those strawberries. Wouldn't we, Sister?''

''Yes, indeed we would, Mr. Tho,'' Ruby Randall answered, just as loudly.

Shelley watched as Lee rose in one graceful, fluid movement, bowed deeply in a show of respect to the old ladies, then took a steadying breath. ''I am honored you deem strawberries worthy of your expertise notice.''

Shelley's mouth dropped open; she'd forgotten just how perfect Lee's English could be when he took the time to slow down or to calm his emotions.

''No need to thank us, Mr. Tho. Sister said only this morning that we needed to buy some of your produce. They are well worth the price. Aren't they, Sister?'' Ruby asked.

''Please, ladies…'' Lee dusted off the last berry, placed it back in the crate as if he were handling a fragile egg, and gave another deep bow, all the while conscious of the stunned onlookers in the market. ''These are the last of today's crop. I would like very much for you to have them with my compliments. A gift for your kindness.''

The two ladies twitted and squabbled between themselves a second before Milly stuck out her hand. ''We thank you, Mr. Tho. I hope to see you here with your beautiful produce more often.'' She turned her head, her nose high in the air, and stared at Nick. ''Do I know you?''

''No, ma'am. I don't believe so.''

Ruby interrupted what Milly was about to say. ''Good! Then you may carry that crate to our car, young man. Right, Sister?''

But Milly's attention was now on Cord and Shelley.

"Your aunt and uncle were fine people, but it surprised everyone in town that they left the management of the produce fields to Mr. Lee. It will take them some time to adjust. And, my dear, you must know how much we miss them?" Her bright blue eyes had wandered in Cord's direction as she talked.

"I'm her husband." He stepped forward a little.

"I see."

"Let me help Nick carry that crate to your car."

"Thank you, no. It doesn't require two men. Besides, you should stay here in case Tinkle comes back." Milly gave an uncharacteristic giggle and hurried off, still talking. "We shall have our handyman, Louis, bring you a strawberry shortcake tomorrow. Won't we, Sister?"

"Oh, yes, Sister. A nice big one, too, for the men. You know how they eat!"

They strolled away, their voices fading as they discussed the merits of making two cakes or doubling a recipe. Shelley smiled, shook her head and looked around the market. No one had missed the ladies' visit and the word would soon spread that the distinguished Misses Randall approved of Lee Duc Tho's strawberries.

Robbie crawled out from under the stall. "Are they gone?" He made a horrible face in the direction the old ladies had taken.

"Robbie!"

"Well, they're always patting my head and saying things like, *'Poor little tyke. Right, Sister?'*"

He did a close imitation of Miss Milly's voice and Shelley had to bite back a laugh.

"Why are they always saying that?"

Shelley knew exactly what he meant. The Randalls

were of a different generation and social station, where illegitimacy might be tolerated, but never truly accepted.

"Why would they do that, Shelley?"

Wanting desperately to change the subject, she said, "You better help Lee finish cleaning the stall so we can leave."

The trip home was quiet and uneventful. No one protested when it was made clear she was going to drive. She loaded her injured warriors, started the truck, put it into gear and drove slowly and safely away.

After a few aborted attempts at conversation, Robbie slumped on Nick's lap. He just couldn't understand why no one wanted to talk about the fight. With a snort of frustration, he crossed his arms over his chest and pursed his lips into a childish pout.

Nick closed his eyes, his expression, like Lee's, unreadable. But every once in a while he moved the fingers of his right hand, stretched them, then made a tight fist.

Cord played with his camera, stopping only once to turn his head to the window and as inconspicuously as possible work his sore jaw.

Lee stared straight ahead, a tiny victorious smile playing at the corners of his lips.

Shelley pulled the truck to a stop at the side of the house and climbed out. Doors slammed and still the quiet persisted. She glanced at the three men, disgust and disapproval shining as bright as a raging fever from her eyes. "Lee, you'd better see to Vo. I'm sure she's heard us arrive and is wondering why we're back so early."

"Yes, Miss Sherrey."

"This situation is *not* funny, Lee."

"No?" He bowed deeply, then trotted off toward his house, whistling a tuneless song as he went, his wooden staff twirling at his side like a long baton.

Shelley watched him go, shaking her head in amusement. Then she turned slowly to the two remaining men. "Both of you follow me."

Robbie filed into the house behind Nick, his mouth unusually severe as he tried to hold on to his elation. His feet almost danced out from under him with anticipation. There was going to be fireworks for sure this time. He loved to see grown-ups lose their cool. Course, he almost never made his mother angry enough to yell at him. She was a goody-two-shoes, and he had to be the man of the house and take care of her, make sure no one ever made her cry like that Tinkle Ferris had one day. He'd have to be as still as a mouse, he knew, or they'd notice him and send him from the room. Like a sly little fox, all ears and eyes, he slipped into a chair at the kitchen table and waited for the fun to begin.

"Sit!"

Cord and Nick sat.

She yanked open the refrigerator door and pulled out an ice tray, emptied half into two dish towels and folded them tightly. Without a word she turned and looked at the two men. They both sat as calmly as toads waiting for flies, she thought, then saw a telltale twitch of Nick's lips. That small reaction was all she needed. With a few quick steps she was beside the men and handed each an ice pack. Pulling out a chair, she sat and stared at them for a second. Nick gazed back, his green eyes dark with some emotion she wished she could figure out. Cord fiddled with his camera with one hand, set the ice pack down, then raised the camera and snapped a few pictures of her. Shelley glared at them. "For people who wanted to keep a low profile, you two sure blew it this morning. Just what did you hope to accomplish? Do you think the entire town won't be talking about this and the fact that the so-called farmhand at Pecangrove Plantation is an expert in karate, judo…whatever you call what you did?''

Cord snapped a few more pictures, set the camera down and picked up the ice pack. He winced as the cold touched his bruised jaw. ''Wasn't my fault.'' He nodded at Nick. ''Our emotionless wonder here flew off the handle when those men started calling Lee names. Told them that Lee fought with us in Vietnam and against the Vietcong, but it didn't matter. They were spoiling for a fight and we obliged.''

Shelley stared at Nick.

He shrugged. ''Damned if I know what happened.'' He stopped and shot Cord a killing look. ''I just seem to have lost my cool and took exception to the name-calling by a bunch of hick cowards who would have found a way to get out of fighting in the war even if they had been old enough to join.'' He dropped his gaze from Shelley's and studied the cold dish towel wrapped around his hand, his next words bringing a puzzled frown to his brow. ''Something snapped.'' His eyes lifted, but instead of looking at Shelley he stared off into space for a moment, then shook his head. ''This place is doing strange things to me.''

Shelley laughed, but the sound was not a happy one. ''It sure is. The two of you ought to be ashamed of yourselves. It's all well and good to take up for Lee, but what happens when my problems are over and you leave? He'll still be here to face the people of this town—''

''Speaking of people,'' Cord interrupted, ''how did

you manage to arrive in time to send the town bully running? I don't believe I've ever seen a man more embarrassed.''

"My mom told us what was happening." Robbie piped up, disappointed that the grown-ups weren't yelling at each other. When Shelley didn't immediately take up the story, he jumped in eagerly. "She works at the bank and heard some people talking that Mr. Ferris was going to beat up Lee. She told Shelley to call him Tinkle in front of everyone and it would make him real 'barrassed.''

Cord chuckled. "Well, it certainly worked. But why 'Tinkle'?''

Shelley rose and pulled out a cookie sheet, some flour and butter from the cabinets. She paused and turned with the canister of flour in her hand.

"Shelley! Let me!" Robbie jumped to his feet, laughing as he rushed to her side and jerked at her shirttail. "Please, let me." When she nodded, Robbie twisted around to his audience and took a deep breath. "When Mr. Ferris was a boy he wet the bed. Mom said he used to beat up on his sisters and the only way they could get back at him was to tell everyone what he did. So, every time he was mean to them in school they would call him Tinkle and make him cry." Robbie was laughing so hard he could barely catch his breath. Then he sobered and continued, "He said something to my mom once and made her cry, but I kicked him in the knee the next time I saw him. I bet he'll never do it again. Will he?''

"I bet he won't, either, Robbie," Cord said.

Shelley watched the two men as they listened to the boy. The tenderness she saw in both their expressions brought a painful lump to her throat. "Robbie, you better go see if you can help Vo."

"Aw, Shelley." But he didn't argue further; he just stomped out.

"Now, Nick..." She scattered some flour on the counter and reached for the bowl of dough she'd left to rise. While punching down the dough, she went on talking. "That little show of strength earlier certainly made us inconspicuous, didn't it?" After greasing a cookie sheet, she pulled baseball-size hunks of the dough, rolled them between her hands then set them on the pan. "The admiral told me you wanted to force the people looking for Anthony's belongings to work for their information." She made her tone as condescending as possible. "I distinctly remember him saying that by making them form an all-out search they would inadvertently show themselves and we would be forewarned of their movements." She dampened a length of cheesecloth and laid it over the sourdough rolls before putting them aside to rise once more. "And since you cut short my shopping in town this morning, you can go to the store for me." She dusted off her hands, reached into the pocket of her jeans and handed him a rather long sheet of paper. "You may have to drive to Houston to obtain some of the ingredients I need. And you needn't get that look, either. If I'm going to be a prisoner, I'm going to have something to do—cooking just happens to be a hobby."

Nick sighed, his expression stubborn but resigned. "Did I thank you for the meal the other night?" he asked, hinting for another invitation. "You're a marvelous cook."

"Yes. But you knew that, didn't you? You know everything about me. I bet you even know the name of the doll my sister gave me when I was ten.''

"Jazzy, short for Jezebel because she reminded you of Bette Davis.''

A muscle along Cord's jaw twitched. He didn't like the fact that Nick knew more about Shelley than he did. He stared at the intelligence officer, seeing for the first time just what it was that was changed in the man's face. The chiseled quality seemed to have softened, and there was animation and a spark of compassion to the usually lifeless countenance. Something had begun to put cracks in the man's aloofness. He let his gaze shift between Shelley and Nick and tried to discern if there were any vibrations of physical attraction there. Nick was handsome enough, but Cord couldn't feel any change in the atmosphere. Still, it was something he'd have to watch out for.

Nick rose, pushed his chair under the table and said, "I got word this morning that someone's been calling your parents' house in Carmel and your brother and sister in Beverly Hills. The FBI has been closely watching your family, and when the calls were being made about you from an unknown person they sent for Lloyd Martin and the admiral so they could explain the situation.''

"You're just full of secrets this morning,'' Shelley snapped, hating the idea that her family was under surveillance.

"Seems you have your secrets, too. You led us to believe no one knew where you were. But your family knows and has from the beginning, haven't they?''

"Of course. Do you think I could just disappear for weeks without them raising hell? I asked them not to tell anyone where I was.''

"Well, you'll be happy to know that they kept their mouths shut. The only reason they finally admitted to knowing where you were was that your father *demanded* to know why the FBI was watching them. Lloyd and the admiral broke the news to your family that Anthony was dead and told them what was going on here. Your mother sends her love and said to tell you she's anxious to meet Cord.''

Cord gave a grunt of surprise and shifted the ice pack. "They told them about me? Why?"

Nick shrugged and reached for the doorknob. "They thought it best. By the way, Shelley, did you happen to tell Dee Radford anything? Is she, like your family, clam-jawed?"

Shelley shook her head. "I didn't tell her a thing, and I feel awful about that. She's my best friend, and she must be going crazy trying to figure out where I am and what's happened to me."

Nick pulled the door open. "She's been calling your father every day to see if he's heard from you. We finally advised him to tell her that you and Anthony were trying to put your marriage back together."

"More lies. Damn it, was that necessary? Couldn't you have just left it the way it was?"

"No. Your family's telephone is being tapped by someone other than us. We want them to think that you and Anthony are together. It may speed up their search a little." He was almost out the door when he glanced back over his shoulder. "It's time to go through the belongings you shipped out here. *Now,* Shelley. Stop putting it off."

The door shut softly behind Nick. Shelley stared at the empty space. She knew it was time, but God, she dreaded it with every fiber in her body. A chill washed over her and she shivered.

"Hey, are you okay?" Cord got up and went to her, wrapped an arm around her and brought Shelley's unresisting body next to his. "It can't be that bad, can it? Just a bunch of stuff you'd want to throw out anyway. Listen, Robbie told me there's a typewriter in the library and to get to it I'd have to climb over a mountain of boxes. Why don't I help? Besides, it's always good to have a friend along when you have to face an unpleasant task." He could feel her warm breath through his shirt, and his blood quickened as he settled her a little closer. With a jolting shock he realized how perfectly she fit him, the way their bodies touched so intimately, as if they were made for each other. *Damn it, man,* he scolded, *stop this dangerous line of thinking. Before you know it she'll have you tied to her side. What happened to the promises that your knowledge of her would extend only as far as her body?*

He released her abruptly, then took hold of her arm, leading her out the kitchen. "Sometimes if you tackle a problem from a different angle it helps." He guided her through the living room with its big bay windows, high molded ceiling and a wood floor that shone like glass. He had immediately liked the airy room with its floral curtains in white, green and yellow and the Early American furniture that looked well used. He came to a halt before a set of double, carved-wood doors.

Shelley balked, digging her heels in, but Cord's firm hold and the slick floor only made her slide within a hairbreadth of the dreaded door. "I don't want to do this. I'm not ready."

"Ready for what? For Pete's sake, Shelley. What's

in that room that has you so scared? The past, or the fact that you'll have to face the present?''

How could she tell him? He was a man and would never understand. There were pictures, clothes, gifts—all sorts of things tied to her marriage to Anthony. She was afraid to face Anthony one last time. How could she make Cord see that the memories would be painful, but that it wasn't the pain she dreaded? Her heart knocked against her ribs as Cord slid the doors back into the wall and she saw the boxes piled high. Her face paled, her skin grew clammy and she suddenly felt sick to her stomach. ''I can't,'' she murmured.

''Don't be silly.''

She squeezed her eyes shut, inhaled deeply and tried to focus her mind on something else. The feel of Cord's fingers wrapped firmly around her upper arm; the heat of his touch; the scent of his after-shave that brought back flashes of an erotic dream she'd had last night. Evasion didn't help. She took another breath, but the specter of the room still lay in wait. Oh, Lord! What if her worst fears came true? What if she faced the past and realized she was still in love with Anthony? And if it were so, how could she ever come to terms with herself, Anthony's death and her feelings for Cord?

''Come on, Shelley,'' Cord coaxed, leading her to the nearest stack of boxes. He dropped her arm and, with little effort, tore the top container open, never taking his eyes off her strained face.

Shelley gave a strangled noise, clamped her hand to her mouth and fled the room, leaving Cord looking after her with a baffled expression.

He gazed down for the first time and flushed in anger. ''Shit. Just my damn luck.'' He'd managed to catch a corner of a carefully wrapped picture frame and had torn the paper as he opened the box. Nestled there in the newspaper packing was Shelley's wedding picture. Cord studied the man in the photo and felt an eerie sensation creep across the back of his neck, making the fine hair stand on end. It was not a pleasant experience to see one's very image wedded to the woman *he* was after.

Like Shelley, Cord fled the room, slamming the double doors behind him. Heading for the back door, he admitted to himself that it was anger, not fright, that was making him flee. But once outside and away from the house, he slowed his steps and finally confessed that he'd run because he was jealous. He gave a bitter laugh. He was jealous of his mirror image, another man—a dead man! A man who had held the woman he intended to have in his bed. Cord squinted up at the sun. God, the hot Texas weather was making him crazy. He ducked his head, letting the sun beat down on his neck, and stomped off across the dry unyielding ground. He was not in love with Shelley. Sighing loudly, he felt better for denying the niggling doubts and continued his trek out over the fields, totally absorbed in his thoughts and the mental tug-of-war.

CHAPTER EIGHT

SLEEP DIDN'T COME EASILY that night for Shelley. When it did, the sweet dreams that lulled her into slumber turned unexpectedly ugly. Anthony grinned from the cockpit of his airplane, his face highlighted by yellow and blue flames that surrounded him and shot high above his head. Slowly he raised his hand and pointed. As if she were his puppet, and though she tried to fight it, her eyes followed the direction of his finger. She gasped and shook her head wildly. Suddenly, instead of riding the fluffy cloud beside Anthony, she was on the ground, pinned shoulder to shoulder in a crowd. She fought frantically to push her way through the masses of people flowing like molasses. Her heart pounded so loudly that her ears ached.

She glanced up. Anthony threw back his head and laughed, a loud demonic sound that sent a knife of fear through her stomach. She had to warn Cord, Robbie, Nick and Lee that Anthony's plane, now a fireball of death, was directed at them and the market stall where they all stood. The sky seemed to be filled with rolling black clouds, then they split open and a blinding flame shot through, heading straight for them. The heat was unbearable, and she raised her arms to shield her face.

Shelley screamed and screamed and screamed again. The vibrations in her chest, the strain on her throat, startled her awake. Jerking upright, she gulped for air, fighting the tangle of covers as she vaulted from the bed and out of the room. The total darkness of the hall met her, and she quickened her steps only to run directly into a warm wall of flesh. The wall grunted in surprise. She gave a strangled squeal of fright before she realized who had caught her, then collapsed in Cord's arms.

"What's wrong?"

"Dreams," she whispered hoarsely, and pressed her cheek harder against his chest. Her body shook all over until she wondered if her knees would hold her up much longer.

"You scared the hell out of me." His voice was rough with emotion. When he realized the uproar was nothing more than nightmares, his fertile imagination returned to its previous machinations on how he was going to get Shelley in his bed. Now here she was, all soft and trembling and trusting in his arms. He couldn't believe his luck. Like a prime plum, she'd dropped into his lap. "Poor Shelley, you've had a rough day, haven't you?" She nodded and his arms tightened around her, drawing her closer as he grinned into the darkness. "Come with me." When he felt her stiffen he swiftly overrode any protest, scooped her up in his arms and marched to his bedroom. Each step was too slow, too much effort. There seemed to be a huge pump in his chest, pushing the blood faster and hotter through his veins. *Easy, old man,* he cautioned the other half of himself, the half that didn't care how or when he relieved his passion just so long as he did it soon. *Don't blow it now with your impatience. It wouldn't take much for this woman to wise up and turn on you. Then things could really get ugly.*

Cord settled Shelley in his bed, pausing only long enough to retie the drawstring of his white cotton pajama bottoms so they would fit securely around his waist instead of hanging dangerously low on his hips. Then he slipped between the sheets, rolled over on his side and gathered Shelley next to him. She trembled and he stroked her hair, letting his fingers run through the short, silky cap before his hand slid down her back. She burrowed against him as if she wanted to melt into his very bones. A low throbbing started in his loins, a tingling shot along his nerve endings. He inhaled deeply, more to calm his ragged emotional state than to take in the sweet scent of her.

He wanted to touch her, to taste her, to fill his hands with her breasts. Was he doing the right thing? The doubt brought a thundering frown; determinedly he pushed the thought away. A picture in his mind of long shapely legs wound around him made the fire in his veins lick higher. She was so helpless. He wanted to hear his name on her lips, and he'd make sure it was his name she moaned. Was he taking advantage? Damn! A tiny sob muffled in the curve of his arm brought his wandering hand to a stop. *You're a fool, man,* he scolded himself. *She's here. Take her.* But the voice argued in the back of his head. His teeth clenched. Her whispered moan of anguish and continued trembling worked like a douse of ice water, deflating his desire like a pin-pricked balloon. Cord sighed gustily, a long-suffering sound of frustration. *You'll regret this in the morning, Lowell.*

He freed his arm, reached over her and flicked the bedside lamp on low. The room came to life with a warm golden glow, chasing away the shadows and easing some of Shelley's fears. "What's this?" He touched the material of her extra large men's T-shirt, rubbing the soft, royal blue fabric between his fingers. "Country chic?'' He gently pushed her away a few inches. "And just who or what is JCP?'' Tracing the large white letters on the front of the shirt, he could feel her grow taut and immediately stopped, then cuddled her once more in the security of his embrace. After a few comforting pats on the back he felt stiff lettering there and folded her closer. He peered over her shoulder. "John Crowe Productions,'' he read. "Not, I hope, an old flame? I do hate to be in the same bed with another man's name plastered on my woman. A company doesn't bear thinking about, Shelley.''

She gave a mute laugh, and her shoulders shook.

"Not talking? I didn't make you have bad dreams.'' There was a small movement of her head and he amended his words. "Well, maybe I contributed to them.'' He looked down at the shining mink-brown head tucked under his chin and smiled. Never had he felt so tender and protective toward another human being, especially a woman. He stared into a dark corner of the room and wondered what was happening to him. He knew; he just refused to put a name to the emotions. Hadn't he vowed not to leave himself open for the hurt he was certain was inevitable? God help him, but this time he couldn't walk away before it happened.

"Talk to me, Cord.''

"What about, love?''

"Anything. Just talk. Your life—tell me about your life. How old were you when you were adopted? Tell me about your family.'' Her eyes shut, locking out the light and the reality of Cord's nearness. Somewhere in the back of her mind she acknowledged his lack of physical response to her and stored the information away to take out later and examine.

"I was only sixteen months old when I was adopted,

so I can't enlighten you as to why Anthony and I were separated. I'll tell you this, though. If my adoptive father and mother had known that I was one of a twin, they would have taken Anthony, as well. They were older when they got me and had daughters of their own. When I was about four they applied for another boy, but were told that they were beyond the age group for desirable adoptive parents. They would have taken Anthony, Shelley, if they'd known. It bothers me to find out now that somehow we were separated. Someone made a mistake or did it on purpose maybe, thinking that the two of us together would be harder to place. That's not right, and I plan to look into it if I ever get off this godforsaken farm.'' It was strange, the anger behind his statement, and it shocked him. He would have loved to have had a brother.

Shelley knew what he was thinking and wondered if the brothers had been raised together, would Anthony have turned out differently? Would he have been the same, done the same things? Suddenly she knew. "Your family wouldn't have changed the outcome of Anthony's life or his death. He would have been the same." She paused. "What kind of life did you have? Were your parents good to you? Your sisters—did you get along with them?"

Cord chuckled, his memories flying back over the years of love and happiness, and, yes, the fights and tears. "Mary is ten years older than me and is the mother hen of the family. My mom thought she was never going to get her out of the nest and off to college. Mary did fine, though. She ended up a top-notch editor for *Time*, then I started *International News Review* and sweet-talked her into joining the venture. She runs the entire operation when I'm gone.''

"So that's why you've not been very concerned about the time spent here?"

"Right." He settled into a more comfortable position, shifting Shelley so her head rested on his chest.

"Am I too heavy?"

"Fine. Stay where you are."

"You're sure?"

He yawned. "Very."

"Are you sleepy?"

Cord almost laughed when he realized it was actually true. Here he was, curled up with the woman he'd spent days fantasizing about, and he was exhausted. He'd like to tell someone the joke, except the joke was on him, and the more he thought about it, the less funny it became. His brow took on a confused frown.

"Your other sister, Cord—what's her name? And your parents, do they work?"

"You don't plan to let me get any sleep tonight, do you?"

"No, I'm too upset."

He planted a light kiss on her forehead, then dropped his head heavily on the pillow. "Nightmares can be the very devil." God knows, he thought, he'd had his share of them. Cord was quiet for a long minute. When she stirred beside him, he began to tell her about the rest of his family. "My other sister, Helen, is seven years older than me. She's an attorney and an acid-tongued feminist who champions women's rights within the male-dominated criminal judicial system. Surprisingly to everyone, she's married and has two children. But then her husband, Ralph, is also a lawyer and an advocate of the women's movement. So they live a fairly peaceful life...until Helen decides to protest for one of her many causes. Then all hell is liable to break loose and it usually involves the entire family.''

"Then your older sister, Mary, isn't married?"

"She's a widow. Frank died six years ago from cancer.''

Shelley rubbed her cheek against his chest in a gesture of sympathy. "Did they have any children?"

"Five.''

He said the number with so much joy in his voice that she lifted her head and stared at him. The smile tinged with happy memories filled her heart with sadness for her own childless state. She had to duck her head to keep him from noticing the tears. Lord, to think of the times she'd begged and pleaded with Anthony to let her start a family. She squeezed her eyes shut. "I'm surprised you and your wife didn't have a houseful of children. You'd make a wonderful father. I bet your nieces and nephews can't wait till you come over. You probably spoil them rotten.'' She paused for a moment. "I would have liked to have had a houseful myself.''

Cord's lips tightened and his free hand clenched into a tight fist. He had to consciously control his breathing before the question left his lips. "Why didn't you have any children? You'd been married long enough.'' His voice was rough and hard, and he knew she picked up on the change. But he couldn't help his feelings and wished the subject had never come up.

"Anthony never wanted children. Before we were married he led me to believe he would love to have a family, and there was never any doubt that I wanted children. I made it very clear. But he saw to it that it didn't happen.'' The pain of the past reared up, and she only wanted to change the subject before Cord asked the question she dreaded. But she knew it was too late.

She could feel it coming and braced herself to lie. The humiliation of the truth was too great to face or to share.

"What did he do?"

She shook her head and tried to pull away, but Cord's arms tightened around her. "I don't want to talk about it."

"Why? Tell me, Shelley."

The word with all its horror seemed to leave her mouth in a rush of air. "Vasectomy," she answered. Then, for the first time in a month, hate and anger set in, taking away the pain and, yes, a little guilt that just possibly she'd nagged Anthony so much he had had it done. "More than a month ago he told me he'd had a vasectomy. That was right before I caught him in Mr. Martin's office with a camera." She gave a pitiful, strangled laugh. "One day to be exact, right after we'd made—"

"Bastard," Cord exploded, cutting off the rest of her sentence, and not by accident. He didn't want to know that his brother, even if he had been Shelley's husband, had made love to her.

"Next time, if there's ever a next time, I'll have my future husband sign a document saying that he's physically fit and has never had a vasectomy nor will he ever without consulting me. That would be fair, wouldn't it, Cord?" She'd said something wrong. She could feel it in every line of his body. His skin went cold under her touch, and the heavy beating against her cheek seemed to speed up.

"Cord?"

Silence weighed heavily in the room, magnifying the squeak of the overhead fan. Shadows moved, skirting the limits of her vision, making the gray light more menacing than the darkness itself. Shelley leaned up, propping her chin on her palm. He lay there with his eyes shut, his breath coming so softly she stretched forward a fraction just to make sure he was really breathing and hadn't died on her. "Cord. Are you all right? Cord, speak to me. Did I say something wrong?"

He couldn't let her think his reaction was her fault. But, Lord, her words nearly broke his heart. He opened his eyes, struggling for a smile. "It must be the twin syndrome. I felt your hate and contempt for Anthony and thought just for a second it was for me."

"Oh, that's silly." She settled back down, relieved that he'd explained his strange behavior. "Friends again?"

"Of course. By the way, Shelley, when did we become friends?"

"Why, when you rescued me from my nightmares."

"A prince of a guy, huh?"

"Well, not quite, but close." Without a thought to her actions, and as if it were the most natural thing in the world, she began to slide her toes up and down his foot, playing a lover's game of footsie. "Tell me more about your mother and father. What did your father do for a living? What did your mother do?"

Cord grunted in feigned annoyance, reached over and flicked off the light, plunging the room into total blackness. "Dad owns a swimming-pool construction company in San Francisco and mother has always stayed at home and raised us."

He yawned hugely and stretched as much as he could with Shelley half draped across him. "Shelley, you better stop with the toes. It's not a healthy game with me right now. Go to sleep, will you?"

"But, Cord, I'm not the least bit sleepy."

"Count sheep."

"How about a slice of chocolate cheesecake?"

The mention of the chocolate perked him up, but his exhaustion won out. "No. Sleep, Shelley."

Once more a quiet fell over the room, but it was soon broken.

"Cord."

"What?"

"About your wife. You've never said a word about her."

"You're stretching this friendship, Shelley."

"But Cord, it's only fair, if you stop to think about it."

"Listen. I don't want to think. I want to sleep."

"You know almost everything about me, my marriage."

"Maybe mine's not worth talking about. After all, my wife wasn't caught with her hand in the cookie jar, so to speak." It was a cruel thing to say and he could have kicked himself. Opening one eye, he gazed at her expressionless face and sighed. "Sandra couldn't cope with my absence."

"Is that all?" she demanded, feeling cheated, but not knowing why.

"No!" Cord worked his arms free and tucked them behind his head as he stared up at the ceiling. "She wanted a typical family and home, complete with a husband who was always there. A husband to cut the lawn on Saturdays, to go to church with on Sundays. A husband who worked from nine to five. I was gone for weeks, sometimes months at a time, with my job. But I think it was the constant danger of my assignments that helped do our marriage in. She would get physically sick every time I told her I was going to South America, Beirut, Libya, Ireland, Africa, et cetera. So I stopped telling her where I was headed and she worried and nagged even more. I'm a photojournalist. Where did she expect me to be? The White House?''

He pulled his arms out from under his head and curled them around Shelley's shoulders. ''You knew the dangers of Anthony's work. The fine edge of death he walked every time he climbed into one of those experimental planes. I bet you didn't fall apart. You knew what had to be faced. How did you cope?''

''He loved to fly. Like most men who do, it gets in their blood—the speed, the disregard for their life, the sheer joy of being free and close to something up there that most of us couldn't even conceive of. It was his job, his life. I had to accept it and the consequences, learn to live with the unexpected. But never doubt that it was hell at times. I just never let on to Anthony. Dee's shoulder was the one that got wet with the tears of worry.''

''Smart,'' Cord whispered. ''I couldn't even talk to Sandra. Towards the last, whenever I tried to explain, we would end up at each other's throats. There wasn't anything left that I could give her, so she found someone else who could.'' Cord didn't want to tell Shelley that though it was over it still hurt to remember how he'd found out. Coming home earlier than expected one day, he caught her in the age-old nightmare every man dreads: his wife was in bed with another man. ''Last I heard she had a nine-to-five husband and two children.''

''If you'd had children it might have helped your wife cope with the loneliness and maybe you would have stayed home more.''

''Would it have helped your marriage?'' Cord snapped, a vicious edge to his tone. ''Kids are not the all-purpose cure for a failing marriage. It doesn't take a five-year-old to figure that out! For…'' He trailed off. ''Sorry. I'm tired, Shelley, and saying things I don't mean. Go to sleep.''

She tried, but it was hard in light of what had just happened. What had caused the explosion? She lay there, replaying their conversation in her mind, trying to decide if he was still in love with his ex-wife, and wondering why that possibility hurt more than she was willing to admit.

AWAKENING SLOWLY, Shelley's eyelids fluttered open, the tortured look of her nightmares gone from the jade-green depths. She felt warm, secure and strangely content, almost loved. Her eyes lost their misty dreaminess of deep sleep and focused, then widened as she realized where she was. Wrapped in a tangle of Cord's arms and legs, he held her so close she felt welded to his body. To have lain like this all night and not awakened once was unthinkable. Her pulse beat erratically, sending the blood pounding in her ears. This position was more seductive, more intimate than she'd ever experienced. *Now that's a silly thought.* He was just a man, a warm body next to hers. But Anthony had never held her in his arms all night. Anthony had never clung to her as if she were something precious, something to be cherished. Nor had he ever held her as tenderly as Cord was holding her now.

Shelley's eyes lifted and she deliberately studied his face. So like Anthony, so unlike him. It was scary how two men who looked almost identical could be so different. There was no longer any confusion in her mind between the two, no overlapping of personalities in her mind. It scared her more than she thought possible. She had an irresistible urge to reach out and stroke his face, to feel the prickly stubble that darkened his jaw. She ached to run her fingertips across his lips, then trace the lines beside his mouth that she knew could accent a smile capable of breaking hearts. She desperately wanted to do all those things. But, instead, she tucked her hand between them, turning the palm inward so as not to feel the heavy vibrations of his heart.

She didn't want him! But her eyes betrayed her, and she thanked her lucky stars that he wasn't awake to see the desire there. Then, suddenly, she wanted to close her eyes, to tear her gaze away, to hide. Cord *was* awake and watching her, his blue eyes as dark as a sea at midnight and as dangerous as a raging storm. His gaze was bright, glittering like a beacon of hope for a drowning victim. This time she reached out, her fingertips touching his warm lips. It didn't make any difference now, she was lost in that look and would willingly give up the fight and drown.

His mouth descended toward hers and she closed her eyes. So close were his lips she inhaled his very breath. Lightly, his tongue touched her lips, tracing them, moving back and forth till she parted them in welcoming invitation. The invasion was sweet and hypnotic. She sighed, feeling all tension melt away. He pulled back, and she made a sound of protest.

"What's my name?"

His breath cooled her moist mouth, bringing her slowly back to reality. Her eyes opened, the lids heavy as she stared at him a second before his words sunk in. "Cord." She gave in to her urge to touch his hair and lifted her hands, allowing her fingers to feather the chestnut thickness. Then her fingers clenched and she forced his head, with little resistance, down to meet her lips. She gave as good as she got, then it was her turn to pull away. "What's my name?"

Cord chuckled, a deep raspy sound laced with desire and humor. "Shelley."

"Now that we have that settled…" She deliberately left the sentence hanging between them.

"I just wanted to make sure that somewhere in the back of your head you didn't have me mixed up…" This time it was Cord who trailed off as she forced her mouth to his again.

After a long heart-stopping minute, they came up for air. "I never kissed what's-his-name like that." She smiled.

Cord felt an invisible weight lift from his shoulders. "You don't need this, do you?" He touched her T-shirt and with a quick shake of her head she reached down and slipped it off. His eyes followed each move, each inch of material as it crept up over the smooth skin till he thought his heart would explode. Lord, but she was a beauty. Not necessarily soft, but firm muscles under satin skin. An athlete's body. Like him, she took care of herself. The running and exercise paid off. With slow deliberate moves he ran his hand from her calf to her hip, savoring the feel of flesh that invited his caress. But his eyes were glued to the high pointed breasts; the small nipples pink and taut. He quickly loosened the drawstring of his pajamas, worked them down, then kicked them away.

Shelley sucked in a huge breath as he started to arouse her. He puckered his lips as though to whistle, but instead he blew a steady stream of air around her breast. He circled each one, moving slowly, then breathed an exciting design down her chest to her stomach, then on to the inside of her thighs. The light touch of air was more electrifying than anything she'd ever experienced. She couldn't stand it, tried to stop the moan before it forced its way up her throat and escaped her lips, but it was useless. She moaned and arched her body to meet the stream of air as it retraced its pattern upward.

Cord's mouth was on one breast, tasting, sucking the sweetness, while his hand massaged the other one. The more she squirmed against him the more he had to fight for control. He knew she was ready for him, but he had to make her crave him as she'd never craved any man before. He wanted her to call out to him, wanted to hear his name on her lips. His hand moved downward, lightly caressing her inner thighs, moving back and forth from the knee. Then, without warning, he touched her, sinking into her with a quickness that made her shudder. He played with her, his mouth bent to her breast, his eyes closed as he soaked in her soft sounds of pleasure. Sounds so sweet and seductive to his ears that he was forced to bring his head up and inhale deeply for control.

He saw her face then. Her lips were parted, her eyes were closed, and he mastered himself, suddenly knowing he could go on forever, just watching her joy at being touched. He'd suspected that this woman was meant to be loved, now he was sure. He began to place light kisses on her neck, testing the area for response.

She was lost in a world where nothing mattered but her feelings. She was as high as the clouds, floating in a sea of sensations. In some ways it was frightening, feeling she'd lost control of her body and mind. They were totally in someone else's hands and care. But, oh, what hands. She bit her lip and shuddered, feeling the release down to her toes. "Cord...Cord," she murmured in a breathless whisper. She'd never reached those heights just by the touch of a man's hands, and it felt wonderful, different. Now she wanted to experience it again, but with him buried deep within her.

"What do you want, Shelley? What do you want me to do?" He could barely talk; his words were a husky growl.

Her eyes were slitted and she fought to keep them open sufficiently to see his face. "You, Cord. I want you." Wrapping her arms around his neck she pulled herself up enough to maneuver under him. She reached between them, clasping the long, velvet length firmly in her hand and guided him to her entrance.

Cord grinned, kissed her deeply and at the same time eased into her. He almost lost his reason as she wrapped her legs around his waist and moved him deeper into the wet darkness. "What do you want now?"

He wouldn't let her increase the rhythm of his movements, but kept it easy and tantalizing.

"Cord, don't tease. I need you."

The playing had come to an end. Cord realized that the plea in her words and the sound of his name were more than a call for release. She did need him, and maybe, just maybe, he needed her in the same way.

Shelley closed her eyes and let herself go, feeling the fire licking across her body, the ripples of pleasure growing larger and larger. Finally she called his name again, her voice a soft explosion as she collapsed, barely able to breath. Then she felt him increase his pace, striving for his own release. Tightening her legs around him, she ran her hand up his back in a hard, pulling-pushing motion that made him groan out loud in release. He stiffened, then relaxed before rolling onto his side, taking his full weight off her, but still keeping himself buried deep inside.

Cord opened his eyes, blinked and smiled. ''What's my name?''

''Harold P. Jones?''

''Nope.''

''Samuel Carp?''

''Wrong.'' He gave his hips a small thrust. ''Guess again.''

''Cord Lowell.''

''Give the lady a chocolate Kewpie doll.'' His smile grew. ''I couldn't talk you into going down to the kitchen and getting me a big slice of cheesecake, could I?''

''No!''

''I didn't think so,'' he murmured sadly. ''How about some sleep?''

She snuggled closer, moving her own hips and causing his eyes to pop open and widen. ''That sounds good. Sleep I mean.''

''Yes, it does. Just be still or you're liable to get more than you bargained for.''

She thought for a second, wondering if she should just leave things as they were. There was so much she wanted to talk to him about, so much she wanted him to understand. But not now. Maybe in a few hours she'd have the nerve to deny what had happened between them.

CHAPTER NINE

IF ANYONE HAD TOLD HER a couple of days ago that she would do something so asinine, so stupid as to crawl in bed with Cord Lowell and allow him to seduce her, she would have laughed in his face—just before she slugged him. Oh, Lowell, he was a crafty devil, allowing her to fall asleep in his arms, making her feel secure and complete. She shook her head, deliberately pushing aside the memory of her own reaction, her eager response. Stupid? How could she have been so stupid—and weak?

Shelley dropped the wire scrubber into the sudsy dishwater and let go of the mammoth roasting pan. She gazed out the kitchen window, her fingers bone-white as they gripped the edge of the sink. The morning sun was just beginning to lighten the cloudless sky and already the glare hurt her sensitive eyes. How could she have done it? The man meant absolutely nothing to her. She gnawed at her lower lip. It wasn't Cord who upset her, it was the fact that she'd let her guard down, allowed herself to feel again. Hadn't she warned herself after Anthony that her emotions, her judgments, the very instincts that she'd always relied upon, were not to be trusted? After all, if she could have been taken in and lied to and made a fool of by Anthony, then anyone with good looks, a charming smile and a convincing

line would make her easy prey. And easy was something she never intended to be again—ever.

Then what about last night? a vicious little voice
mocked. With a groan of pure agony, she bent forward
and rested her forehead on her hands. She hadn't even
protested. Life, she concluded, wasn't fair at all. Just
when she believed her self-confidence was returning
enough for her to leave her self-imposed exile, Cord
dropped into her life, turning it upside down again and
making her doubts rush back in a flood. She felt adrift
in the emotional upheaval he'd caused. She should hate
him. Her teeth worried her lower lip again. Yet... She
plunged her hands back into the hot dishwater, found
the steel-wool pad and began scrubbing the old roasting
pan, destroying years of accumulated grime.

Her lamb had turned into a ram, literally. She chuckled, then scolded herself. *Really, Shelley!* That was not
the least bit funny; it was crude. But there was so much
truth in the thought that she smiled; a dreamy twist of
her lips as the night flowed back in snatches of heart-
stopping detail.

Her daydreams were shattered when she heard the
sound of footsteps on the stairs. She stiffened, ducked
her head and began scrubbing furiously, all the while
trying to master her pounding heart.

"Good morning." Cord came to a halt, and his smile
of greeting tinged with male conquest died slowly as he
took in the stiff back and lack of response. There was
an insatiable hunger within him, a deep yearning to
sweep her into his arms, to kiss her, consume her. He
wondered if women ever had sudden erotic images the
way men did. Cord sighed. This wasn't going to be
easy. He knew exactly how she felt and could sympathize with her. As he watched her apply more pressure

on whatever she was doing, her bottom bounced enticingly in the skimpy jogging shorts. "Have you been running this morning?"

Shelley couldn't ignore him; besides, it was best to get what she had to say out in the open. "No. I'm going in a few minutes." She quickly rinsed the stainless-steel pan, struggling with its awkward bulk for a minute before she balanced it on the partitioned porcelain sink, yanked up a dish towel and started to dry it. Finally, flipping the damp towel over her shoulder, she gripped the oblong pan by its handles, walked over to the table and set it down. "Cord..."

"Yes?"

"Cord, what happened last night was—"

"Wonderful."

"No!" She wanted to throw the pan in his face.

"No?" Cord's lips curled up at the corners, giving her a glimpse of perfect white teeth.

"No. Yes. Damn it! What happened last night was...was..." She glared. "There was nothing to it." As she watched for his reaction, he rose and a pulse began to beat frantically in her throat. Every muscle tightened as he walked toward her. But he stopped, reached in an overhead cabinet, pulled down a mug, picked up the coffeepot and filled the cup. Just as quietly he returned to his chair and looked at her, his expression innocent and inquiring.

Smug bastard! He thought her embarrassment and fumbling for words were funny. "This doesn't mean we're involved. What happened between us was just physical attraction." She punctuated each word by slamming the roasting pan repeatedly on the table.

Cord's blue eyes glittered as he let his gaze move from her face to the thumping pan, then back to her earnest face. "Oh, Miss Calm and Collected. I'm so glad to see you never lose your cool."

"It was purely physical."

"If you say so." He took a sip of coffee, watching her closely.

"I do."

"Fine with me."

"Good!"

"Right!"

They both knew they were lying.

"It meant nothing," Shelley snapped.

"Oh? I have to draw the line there. It meant something to me."

"Nothing." She looked at him through lowered eyelashes.

"You're sure?"

"Yes."

"You *felt* nothing?" he asked, a wicked gleam in his eyes. "Liar," he whispered.

"I didn't say that.... I said it meant nothing."

"Big difference?"

"Yes."

"Fine."

"Good!" She stomped over to a cabinet, opened the bread keeper, yanked out a box, then slapped it down in front of him. "Robbie brought over his day-old donuts. He knew you loved the chocolate-covered ones, and he didn't want to let them spoil since he has to go to Houston today with his mother."

Cord studied the two donuts through the cellophane window with a peculiar look on his face. He swallowed hard, then cleared his throat. "One's half-eaten."

Shelley couldn't help but laugh at his expression. It was a mixture of tenderness and humor, and yes, there was even a tinge of sadness in his eyes. "Well, what did you expect from a small boy who walked all the way from home? I suspect somewhere between here and his house hunger struck. Besides, you know how Robbie is about sweets. You're the same, and I'd guess they would have arrived in the same condition if you were the one bringing them, wouldn't they?"

"Guess so." He chuckled, then sobered. "Is this all I'm getting for breakfast?"

"No, you can have anything you want. Only you'll have to make it yourself and clean up your mess. I'm going to put these ribs in to cook, then I'm going jogging." While she'd been talking she'd unwrapped two huge slabs of beef ribs and rubbed them with salt, pepper and crushed garlic. She flopped them onto the wire rack in the bottom of the roasting pan, poured some water in, covered them with foil, then took a deep breath, grasped the pan's handles and yanked. She staggered and immediately set the pan down.

"Heavy?" Cord asked politely.

"A little."

"Need some help?"

"I can manage, thank you." She was ready to try once more and tensed her muscles. But Cord was up and taking the heavy pan from her hands, pushing her aside.

"I love barbecued ribs, and it would give me nightmares if they landed on the floor." He carried the pan to the oven and waited while she opened the oven door. Warm heat caressed his face as he watched her. When she met his eyes and blushed, she dropped her gaze, and he slid the ribs in. "Last night meant nothing?"

She turned her back to him and began adding potatoes to the huge pot of water simmering on the stove.

The inside of her cheek was sore from where she'd bitten it to keep from losing her temper. He was teasing her, and she resented that he could take their lovemaking so lightly. Suddenly the contradiction of her thoughts dawned on her, and she wanted to laugh at her confusion. "I told you, what happened was just a physical thing. You were restless and hungry—"

"And you? What were you?"

Shelley dropped in the last potato with a force that sent water splashing over the sides of the pot. She whipped around. "Listen you…"

"Are we going to have potato salad with the ribs?"

"Yes. I don't want to get into a fight with you, Cord. But I would appreciate it if you would stop teasing me about last night. It's over and that's that. If you're not man enough to take the truth, then I suggest that you take a good hard look at yourself and decide if it's your ego that won't let you accept the fact that I'm not attracted to you."

She turned her back to him once more and he stepped over to her, leaned down and whispered, "Little liar. Don't try and start something with me just because you didn't have the willpower to stay out of my bed."

"Willpower?" She inhaled the word, then almost strangled on her anger.

Cord grinned and his eyes sparkled as he watched her cheeks grow pink. He wanted nothing more at that moment than to take her in his arms.

Get control of yourself, Shelley. She took a deep breath, glared at him and said, "I'm going jogging."

"Wait!" Cord wasn't through with his tormenting and felt deprived that his prey was getting way.

Shelley was halfway out of the kitchen and threw

over her shoulder, "If you want to join me, you'd better hurry up."

SHE NEVER EXPECTED him to take her up on her offer, but just before she turned off the blacktop lane onto the dirt road, she heard his pounding footsteps behind her. A cruel smile touched her lips. He'd been ill and was probably in no condition to keep up. She picked up speed. The sudden thought that he'd also get a firsthand dose of Napoleon sent her feelings of smug satisfaction soaring. She'd show him.

He caught up with her on the dirt road. She glanced sideways, liking the easy way his body moved along, the confidence and grace in his stride. The morning sun touched his chestnut hair, bringing to life the red highlights, and she wondered if it was true that redheads were hot tempered. Anthony had very seldom lost control, but maybe that was because he didn't care enough about anything to get upset. After a while they came to the end of the road before it intersected with the main highway and turned around, heading back the way they'd come. "How many miles is your route?" Cord asked.

Shelley frowned. He wasn't in the least breathless and she increased her speed some. How long could the man last? "About five miles." Cord nodded and her eyes narrowed. "Do you run much?" She consciously kept the breathlessness from her voice. Sweat rolled down her sides, her headband was soaked and her eyes stung from the salty moisture that escaped the thick cloth.

"Oh, I only jog a couple of times a week."

"How many miles?" she snapped.

"Eight, maybe ten. I play a lot of handball, too."

Shelley slowed, realizing it was useless to try to wear him down. She should have guessed, should have known by the way he was built. A body like his didn't come from sitting behind a desk or going to the gym a couple of days a week. But it galled her that she couldn't get the better of him. Then she heard it, a quick snapping of dry twigs in the bushes alongside the road. The sound gave her an extra spurt of energy. Napoleon was stalking them. Now Cord would see what a vicious creature he really was.

She tore her gaze from the rutted road and hurriedly glanced ahead to get her bearings. The turn to the black-top lane that led to the house was just ahead. Her eyes darted past Cord, following the line of the dry gully that bordered their path.

The muted sounds of morning were nothing more than nature's whispering, making their heavy breathing and the rhythmic noise of their feet hitting the hard-packed dirt road seem jarring in the stillness. Small puffs of dust rose from their steps, leaving the road behind dotted with rising clouds. Was that a flash of white along the line of bushes? It was. The damn gander was heading for his usual position of attack. A silly smile bloomed on Shelley's face, and she struggled to get it in check before Cord glanced over and saw.

They were almost there. Their shoes just touched the black surface of the lane when she got a clear view of her feathered nemesis…but something was terribly wrong. The white monster was just squatting there, quaking like an imbecile as they pounded by. Where was the attack he'd inflicted on her every morning? Where was the honking, the hissing, the snapping at her heels that drove her crazy with fear?

Cord's laughter snapped her head around. She glared

at the gander and yelled over her shoulder, "Peking duck!"

Napoleon honked, hissed, then disappeared back into the brown-tipped bushes.

Shelley threw another look at Cord and found he had stopped some ways back, laughing so hard he couldn't go on. She jogged in place for a few minutes, trying to think of something clever to say. Nothing came to mind that wouldn't make her appear an even bigger idiot, so she spun around and sprinted to the house.

The instant the echo of the front door slamming had died away, Cord followed Shelley into the house. By sheer willpower and a healthy amount of male pride, he bounded up the stairs, down the hall, through his bedroom and into the bathroom. Once the door was firmly shut behind him, he collapsed against its cool surface, closed his eyes and slid to the tiled floor.

He expected his heart to burst from his chest at any moment. Sweat literally poured off him in small rivers as he crawled toward the shower and reached for the cold water knob. He was going to have to find a way to reward that damn gander. Just a few more steps at the pace Shelley had set and he would have keeled over on his face.

The icy spray switched to tepid far too soon. Cord rose shakily to his feet. He definitely wasn't going to get conned into another race with Shelley until he was in better shape. As he stepped out of the shower and began to towel off, his thoughts flew back to last night. He really shouldn't have lost control and made love to her. Shelley deserved better than he had to offer—if he had anything to offer at all.

The past had been ideal for him to hide behind. He'd managed to shove his troubles away, and that had all but ruined one marriage. Shelley had the right to know what she was getting into. He slipped into his jeans, quickly pulled a multicolored polo shirt over his head and left the room, tucking in the material as he went. What he had to tell Shelley was going to be the hardest thing he'd ever done, especially knowing her views on the subject of marriage and family.

SHELLEY, CLEAN AND REFRESHED from her run and bath, stood before the library door. She ran her hands nervously up and down her thighs, feeling the soft worn material of her jeans warm under the friction. The door remained shut and she continued to stare. Then, as if a dam of emotions were let loose inside her, she relaxed and sighed with relief. Somehow, making love to Cord had severed her last remaining ties to Anthony. There was little sense in the way she felt or the reason behind it, but there it was—she was rid of him for good. The fear, the love and the agony had all been washed away last night. Now she could face the room of unpacked boxes, knowing she no longer harbored any secret yearnings for Anthony.

She reached out, clasped the cold brass knob, turned it and pushed the door open. One step, then another, and just as she was about to take the third she stopped, her mind suddenly assailed with doubts.

Cord eased up behind Shelley, watching as she gathered her courage. When he saw her pause after her first couple of steps, he gently laid his hand on her shoulder, letting his fingers smooth the lime-green material of her tank-top.

Shelley relaxed under his touch, reached up over her shoulder and grasped his hand like a lifeline. The past was fading, her future was standing right behind her.

She froze, her eyes widening at what she had just admitted to herself. It couldn't be! One night couldn't make that much difference, could it? It was too fast, wasn't it? Coming on the heels of everything that had happened to her, that was still happening, she couldn't allow her hormones to run wild or let her emotions get out of hand. She needed time to think clearly, to analyze the situation.

Yet, space and freedom did not have first priority on her agenda now, nor would they anytime soon unless her search turned up Anthony's records—or the lack of evidence that would dispel Nick's theory. Then Cord wouldn't have a reason to stick around; he'd be gone, back to his own life and friends...and women. Now why did that thought make her insides tighten with a sick dread?

Well, Shelley my girl, this is another fine mess you've gotten yourself into. No sooner are you out of one disastrous relationship than you jump feet-first into another. You don't care one little bit for Cord. As much as she tried to convince herself of that, the wonderful feeling was there, warm, secure and growing inside.

"Where's the typewriter?"

She shook herself out of her thoughts and laughed. "Somewhere behind those boxes. If you'll move one for me, I'll start going through it." Thirty minutes later she was sitting on the floor, the contents of the carton spilled around her as she listened to the steady clicking of the typewriter.

"Hey, Shelley," Cord called out, never stopping the flow of words onto the paper. "Is Milly and Ruby's last name spelled with one *L* or two?"

"Cord, you can't use their names in your article. They'd die!"

"I'll clear it with them first. But this story is about more than just prejudices, Shelley. It's about small towns in general. I'd forgotten what a delight they are. The state might change, even the country, but small towns basically stay the same. There's something special here. I want to capture its essence and let my readers see the other half of life away from the city. Maybe some of them need reminding of where they came from and how to return to some of those old-fashioned values."

She picked up a folder containing a year's bank statements and began to thumb through them. "That's all well and good, Cord, but you still can't use Milly's and Ruby's names. They'll never allow it."

"I think you're wrong. They'll be thrilled to be mentioned in an international magazine. I'll talk them into it."

Shelley sighed and shook her head at his self-confidence, or was it arrogance? "You'd best do a lot of research before you write that article. You know absolutely nothing about small towns."

"I *have* traveled all over the world."

"Makes no difference. You still don't know about people who have lived in tightly knit communities all their lives."

The typing stopped. "Okay, I'll bite. What makes you think Milly or Ruby wouldn't like to be in my article?"

"Because they're ladies to the tips of their white gloves and sensible shoes, Cord. They're from a different generation. A generation who believed the only time ladies' names should appear in the paper was at marriage or death."

The typing resumed without further comment and

Shelley went back to what she was doing. She dumped all the papers in the box, closed it and pulled over another one.

Cord continued making the necessary notes for his article—points to check and names of people to talk to. "You seem to know a lot about small towns, this one in particular. Strange, considering you're from California."

"Ahh," she breathed, grinning to herself. "But you forget, *old world traveler*. Carmel is a small town and I'm a small-town girl. Besides, I came here several times with my mother when she visited her sister. When I grew older my trips weren't so frequent, but my aunt wrote us faithfully every month and filled us in on all the gossip. We always looked forward to her letters. You should have seen the commotion around our house...."

Cord's head snapped up when he realized that she had trailed off. A second later he heard a watery sniffle, and shoving back his chair, he quickly maneuvered around the stacked furniture and boxes. Another sniffle reached him as he rounded a wooden crate marked "Fragile."

"Shelley?" She was sitting cross-legged on the floor, her back to him and her head bent over an open album on her lap. "Hey, what's the matter?"

Shelley swiped at her wet cheeks with the back of her hand. "My wedding album," she explained as he hunkered down beside her. "I just realized that I'm homesick."

The constriction around his chest loosened. She wasn't crying over Anthony, but her family. Looking down, the muscle along his jaw began to work spasmodically as he looked at the picture. His gaze didn't take in the people in the family photo; instead he homed in on his twin brother. "What was he like?"

Shelley turned a page in the book showing her and Anthony standing, smiling happily as if they had just finished their vows. "Charming, loving, funny. Self-centered, unfaithful, cruel." She turned another page. They had cut the wedding cake her father had made and were feeding each other. "Intelligent, fearless, reckless. A coward—"

"Shelley," Cord interrupted gently, afraid his questions would break the thread of communication between them and send her back into herself. "You've repeatedly contradicted yourself."

"That was Anthony. Impossible to pin down, to understand or to figure out."

"Why did you stay with him?" He had promised himself he wouldn't ask about her life with his brother, but he couldn't go on not knowing what it was that made a woman as savvy, as strong as Shelley, marry a man he considered a weakling. His next question was asked with a hard edge to his voice, an anger he found hard to conceal. "After you knew what he was, that he was being unfaithful, why the hell didn't you kick him out? It seems so out of character that you'd take that sort of humiliation."

She looked up from the book in her lap, her jade-green eyes dark with confusion. "It's hard to explain. Harder even to believe how Anthony could manipulate people and their emotions. I would confront him with his infidelities and somehow he'd make me feel that it was my fault, that if he strayed it was because I wasn't the wife I should be. Mind you, he would never accuse me openly. It was what he didn't say, his clever use of words that could make me doubt myself. If I caught him in an outright lie, one he couldn't back out of, he'd tell me he lied because he didn't want to hurt me or make me feel guilty, which of course would immediately make me feel as guilty as hell.

"Then there was another side to him—the clown. I could be so angry with him I'd want to kill him. Somehow, when I was on the very edge of losing my cool and walking out on him, he'd do some crazy thing and make me laugh. He could always make me laugh." She shook her head, still puzzled at how she'd been taken in and used. "It would take me days to get some perspective and realize what he'd done, but by that time it was over and there was usually something else he'd done and was trying to wriggle out of."

Shelley glanced down at the album, feeling that her explanations were inadequate. No one could verbalize how Anthony could bend people to suit his purpose without them being aware they were being made puppets. Yet, there was one act he'd committed that he could never have talked his way out of—treason. Treason had ultimately cost him his life.

"Were you very much in love with him?" He didn't want to ask, but had to know.

Shelley looked away from Cord, trying to hide her own faults and weaknesses from this man who had burst into her life and turned it upside down. "In love? If you had asked me that a year or even six months ago I might have said yes. Now, I wonder if I was only in love with the idea of love and of having an old dream come true."

"What dream was that?" Some instinct warned him what was coming and a nauseous sensation hit his stomach.

Her eyes cut sideways and her mouth quirked up at one corner. "You promise you won't laugh?"

"Cross my heart."

"All my life I've wanted nothing more than to be a wife and mother. Now don't have a heart attack or tell me that all womankind will come and lynch me if they discover I've betrayed them. I know all the arguments, the scorn, the ridicule. I heard it all when I was very young. As a matter of fact, I think I heard it so much from my friends that I developed a complex and learned to keep my mouth shut. So, I went to college, became an overachiever, studied and worked hard, and graduated with an MBA at the top of my class.

"Like all my contemporaries, I charged out into the business world, married and for a year became Superwoman. That's no easy task, Cord. I worked long physically and mentally exhausting hours, cooked, did the laundry, paid the bills and tried to be a loving and exciting wife. I hated every minute of it, too. Don't get me wrong. I admire women who can accomplish all these things, but I'm just not cut from the same cloth. I wanted a loving husband and a family, not a full-time career and an empty life."

"Did Anthony know how you felt?" He reached out and turned the last page of the wedding album.

Shelley's voice turned cold. "Yes. I made it clear before we married. He convinced me that he wanted the same. It wasn't till after we were married awhile that I learned differently. I should have left him then." She smiled, her mouth thinning into a cynical line.

"Anthony and Sandra sound as if they should have met. She knew about the ups and downs of my job, the travel, the out-of-the-way places. I made the mistake of assuming that because she was a military brat, used to moving around the country, she was willing to come with me whenever it was possible. I also made it crystal clear before we married that I didn't want any children.'' He grimaced, remembering his foolishness. ''I married one woman, but left the church with another. She started putting down roots, complaining of loneliness when I was gone, yet refused to go with me. Then she started harping on wanting a family. God!'' Cord ran his fingers through his hair in frustration and anger. ''I was at the height of my career and she demanded I find another vocation so I could stay home and father children.''

A stillness fell between them. Cord stared off into the distance, lost in his thoughts, tortured by what he knew he was going to have to tell Shelley. How had things progressed so quickly without him realizing? Lately he'd been living on his emotions, a luxury he hadn't afforded himself for years. He realized at that moment he despised Sandra for making him feel less than he was. Now that hate was shared with Anthony, also. He hated him, his brother, a man he'd never known. He'd learned to live with his memories of Sandra, but now there was Anthony and his own feelings for Shelley. The truth would have to come out or he would have to sever the relationship before it really got started. *Easier said than done, old man,* he mocked himself. *Especially when you've hidden behind the truth most of your adult life, telling yourself it didn't make any difference. But it does—it did with Sandra so much so that she divorced you.*

Shelley snapped the album shut and tossed it back in the box. ''I've had enough for today.'' Without another word she rose stiffly and rushed from the room.

He retrieved the big leather book and turned to the last page, wanting to take a good look at his brother and also to study the people in Shelley's life, the people she cared about. He scanned the line of elegantly dressed wedding guests, picking out family members without any trouble because of their obvious resemblance. His gaze stopped at an exotic-looking, dark-haired woman. Slanted jet eyes stared out of a sultry face. Wide lips smiled slyly, pulling creamy skin over Slavic cheekbones. Dee Radford, he thought, and wondered how he knew. The woman was a sexy piece of work, yet there was something in her expression that he didn't like—a look of deceit. Remembering a couple of pictures farther back, he hurriedly flipped through till he found what he was looking for. They were of Shelley, Anthony and Dee. The trio were happily smiling, but it was Dee's expression, the way she was looking at Anthony, that made him draw a loud breath. He wondered if Nick suspected that Anthony and Dee Radford had had an affair. My God, did Shelley have any idea? He decided she didn't. There was no doubt in his mind, though. He'd made a life's work of studying people through a camera lens, of catching what they tried to hide.

Cord rose, stopping only long enough to massage the cramps that knotted his calf muscles. When he finally relieved the pain and ceased cursing the pride that had forced him to overdo this morning's run, he set out to find Shelley. Ten minutes later, after searching the house, he heard a faint clink of glass hitting glass and the tinkle of ice. He followed the sound out the front door to the side porch and the only pool of shade around. She was curled up on a white wooden swing suspended from rafters, holding a sweating glass filled with ice cubes and lemonade.

Shelley looked up, pointed to the big pitcher and another glass and resumed her swinging.

The swing squeaked and groaned with his weight. He propped his bare feet on the porch railing, took a gulp of the sweet-tart lemonade and closed his eyes with the gently rocking motion. Now was the time to tell her, but the words wouldn't come. He opened his eyes and stared off into the distance. Disgust at his own cowardice lined his brow. Then movement caught his attention and he straightened a little. "Shelley, there's a car coming down the lane." He strained through the glare, finally shading his eyes to get a better view. "Would you look at that!" He leaned forward, his gaze glued to the shining black car coming to a stop in front of the house. "A mint condition 1949 Cadillac." As he watched, the door opened and a tall, thin old man slowly eased out. The contrast of nappy, snow-white hair and skin the color of milk chocolate was startling, bringing Cord to his feet. This was no Russian enemy.

Shelley stood beside Cord, smiling. "Hello, Louis. How are you today?"

"That you, Miss Shelley?" He didn't wait for an answer. "I'm tolerable."

"Sure is hot," she said.

"It be that. Why, on the way over here I saw two trees fighting over a dog." He ignored their laughter, leaned back into the car and carefully pulled out a large cardboard box. "Weather be hot as the devil's breath." He moved slowly toward the porch steps and Cord met him, relieving him of his burden. "Miss Milly and Miss Ruby sent you that strawberry shortcake they promised. There's some strawberry jam for Mr. Tho and his wife."

"Louis, this is Cord, my…husband."

Louis shook Cord's hand and studied him with alert velvet-brown eyes. "Heard about you."

"Did you? I bet the Misses Randall are a well of information?"

"Yes sir, they're that." The two men smiled their understanding, then chuckled together.

She was piqued. It had taken years of visits to get more than ten words from Louis. Here Cord was practically bosom buddies after only a few minutes. "Would you like some lemonade, Louis?"

"No, I thank you, but Miss Milly said she had a bad feeling this morning. Something ugly was brewing and I was to get to town and put my ear to the ground." He clucked his tongue at them as he made his way back to the car and climbed in. "You shouldn't have shamed Tinkle Ferris in front of the townsfolk. He's a real peckerwood, Miss Shelley. You sure be careful when you're alone, you hear?" He didn't wait for an answer, but started the old car with one try and drove off down the lane without a backward glance.

Cord balanced the box on one arm and dipped his finger into the thick whipped cream. He poked his finger in his mouth and closed his eyes, making sounds of ecstasy as he slowly pulled it out.

"Stop that and go put it in the refrigerator," Shelley snapped, angry with her reaction to the suggestive sounds he made. Her thoughts were absolutely lascivious! When Cord came back outside and resumed his seat at the end of the swing, she turned her head, pretending she was interested in the line of trees and thick vegetation in the distance.

"Do you want to talk about last night?"

"There's nothing to say. I told you before it meant nothing."

Cord sighed irritably. He was tired of playing games and had decided to have it out with her before she actually convinced herself that what had happened between them was of little importance. He was just about to blurt it out when Nick rounded the corner wearing a grim expression that could only spell trouble. Cord dropped his bare feet from the porch railing and sat up expectantly.

"Get your shoes, Cord. Some neighboring cattle have broken through a fence and are attempting to drain one of Lee's water reservoirs. That water's crucial to the produce crop and the pecan trees."

Shelley came to her feet and was in motion toward the door when Nick's voice snapped her to a stop.

"There's no sense in you coming, Shelley. We can handle it. Besides, it's too damn hot for you to be running after cattle that are dropping from thirst and could stampede at the slightest noise."

She bristled. "I'll have you know—"

"Later. Just this once do as I damn well tell you."

"Nick..." Cord warned.

"Ah, crap. I don't have time to soothe her ruffled feathers. Just please do as I say. Go in the house, stay cool and lock the doors till we get back." He glanced at Cord, his green eyes as sharp and hard as ice. "You coming?" He didn't wait for Cord's answer but took off at a run.

Cord watched Nick disappear around the side of the house, then he made a dash through the door, retrieving his running shoes and ran down the steps. "You'll do as Nick says?"

"Yes." Her next words stopped him in his tracks. "Cord, I don't take birth control pills."

Cord froze. His silence and stillness was like a vise around her throat as she waited.

Then, as if life had suddenly been breathed into his

body, Cord shrugged. "No problem. Don't worry about it." And he was gone, putting as much distance between them as he could.

Shelley stared numbly after him, totally floored by his lack of reaction. Then a flash of white caught her attention, erasing all thoughts from her mind. Napoleon had come out of nowhere and was running beside Cord, his honking audible even from where she stood. Shelley grinned, her heart leaping with the thought that Cord was finally going to find out what it felt like to be attacked by that feathered Lucifer.

She raised her hand, shielding her eyes from the sun's glare. The damn gander wasn't after Cord. He was going to join the men in their game of chasing the cattle out of the field. Unable to stop the childish reaction to her spurt of disappointment and anger, she cupped her hands around her mouth and yelled at the top of her voice, "Fricasseed goose!"

Napoleon suddenly leaped higher in the air, as if someone had touched him with an electric prod. His wings flapped wildly and his quacking was louder than usual.

Shelley snickered. With a satisfied smirk on her face, she picked up the pitcher of lemonade and walked into the house.

"WHAT DO YOU MEAN, the fence was deliberately cut?" Shelley's gaze shifted from Nick to Cord, but her demand lacked conviction as she grinned at the two men opposite her. They both were somewhat worse for wear; tired from their long hours running thirsty cattle away from the water reservoir, well fed, as evidenced by the high pile of barbecued rib bones stacked on their plates, and less sober than they would have liked from the cold beer Shelley plied them with. Nick belched, covered his mouth and apologized profusely for his rudeness. "Another beer, Nick?" She was out for information and smiled sweetly, but her jade-green eyes had deepened to emerald with frustration at the two close-mouthed men. She hadn't figured out yet if they were being pigheaded in not telling her all or if they were just teasing her. "More beer, Nick?"

"Sure. Why not?" He accepted another frosted glass and cold bottle, making a production of carefully tilting the glass and pouring the amber liquid down the side. "I haven't had this much to drink in ten years. And that time was a disaster." His eyes narrowed suspiciously on Shelley. "Are you trying to get me drunk?"

"Of course."

He looked at Cord, grinning crookedly. "Won't do her any good. I don't talk, drunk or sober. Course, if history repeats itself, I wouldn't remember if I did talk. No tolerance to alcohol at all; that's why I don't touch the stuff anymore—causes dreams. Lovely dreams of an angel with the sweetest smile you've ever seen and a soft voice that could lure the devil from hell."

Shelley coughed, trying to cover her laughter at Nick's uncharacteristic behavior and loose tongue. "You're drinking now. Maybe your dream will come back."

"Not likely—don't deserve it." He frowned at his plate, set down the half-empty glass and rose slowly to his feet. "Wonderful dinner, Shelley, but I think it's time I left." He wobbled carefully to the door, then was gone.

Shelley and Cord burst out laughing.

"You did that deliberately, Shelley. I saw how many times you exchanged his empty bottle of beer for a full one. Nick's going to realize your trickery in the morning and there'll be hell to pay. He's a dangerous man, honey, and you'd better stop picking on him.''

She crossed her arms over her breast and tried to look severe. "Are you going to answer my question? Every time I've asked, either you or Nick have changed the subject.''

"What question's that?"

"Cord!" she snapped, exasperated with his calculating manner.

He grinned, placed his elbows on the table and rested his chin on his folded hands. "Are you referring to the loose cattle and the fence?''

"You know I am."

"There's not much to tell. Nick and I found the hole where the cattle got through. He showed me the three strands of barbed wire that had been cut. Someone tried to sabotage the plantation. From what Lee told me those two water reservoirs are absolutely vital to the crops if it doesn't rain soon.''

Shelley pushed back her chair and climbed to her feet. "I guess there's no doubt who cut the fence?''

"None, as far as Nick, Lee and I are concerned. Nick is going to have a talk with the sheriff in the morning. He's not exactly thrilled about having to deal with town problems, nor does he want anyone snooping around where they don't belong. Hey…where are you going?'' He'd gained his feet hurriedly as she turned her back on him and was leaving the kitchen.

Shelley stopped, glanced over her shoulder, a smile of mischief lifting the corners of her mouth. "It's been a long day. I'm going to bed.'' The smile broadened as her gaze swept the kitchen. Dirty pots, pans and dishes were stacked in the sink. The roasting pan with barbecue sauce that had turned to red glue was sitting on the counter along with the rest of the dirty dishes. It was a fine mess. "Looks to me like you'll be a while cleaning up the kitchen. So, I'll say good-night now." With that she quickly left the room, but not before she heard the low groan and the whispered cursing.

COOL SHEETS CARESSED HER, the softness as seductive as a man's hand moving in light circles over her stomach, then slipping downward. She wanted to shut off her outraged thoughts at the invasion and continue to float in the sensations that coursed through her body. Strong fingers touched her, meeting the warm wetness they had invoked, and she sucked in air at the heat that raced through her. Shelley forced herself to roll over, her eyes glittering with a warring mixture of desire and anger. "What do you think you're doing?"

"Obvious isn't it? I'm trying to make love to you."

"You're in *my* bed."

"Well, yes, Shelley. To make love I'd either be here or you'd be in my bed."

"That's not what I mean. Stop that!" Her hand dived under the covers and grasped his wrist. "I didn't invite you—"

"Did you think you could cut me off? Push me aside and forget what we'd had? It's not that simple, Shelley. I'm not a pubescent boy to be taunted or led around by his zipper. You can't just switch your feelings off like hot and cold running water…not on me." He planted light kisses along her shoulder, up her neck, then claimed her mouth. "You don't really want me to go, do you? Even if it means nothing to you, you don't want me to stop, do you?"

"No." She couldn't lie, not with her body turning

her protests into soft whimpers of pleasure at his every touch. Besides, she wanted him, suddenly knowing that his being here meant everything to her. She wanted to wake to a new day...and a new life in his arms.

CHAPTER TEN

FOR THE FIRST TIME in her life she was content.

In the past seven days, ever since Cord crawled into her bed demanding she accept his presence there and in her life, she was happier than she'd ever been or dreamed possible. Her life with Anthony was now only fading memories; the future something to look forward to with eager anticipation. It had all happened so fast, this change, but surprisingly even to her, there were no lingering doubts to ruin her joy.

Shelley cocked her head, smiling as she listened to the far-off sound of a typewriter clicking away at an astonishing speed. The male myth never prepared her for such efficiency at a keyboard. Then she scolded herself for being a female chauvinist. Gingerly she poured lemon oil onto a folded cloth and began moving it in long fluid strokes over the oak dining room table. She always did her best thinking when she was dusting.

The typing stopped and she paused, her breath hanging hopefully in the back of her throat. When the pecking resumed, she sighed with disappointment. The intimacy between her and Cord had gone far beyond a physical relationship and she knew, though he was hard at work, that he had thought about her in that moment's pause.

Strange how they had found sheer joy in discussing and arguing every topic that came to mind. Even their silences were comfortable, without strain or awkwardness. There had been no talk of tomorrows, yet there was an unspoken understanding they both acknowledged. For the past couple of days they seemed to have fallen into the habit of talking in terms of ''we'' and ''us'' instead of the singular ''I'' and ''me.'' Soon the silences would no longer be enough, and they would have to speak their thoughts aloud.

She needed a commitment, an open declaration. But that would come in time, and she was determined not to rush it. She'd take one day, one night at a time until the business of Anthony and what he'd done was cleared up. Then she and Cord would talk about their future.

Shelley paused in her work, staring off into nothingness, biting her lip in thought. There was only one major problem: Cord had said he didn't want children. She couldn't understand why—he was so good with Robbie. The frown that lined her brow deepened over the puzzle. Had his first wife's constant nagging turned him off the idea? Her fingers tightened on the cloth she was holding. Damn it, she wanted children so much. Maybe what's-her-name just went about it all wrong. It wasn't a subject to bring up in the heat of an argument, and from what Cord had said that's about all they did. She was sure Cord would change his mind someday, but it was definitely a subject that had to be explored as soon as possible.

The oven timer went off. She gathered up her dust cloth and the bottle of lemon oil and headed for the kitchen. The aroma of chocolate cake had begun to invade the entire house, and she knew it wouldn't be long before Cord was seduced from his work to lick the icing from the spoon and the bowl—if he could beat Robbie to it.

Once the two round pans were cooling on a wire rack Shelley let her thoughts drift again, chuckling to herself, thinking that daydreaming had become second nature to her lately.

Anthony had made her laugh, but Cord was *really* fun. Because she was feeling totally herself for the first time in years, she was starting to do outrageous things. As the boredom of farm life began to grate on her nerves Shelley took it upon herself to get into as much trouble as possible. She finally made Cord admit that the forced imprisonment was getting to him a little, even though he was occupied with writing his article. But Nick, when faced with their dilemma, proved to be unsympathetic. Because of his scorn Shelley had begun a campaign to drive the hard-bitten man as crazy as she was becoming. At first Cord was reluctant to go along with her tricks, but he soon joined in, supposedly to make sure she didn't get into any real trouble.

They started by taking long walks at odd times of the day without telling their warden where they were going. The first couple of times Nick had found them and they'd returned to the farmhouse. Later he would only meet them at the door with a daunting scowl and a few very original curse words.

One day Cord had managed to hot-wire her car and they'd gone to town and the ice-cream parlor. Nick found them there indulging in banana splits and drove them home, his silence and ominous glares something to behold.

The topping on the cake, the coup de grace, was when Shelley decided they would once again steal the car. But this time they would venture farther afield. She was sick and tired of her own cooking and hungry for a different environment, starved for people around her. She desperately wanted to dress up, feel feminine again, so she talked a none too reluctant Cord into going to Houston. It took an hour of sweet-talking, but she managed to get him to call a restaurant and make reservations.

Cord had realized if he didn't accompany Shelley, she would take off on her own, and though she shrugged off the danger they might be in, he never forgot. Better that he be around to act as her guard than for her to execute her schemes all alone. They would have to leave early, he had told her, so he could stop at Neiman-Marcus and buy himself a suit. He'd only brought casual clothes. Because of Nick's constant prodding and his earlier illness he hadn't thought to pack anything more formal.

For days they planned, trying to hide their smug elation from Nick until they thought they would explode with laughter. Then, toward darkness on the appointed evening and dressed fit to kill, they arrived at Tony's, one of Houston's most exclusive restaurants. Each morsel was savored with a sinful enjoyment. They had reveled in the service, the atmosphere and the quiet, elegant crowd. They had been in heaven…until Nick arrived.

Still dressed in work shirt and jeans he had pushed his way past the maître d' without a word or a care for the outraged glances from the elite clientele. Pulling out a chair, Nick had joined them. Not a word passed his lips, none was needed.

She had never seen a man look so coldly dangerous. His crocodile grin barely hid the turmoil and anger brewing beneath the surface. Within minutes they had left the restaurant with Nick following them home, his truck's bumper only inches from theirs.

"What are you smiling about?"

Shelley jumped and swung around. "I was just thinking about our wonderful night at Tony's."

"And Nick?"

She laughed. "Yes, and Nick. Is he still very angry?"

Cord shook his head and gathered her into his arms. "Shelley, Shelley. You must ignore these urges to take digs at Nick. I don't think you realize your last trick just about pushed him to the limit. To send him to a lingerie shop in Houston to buy you some underwear and a bra was one thing, but to send him to the store for tampons! He almost choked over having to go. You went too far with that one, my girl. He told me to inform you that one more of your tricks and he'd see to it *personally* that you'd remember him for the rest of your life. What the hell possessed you? And don't give me that innocent look. You didn't need the things you sent him for, you did it just to be mean."

"I know," she whispered, and snuggled closer, "and I'm mortally ashamed, too."

"Liar!"

Shelley threw back her head and gazed up into navy blue eyes sparkling with laughter. "I'm just trying to humanize him some."

Cord couldn't hold back a deep chuckle as he set her away from him. "The man's mortified, Shelley, that's what he is."

"I think when he was young, his life must have been a living hell with his father. I bet every time he was hurt, a little of him died inside until he realized if he didn't do something about his life he was either going to end up destroying himself or killing someone else.

He escaped his environment and changed, built a wall around himself, but he went from one extreme to another. Cord, there's a sensitive man beneath that iron exterior.''

Cord snorted in disbelief.

"It's true. Just look at the changes so far—the way he's been with Robbie and Lee. Nick needs a wife and children to soften him up.''

"Another one of your cure-alls, Shelley? Stop trying to understand a man like Nick. Just stay away from him and quit needling him.''

She cocked her head, looking at him with laughing eyes. "Jealous?''

Cord dismissed her question with a quirk of his mouth and his gaze quickly bounced away from hers. He decided to change the subject and eyed the cakes on the counter. "Are you going to ice those soon?''

"Not until they cool, why?''

"You haven't seen Robbie around, have you?''

"Cord! He's just a little boy.''

"With a huge appetite! Speaking of appetites…'' He reached for her and managed to grab the tail of the shirt she'd stolen from him. "I wonder why women look so sexy in men's clothing?''

She snatched the material from his hands. "Are you going to help me go through those boxes of books or not?''

He gave her an intent look that let her know what he'd really like to help her do. She danced out of his reach. He sighed. "Lead on.'' Shooing her ahead of him, he watched the sway of his shirt and the way the skintight jeans hugged her thighs. He would never get his fill of her. What amazed him more than anything was the change in Shelley. He wondered if she even realized the metamorphosis. What was it she had said? That she was the calm, cool one in the family. He wanted to laugh and hand her a mirror when she was involved in some discussion. She was volatile, expressive, full of passion, and he loved her dearly.

"Must we go through the packed books, Cord? If I haven't found anything by now, I really don't think I'm going to. Anthony would never have hidden anything in my books. He knew I was always reading or rereading."

"Nick says everything, every page. Let's humor him for a while, okay?"

"Nick! 'Nick says,'" she mimicked sarcastically over her shoulder as she approached the library with Cord right behind her. "He won't even let me answer the telephone. I can't even pick it up and say hello!" Throwing open the library door, she grabbed a heavy box, scowled at Cord when he tried to help, dragged the carton over to a clear space and flopped down. "Ever since the cut fence and Nick's visit to the sheriff the phone has all but rung off the wall. It's torture, Cord," she wailed. "To think that just a few steps away lies a whole world of people—voices, someone to talk to."

Cord laughed, sat down beside her and began tearing the box open. He handed her a book. "Fan through this and don't think about it."

She snatched the book from his hand, giving him a hateful glare. "I'll bet everyone in town has called here." The small community had heard of the fence-cutting incident and were taking sides. The tide of emotions had turned. For years, most of the townspeople had been as hostile toward Lee and Vo as the small group that kept the hatred high. Later, Shelley sensed an atmospheric change to a wait-and-see attitude as Tinkle Ferris and his rabble-rousers harassed the Vietnamese couple. The townspeople neither condoned nor interfered.

Then the fence-cutting episode, combined with the heat, the near-drought conditions and the community's inbred respect for water and land had been the last straw. Tempers flared, sides were taken. After all, the townsfolk told Cord and Nick and anyone else who'd listen, Shelley owned the plantation, Lee was simply the foreman and he only leased the produce fields. They could accept that. The wind of prejudice had shifted, blowing with Lee and Vo instead of against them. Well, almost. There were still a few townspeople and Tinkle to worry about.

Shelley picked up another book, fanned through it and tossed it into a nearby box. "You even get to call your office and family," she mumbled. "But not me."

Cord tossed her another book. "Buck up. Surely we'll find something soon, if there's anything to find. Either way we're getting close to leaving this hellishly hot place."

Shelley smiled thinly at his placating attempt. "I seem to have lost my cool lately, haven't I? Maybe I'm more like my family than I thought." She sent him a mock scowl. "Or maybe you bring out the worst in me."

"The best."

"Could be." Their gazes locked and Shelley felt her cheeks turn hot with the first flush of pure lust. Would she ever get enough of him? She hoped not. "How's the article coming along?"

Cord acknowledged her attempt to get their minds off their desire for each other and clucked his tongue at the intervention. "Fine. You were right about the Misses Randall. They were horrified at the thought of their names being mentioned in my article. One good thing has happened, though. Writing down Lee's struggle to get out of Vietnam and to America was enough to make him decide that this time he was going to take a stand. He and Vo are not running anymore."

"Good." Shelley picked up a book and flipped through it, then slammed it shut. "Cord, what are you going to do when this is all over?"

"First of all, get my company straightened out. I keep having nightmares of what my competent sister is doing. I've left her in charge before. She tends to make changes without discussing them with anyone else in the company."

Shelley's forehead began to line with concern. The answer wasn't what she'd hoped for. His next question made her feel as if something heavy and solid had settled in the middle of her stomach.

"What about your job? Are you going back?"

She looked down at the book in her hand and absently fanned the pages. "I should, but I don't think I can." Shaking her head, she said, "I don't know what I'll do. So much has happened." She glanced up, trying to hide her feelings. "Maybe I'll go home for a while."

Cord laid aside the book he held, folded his arms over the top of the box, resting his chin on his hands. "Your family will be glad for the visit. Maybe I could come along. I'd like to meet them."

The pain around her chest eased up a little, but she didn't want to appear too excited in case his invitation wasn't what it seemed. "You could. Dad would take you on a tour of the restaurant and make you taste everything. He'd want to tell you all about my childhood.

He'd lie to you and tell you I was an angel and his favorite, even though I'm not creative.''

"We could go see my family afterward." Cord grinned as Shelley set aside her book and, like him, folded her arms on the top of the box, resting her chin on her hands. "My dad will love you. Mom will hover, wanting to wait on you hand and foot. She'll call everyone, and the kids will drive you crazy with questions. My sisters will give you a hard time, they love to tease. But you're not to believe all the stories about how mean I was. They love to embarrass me."

"So do my brother and sister." She smiled dreamily, her head light with the picture he was painting.

"We could stay in San Francisco. That is, if you come. I'd take you to my office, introduce you around."

"I'd like that," she whispered.

"You'll like living in San Francisco. There's so much to do."

"We could go to the theater."

Cord grinned. "Of course. And the opera."

"The ballet."

"We could stay home, build a tremendous fire and make love." Cord waggled his eyebrows.

"And eat."

"And get fat."

"Never," she wailed. "We'll run."

"Would you mind living in a city that you need jogging shoes just to get around?"

"With you?" she asked bluntly.

"Of course. What have we been talking about?"

"I don't know really. Spell it out for me. Please, Cord, don't make me fill in the blanks. I need some solid emotional ground to stand on."

What had he done? Lord, how could he have let his

tongue run away with his head? Now was the time, he thought. Time to tell her and see if she ran or stayed. He sat up, leaned across the box and clasped Shelley's hand. "I shouldn't have let things go so far between us without telling you." He stopped, swallowed, realizing this was going to be the hardest thing he'd ever done. "Shelley, the reason my marriage fell apart was that I never told Sandra…I never saw any reason to tell her, she always said she didn't want any…damn." He'd never had such a difficult time getting words out of his mouth. "Shelley…I'm sterile. I have been since I was thirteen and got the mumps."

For a long second she inwardly flinched, grieving for the child she and Cord would never have. Then the remorse passed, and she was horrified remembering how she'd complimented him on his treatment of Robbie and the times she'd told him he should have his own children. She squeezed his hand. "Do you have anything against adoption?"

He was stunned. Her easy acceptance of the problem floored him. "How could I object to adoption? I'm adopted. But, Shelley, you'd better take some time to think about this—about us. You've wanted your own children so badly. You deserve everything life has to offer you."

"Cord. It's okay, really it is."

He couldn't believe his ears. There was a sharp stinging behind his eyelids, and he blinked to release the pain and fight any hint of moisture from surfacing. "Sandra wanted to experience being pregnant. She said it was every woman's desire to have a child."

There was so much raw hurt in his voice that Shelley wanted only to hold and comfort him. Pushing the box from between them, she scooted over and was immediately clasped in his arms. "Don't punish yourself, Cord. Not being able to produce a baby doesn't make you any less a man."

"Of course it does, Shelley. I'm physically incapable of giving you children, and there's no use wishing for a medical breakthrough. It will never happen for me...for us."

She touched his face, lightly tracing the lines of stress, wanting only to wipe them away and have him smiling at her again. "It doesn't matter."

"Now, maybe. But what about six months, a year or five years from now? Can you in all honesty tell me it won't matter then, that you won't be sorry?"

She let her fingertips linger over his lips a second, then pressed them against his mouth wanting to stop the flow of words. "I can't promise you I won't think about having children. No one can predict the future. I can't even say there won't be times when I'll regret never being able to have a child. But those will be fleeting moments, Cord. Surely you see that I'm only human, with all the human frailties? Problems can be worked out, Cord. If you really want to."

"Sandra—"

"Screw Sandra!"

"Shelley!" he scolded, but there was laughter in the gruff voice.

"I'm sick of that woman. She really did a number on you. It's obvious she wanted out of the marriage and used your sterility just to get her way."

Cord laughed out loud. She made him feel whole and more alive and vital than he had in years. His hands cupped her face tenderly, tilting her chin up. "You're sure about this?"

A stillness hung in the room; a hovering suspense

tightening her nerve endings till she wanted to scream, *Say it, say you love me!*

"Shelley…"

"What?" She tried to keep disappointment from lacing her voice.

"Are you sure?"

"Yes."

His mouth captured hers, his tongue a persistent invader as it explored the moist depths. When he pulled back, his lips only a whisper upon hers, he asked, "Before we take the final step, I want you to take a couple of days and think everything over."

"But, Cord…"

The sudden blare of the telephone shocked them apart. Shelley said a cuss word that made him laugh. "Let me answer it, Cord. Please." The ringing went on. "Please."

"No." He tried to get up, but Shelley held him down. There was a determined expression on her face. He grabbed her around the waist as she tried to climb over him, the temptation too much for her. "Shelley…"

"Just one small 'hello,'" she said, panting as she fought to wiggle out of his arms. "I'll change my voice. Listen." She said "hello" in a high little-girlish voice that started him laughing all over again. "Okay, I'll lower it." The ringing continued. "Cord!" she wailed, fighting harder to get out of his viselike hold on her. "I can't *stand* it."

Suddenly his mouth was on hers, both of them breathless from the struggle and their laughter. Under the passion that flared they went still, feeling with every nerve the desire that danced between them, drawing them closer. There was an urgency to touch warm flesh, a reckless disregard for buttons and material under their hands.

Cord's fingers hooked in the open neck of her shirt, pulling the pliant cotton apart with a quick jerk. He sat up, positioning her on his lap, opening the fabric farther so he could watch his hands cup each breast.

The look in Cord's eyes, the pleasure there, was almost painful to see. A tiny smile curved the ends of Shelley's lips as her gaze followed the descent of his head. His hair brushed her skin and she shivered, then she felt his mouth take a budding nipple in and worry it with his tongue. Fire curled in her insides and a throbbing began between her legs. Instinctively she pressed herself against him. He began a path of light kisses from one breast to the other. She arched toward his mouth, her body begging him to return to the hard sucking and the titillating sensation that shot through her with each caress. A low moan escaped her lips.

"Unbutton your jeans, Shelley."

She did as he asked, her fingers fumbling and shaking with their task. "What if someone comes?" Throwing a frantic but excited look around, she realized that the cocoon of boxes acted as a shield for them.

"That's their tough luck," he growled as his hand slid down her stomach, loving the way the flesh moved under his touch. His fingers caressed dark curls, then slipped lower into a wet warmness.

Shelley sucked in a strangled breath as he found her, but the whimper of pleasure died as his mouth clamped on hers. She moved against him and his hand as the unbearable burning sensation intensified.

"Move your hips, sweetheart," he said against her lips.

Dazed and throbbing all over, she opened her eyes,

shocked at the shaft of fierce anger that shot through her when he stopped.

"Your jeans are like a second skin. Help me get them off."

She stood on shaking legs, straddling him. The shirt she was wearing was hanging open, her jeans were un-zipped and yawning invitingly. She stepped to his side, peeled the jeans down and kicked them away. As she shucked her underwear she watched Cord, laying on the floor struggling to get his own jeans off. If she hadn't been so hot and wanting him so badly, she would have laughed at the scene.

Cord's fingers clasped around one of her ankles and she stepped back across him, proud and lithesome with a nipped-in waist and full high-tipped breasts—a body that called to him in the most primeval manner. She was magnificent, but still a mystery to him. He wanted to know every inch of her, to touch and taste and enjoy. Every time they made love he found something new and wonderful in the abandoned way she gave herself to him. His hands roamed up her inner thigh. Then, as he sat up, he brought his mouth to her, tasting her.

"Cord! Oh, Cord. I can't stand it, my legs are going to give out." It was true. Her knees were trembling so badly she felt she was going to fall over. She grabbed for his head, burying her fingers in his hair, torn be-tween pushing him away and pulling him closer. "Cord..." she moaned desperately until an electric shock engulfed her, folding her body and almost melt-ing her bones.

Cord leaned away, catching her and settling her on his lap, making her straddle him. "Sit up a second, Shelley."

She was like a wet noodle, every muscle limp and

unable to budge. Leaning against him, she waited for the weakness to pass. "I can't move, Cord."

He chuckled, clasped her face in his hands and kissed her deeply, then trailed his lips to her breast. The rasp of his tongue on her sensitive nipple made her hiss in her breath. "Lift up, sweetheart."

She felt his hand on her buttocks, squeezing gently, then he was inside her and she wrapped her arms around his neck, rhythmically moving her body with the help of his hands on her hips.

"Lord, you feel wonderful." Cord kissed her again, a wild meeting of their lips. "You taste good, too." He nibbled at her ear, his tongue tracing its shell shape. "Easy, love. Ride me slowly. Make it last forever."

But forever was a joke, a wish only for the chaste, not for two lovers locked together in the heat of passion. Shelley strained against him, then arched, bringing Cord's harsh breathing closer to her ear. Something went wild inside her, an insatiable urge to make him feel what he had done to her and the way blood sang through her veins. She took him in as deeply as she could, and smiled when he gasped her name.

Cord couldn't stand it. He buried himself in her, losing all sense of time and even of the woman straddling him. His world consisted of nothing but texture and sensations, and then, suddenly, it all exploded behind his eyelids.

Like the tattered ends of a storm, their breathing came in small gusty sighs. Exhausted, silent, each savored what had happened between them.

Magic, Shelley thought, *sheer magic.*

Devastating, Cord's mind drifted across the word. He rolled over and gently ran his fingers over her hot cheeks. ''We better get dressed. Someone might come in.''

She began to chuckle.

''What's so funny?'' He sat up, reaching for their jeans, threw hers at her and began to pull his on.

''A while ago you couldn't have cared less if someone walked in on us.''

Cord grinned guiltily. ''Didn't your father ever tell you a man will say anything, tell any lie to get a woman? At moments like that nothing matters but slaking one's desire.''

She shot him an arched look, struggling to get her underwear and jeans on. ''Are you trying to tell me something?''

''Now, Shelley, don't start putting words in my mouth. You know exactly what I was talking about.''

No, she didn't, and confusion marred her happiness. There seemed to be something going on under the surface of his words. ''What's eating you, Cord?''

''I've been thinking...''

The slamming of the back door threw them into a panic. Buttons, snaps and zippers eluded their fingers as they fought to finish dressing. Shelley's name echoed through the house. She cursed under her breath, realizing her shirt was buttoned wrong, her zipper was caught in her underwear and Cord was laying on the floor, completely dressed and laughing at her frantic efforts.

From the kitchen a childish voice chirped her name like an irate chicken hawk. She scrambled on all fours to a stack of boxes that faced the door, using them to conceal her body from the first four buttons on her shirt downward. Propped on her knees, tugging at the jeans' zipper, she listened to the clomping of Robbie's feet through the house. She gave the zipper one last yank, glanced up, then back down, cussing softly under her breath as she tugged at the stubborn metal teeth eating her underwear.

"Shelley…Cord," Robbie called, bounding into the room, then skidding to a stop when he saw Shelley. "What's wrong?" he demanded, a belligerent frown disturbing the smooth forehead.

Shelley placed her elbows on the top box and rested her chin on her folded hands. "Wrong? Everything's just fine. What could be wrong?"

Robbie's frown deepened. "Why's your face all red?"

A hand flew to her cheek, confirming his question. "We've been working hard." She dropped one hand behind the cardboard shield and yanked at the waistband of her jeans just as they began to slide.

"I smelled chocolate cake." His eyes were everywhere. "Where's Cord?"

"I'm over here, Robbie."

Robbie's eyes narrowed suspiciously at the man, then his gaze bounced back to Shelley. "When ya gonna put the icing on?" When it came to chocolate cake he drew the line on friendships. "You'll call me?"

"Of course."

"I can lick the bowl?" he challenged.

"Yes."

"And the spoon!"

"No," Cord shouted, fighting to keep from laughing at the fierce scowl he received. "Spoon's mine."

"Maybe." The boy's hazel eyes were full of mischief. "Nick wants you outside." Then he forgot the cake and his determination to get both bowl and spoon.

"He wants you to help him. He's gonna build me a telephone booth."

Cord and Shelley looked on, confusion stealing away any questions. Then Shelley noticed the child's attire: the large blue bath towel tied like a cape around his thin neck, the blue T-shirt that someone had carefully painted an *S* on with red and white paint. She began to chuckle as she remembered the Superman videos Nick had rented the last time she'd sent him to Houston. All three males had spent hours glued to the set. "I see. Cord's supposed to help Nick build you a telephone booth so you can play?" Her hand slipped down beyond Robbie's line of vision and snatched her jeans as they tried to crawl down her legs.

"Yeah. Neat, huh?"

Cord rose slowly to his feet, stepped around the boxes and clasped Robbie by the shoulder, nudging him out of the room before Shelley lost either her temper or her pants.

"Come on, kid. Shelley's got things to pick up."

Robbie dug in his heels and threw a moon-sliver grin over his shoulder. "I'll be back as soon as you finish icing the cake."

Shelley couldn't help laughing at the boy's eager expression and Cord's chagrined grunt. Flopping onto her seat, she grabbed the nylon panties that were stuck in the zipper and ripped them loose. Then she had to lie down on the floor to get her jeans zipped up. The struggle made her realize that for the first time in her life she was putting on weight. She made a mental note to cut out the sweets. But the thought of the cake waiting to be iced made her mouth water, and she hurried to her feet and out of the room.

From the kitchen window she could see Cord, Nick

and Robbie as they squatted under the shade of an old pecan tree with Nick's plans for the phone booth laid out on the dry ground. She wondered how they could stand the heat and looked up, pleasantly surprised to see white fluffy clouds floating lazily across the sky.

Out of the corner of her eye, movement caught her attention and she glanced back toward the group under the tree. A snort of disgust passed her lips as she spied a white feathered tail among the masculine bodies. A strange overpowering urge took hold of her. Without thought as to what she was doing, she shoved the kitchen window open and yelled as loudly as she could, "Baked Napoleon!" Immediately ashamed, she slammed the window shut and spun away, missing the bird's squeak and the men's laughter.

Where was the cool, calm and collected Shelley she used to be? Granted, she hated the damn gander, but it went deeper than that. She'd changed. Without even knowing what was happening she was allowing emotions to surface that she'd deliberately buried. After years of putting up with her family's volatile personalities and thinking she was the only sane one, she was finding out she was just like them—crazy!

CHAPTER ELEVEN

SHE WAS BACK to where she'd begun.

Just when her fear and guilt had started to fade and confidence in herself had begun growing, time turned enemy and rolled backward. The guilt that rode her thoughts daily now and the fear that simmered just under the surface when the lights were out were of her own making. She had no one to blame but herself. Whatever was necessary to guard against interference, she'd do. After all, it only meant a couple of days delay.

Shelley stood in the utility room beside the white, oblong chest freezer, staring at it as if it were a snake poised to strike. A noise from the depths of the house, a pipe knocking against a wall, perhaps, brought her head up with a frightened jerk. Her eyes widened, the soft jade-green darkening with panic. Her gaze darted everywhere, making sure no one was hiding in the shadows and watching her. Once convinced she was indeed alone, she shivered, feeling foolish for her silliness. But fear was a permanent thing now, a living organism growing hourly. Hesitantly she touched the top of the freezer, wondering for the millionth time if she was doing the right thing. Suppressing evidence could be considered a criminal act. But the circumstances surely warranted just a small delay?

She backed away from the freezer and the package hidden among the other frozen foods. A package she'd

wrapped and labeled "Lamb Chops," using red ink to
distinguish it from the rest. She'd found Anthony's
notebook. A small book filled with letters and numbers
that she could neither understand nor wanted to. Natu-
rally it was all in code, something only a professional
cryptologist would be able to decipher. At least when
she'd found the notebook snuggled in the cut-out in-
nards of her copy of *Grimm's Fairy Tales*, she'd been
rational enough to wrap both books together. What a
perverted sense of humor Anthony had to hide his treasonous accounting in a book of fantasies.

The house groaned and she jumped, realizing for the
first time how alone she was, with Cord and Nick at the
machinery barn helping Lee prepare the insecticide so
he could spray the pecan trees. Being Saturday, Robbie
was at home with his mother, and Vo was most likely
busy tending the couple's personal vegetable garden.
Not until this moment had she fully realized the extent
of Anthony's treachery—the money he took, the secrets
he passed along to his bosses—and the danger she was
in if those men found out where she was. If they had
killed Anthony—and the cause behind the plane's explosion was still unknown—then they wouldn't think
twice about killing her or anyone with her. Everyone
on the farm was in danger.

She should turn the notebook over to Nick. But then
if she did, it would be over and Cord would leave. Oh,
she had no doubt he'd be back or that he loved her.
Only she needed some time, just a few more days until
she could get through to Cord. A more stubborn, hard-
headed man she'd never met.

For some crazy reason he seemed determined to give
her some space and time to decide if she could live with
him knowing he could never give her children. He was

putting her at arm's length so she could reevaluate the situation. He was being rational, levelheaded, noble. But he was keeping her at an emotional distance, too, and it hurt to see him slowly pull away from her.

The decision to let him have his way, to heed his warnings, was difficult, and she'd just as soon not have to do it. Yet, it was for Cord and his future peace of mind and ultimately worth it. Now she couldn't take the chance of his leaving the farm and brooding alone over the problem. She wanted him next to her so they could discuss it, talk it out and come to terms together. She needed time, and by hiding Anthony's notebook she'd managed to buy them some. She just prayed what she'd done wasn't going to rebound in her face. The thought that the people she cared for might pay for her determination to have her way was unthinkable.

The kitchen cabinet at her back stopped her retreat from the utility room. She swung around and entered the kitchen, wondering again if she'd done the right thing. A pyramid of neatly cut squares of fudge caught her attention. She pulled the plate over, stuffing a piece in her mouth before she even stopped to think of her earlier promise to diet. As she swallowed and automatically picked up another piece, she pinched the skin around her waist. A puzzled frown pleated her brow. From the snug fit of her jeans and the way her bra was cutting into her, she figured she'd somehow put on about six or seven pounds.

"Shelley!"

She jumped and whirled, pushing the cube of fudge into her mouth and almost choking on it as she faced Cord. "What?" she managed, knowing something terrible was wrong.

Cord spotted the huge plate of fudge, quickly

snatched a couple of squares and dropped them into his shirt pocket.

"What's happened, Cord?"

"Don't panic and listen carefully. Call the fire department."

"Fire!"

"Listen. Call them, tell them that there's a field fire behind the pecan grove. Nick says it's on the 'old property' acreage. They'll know." He started off toward the hall. "Do you have any old blankets? We can wet them down and beat out the fire."

"I'll get them." She dashed to the storage closet under the stairs and pulled down an armful of woolen blankets.

Cord took them from her arms and turned away, then stopped. "Call Robbie's mother and tell her there's no danger where they are, but for God's sake keep *him* home." He tried to move past Shelley. She stepped in his path. "Nick wants you to go over to Vo's and wait there."

"No way." As she rushed to the telephone and began to dial, she stuffed her feet into her running shoes. Once the necessary calls were made, she looked at Cord who was standing where she'd left him, just staring at her.

"Shelley, do what Nick and I ask." He headed for the door again.

"I'm going with you."

"Damn it! Nick says he thinks this could very well be a diversion to get at you."

She shoved past him and was out the back door and sprinting down the steps before he realized what she was doing. The loud cracking of the back door slamming in his face jerked him into action. "Shelley!" he bellowed.

She climbed in the cab of the truck and slid behind the steering wheel. The engine roared to life. She gunned it impatiently as Cord shrugged resignedly, threw the blankets into the back and got in.

"Why would Nick think the fire could be a ploy?"

He debated what to do first: tell her what he knew or chew her out for being so stubborn. "All the wiretaps and surveillance have been pulled off your family and your boss's home and office."

"Maybe they've given up."

He shook his head and grabbed the dashboard as she left the blacktop lane and turned onto the dirt road. "Nick doesn't think so. More than likely they've found out where we are." He sucked in a breath and closed his eyes a second as Shelley took the corner on two wheels.

"We? You mean me. They're after me, Anthony and his notes."

Cord gave her a droll, rather thoughtful look, then snorted in disbelief. "You forget. As far as they're concerned, I am Anthony."

Long ago she'd separated the two men in her mind, and it was a shock to be reminded that he was Anthony's identical twin. Cord was so different that she no longer looked at him and saw her ex-husband. In a way it was eerie how personalities changed a person's looks.

"Shelley, watch out!" Cord's feet stomped the floorboard as if he were working the brakes. "You're going to drive off the road."

She righted the truck and drove on without comment. Fence posts flew by, the wind was like a furnace on her face and her heart was in her throat as she thought of the damage a fire out of control could do to the plantation—to the community.

"The 'old property' backs up to the original pecan grove. Cord, most of those trees are hundreds of years old. They're still producers and are priceless."

"I know; Nick told me."

She darted a look at him and the corner of her mouth curled up as she watched him retrieve the pieces of fudge from his pocket and plop the candy into his mouth.

Cord caught her gaze. "Want to tell me what's been eating at you these past two days? And don't say me. There's something else. What have you done, Shelley, that's caused the three in the morning baking sprees?"

She bit back a grin, slowed the truck and hooked a turn down a side road. The dust they kicked up followed them, then as they slowed the cloud rolled across the open cab of the truck and stung their eyes. Shelley spat grit from her mouth. She could smell the fire now; the grass, twigs and bushes turned to cinders by the inferno that crawled along the road.

"I thought we promised not to keep secrets from each other?" he prompted.

She gnawed at her bottom lip a second, then threw him a pleading glance. "You won't tell Nick?" He didn't respond and she sighed. "I answered the telephone. Now listen, Cord, before you fly off the handle…" Her words rushed out in hopes of making him understand. "Well, I didn't think it would matter, not after so long."

"When?"

"Three days ago. But Cord…it was the wrong number. As soon as whoever it was heard my voice they hung up.'' The significance of her feeble explanation struck her and she swore under her breath.

"About the same time all the surveillance was pulled off your family and boss? Really, Shelley. What an incredibly dumb thing to do.''

She wiped her sweaty hands, one by one, on her jeans. "Yes, I can see that it was.'' A bubble of laughter escaped her lips. "I guess you realize by now just how weak I am.'' The truck hit a deep rut in the road, sending their heads within a fraction of an inch of the roof.

"This is not a laughing matter,'' Cord scolded, fighting to keep a smile from creeping across his mouth.

"If we know that they know, and we're prepared for them, then that's good, isn't it?''

Cord shook his head, trying to rearrange her question so it was clearer. "Maybe.''

The smell was stronger, burning their throats as a thin plume of smoke drifted through the open window. Shelley spotted the far-off figures of Nick and Lee, working frantically with shovels. She stepped on the brakes and was out the door before Cord could stop her. "Damn it, Shelley, stop!'' The anger in his voice pulled her up short. With his arms full he caught up with her at the edge of the field and tossed the blankets over the wire fence. He grabbed her arm and hauled her close so he could watch every nuance of her expression for any signs of rebellion. "You're to stay back. Do you hear me? I don't want you hurt. If you see the fire's getting out of hand, you're to get the hell out of here.'' His mouth lowered on hers and she wrapped her arms around his neck. The heat of the day warred with the fire rapidly pumping through his veins. "Promise.''

"Yes, Cord,'' she said sweetly, too sweetly, and pulled out of his embrace.

Cord caught the lower strand of barbed wire with his shoe, clasped the second wire and motioned for her to hurry. Once on the other side, she gingerly took his hold on the wire to allow him to squeeze through. She picked up half of the blankets and sprinted for the big water reservoir.

Cord's eyes slitted like a suspicious cat's. He no more trusted that angelic promise than he would turn his back on a mad bull. "I mean it, Shelley. Stay back. Keep us supplied with wet blankets, that's all."

"Yes, Cord."

He gritted his teeth, watching as she dropped the woolens in the water, then struggled to drag the heavy water-soaked blankets out and hand them to him. "Shelley?"

She turned bright eyes on him, and he wondered if the spark was defiance or a glint from the sun. He lifted the blankets, threw them over his shoulders and took off across the field, where Nick and Lee worked at beating out the encroaching fire.

After numerous trips back and forth between the men and the reservoir, hauling the now-smelly wet blankets, contending with the increasing heat, Shelley had a growing realization that the three of them were never going to contain the fire. Once more she dropped the dirty, scorched blankets in the water. Sweat plastered her cotton shirt to her body, and she swiped at the straggling strand of hair that persistently fell back in her eyes. She sighed, grabbed hold of her wet load and took off toward the men.

She was beside Cord, slapping the water-soaked blankets against the ground, beating at the flames as they ate up the grass in a slow rolling motion. If there had been the slightest breath of a breeze, their puny efforts would have been in vain.

"I thought I told you—" Cord broke off, attacking another finger of fire as it shot toward Shelley's feet. "Get the hell out of here."

"Shut up, Cord, and beat."

"Damn fool woman," he grumbled.

Slowly they backed away, out of reach of the flames. The heat blasted against their faces as the fire fed on the dry grass like a greedy animal. Once rich, black, river-bottom soil, the ground was now hard-baked earth with cracks wide enough for a man's three fingers to fit in. Bare spots stopped the fire, then it would spark wildly with its insatiable hunger and pop a hot coal on a distant patch of grass. The fight would start all over again.

"Here." Cord tossed her his and Nick's dry blankets, then flipped the spare he had hanging across his shoulders onto the ground. "Go wet these and be careful. It looks like the fire is shifting, so don't let it encircle you and trap you." He watched her go, his eyes following her every move. It wasn't till Nick hollered a warning that he realized the flames were entirely too close to him.

Shelley dunked the half-burned blankets in the water and fought their weight and her growing exhaustion to haul them out. Straightening, she dropped her soggy load, placed her hands behind her back and stretched. It didn't look as if they had a chance to stop the blaze, and she wondered suddenly where the fire department was. Bending to retrieve her burden, a sound caught her attention and she spun around. People were everywhere. Before her stunned gaze, cars were pulling off the main highway, disgorging bodies, each carrying either burlap sacks or shovels.

A fire truck slowed only long enough to make sure that the wire fence snapped under its weight before it plowed across the field. The big red-and-silver vehicle headed for the pond of water, stopping when it was at the edge of the reservoir. Local volunteer firemen jumped down and made quick work of dropping a hose in the water. A pump was started and the long hose was unwound from the truck. The men stood alert and waiting to see if the long line of beaters that was now forming could put out the flames. Water was for crops, for irrigation. It was the lifeblood of every farmer. This water reservoir was a precious commodity, to be used only as a last resort.

An old Cadillac, the shine so bright it outbid the sun for brilliance, pulled to a stop beside the road along with other cars. Shelley grinned. Women, wives of the men out in the fields, turned to see Louis's snow-white head emerge from behind the Cadillac driver's seat. Moving slowly and with his grandest gesture, he swung open the back door, helping the Misses Randall out. Shelley dropped the wet blankets and trotted across the field, pausing only a surprised moment as Louis assisted a third person out of the back seat—Vo. Shelley's eyebrows jumped and her grin stretched into a huge smile.

"What a tragedy, my dear Shelley," remarked Milly, setting the big straw hat on her blue-gray curls. The sun's rays never touched the elderly ladies' skin. To them it was a mortal sin for a female to have a tan. "The very minute Sally Roads rang to tell us you had called the fire department, we came to see if we could help." She turned away a second. "Louis, please set up the iced-tea table for the workers." She switched her bright gaze to Shelley. "We called Sheriff Jones and he will be here soon. Sister reminded him this was election year and the fire must be looked into. Isn't that right, Sister?"

"Yes indeed, Sister." Ruby strolled away, adjusting her sun hat as she went.

Shelley was at a loss for words as she listened and watched. Ruby was busy fussing around the iced-tea table, giving Louis and Vo orders that were eagerly and happily carried out. Soon all the women and some of the older men were putting up umbrellas for shade, dropping rolled compresses into ice water for the over-heated workers and making sure there were plenty of glasses filled with cool drinks. "Has the entire town turned out, Milly?"

"Why, of course. It's the neighborly thing to do. Also, you must realize if the fire gets out of hand their livelihood will be in danger, too." She stopped her ex-planation a second, using her fan more as a barometer for her emotions than an aid from the extreme heat. "I just pray that my premonition was wrong. I've just wor-ried myself sick. Haven't I, Sister?"

Ruby joined them. "Indeed you have, Sister. You've nearly driven poor old Louis to death sending him to town to listen to the gossip."

Shelley leaned against the bumper of the car, heard a loud cough of disapproval from Louis and quickly pushed off. She shaded her eyes, watching the line of men desperately fighting the fire. "I hope they can put it out without using the water in the reservoir."

"We all do, dear. Your pecans have always been the prize winners at the county fair. Haven't they, Sister?"

"We always buy them." Ruby glanced over her shoulder at Louis. "Careful with that pitcher, Louis.

Harold Clements won that for me at the carnival years ago.''

Louis met Shelley's gaze and winked. ''I know that, Ruby Randall. I lied to your pappy when you sneaked out of the house to meet that boy.''

Ruby blushed to the roots of her silver-blue hair, then adjusted her hat to shield her eyes from her sister's disapproving look.

Milly sent Louis a look and getting only a chuckle in return, she changed the subject. ''Such a nice woman, that Vo. Shelley, you must just love her. So quiet. Wasn't she sweet when we stopped at the house, Sister? She was frantic because she couldn't find you, Shelley, but she never forgot her manners and offered us tea. I told her I just bet you were right out in the field with the men. Sure enough, here you are.'' She lowered her voice to a loud whisper that everyone within three feet could hear. ''I recommended a nice doctor friend of mine to her after I found out the poor dear wasn't crippled with arthritis.'' She touched her elbow and rubbed it a second. ''I suffer from it myself, you know.''

''Sister!''

''Well, yes, but the darling little lady told us those villainous Vietcong captured her and Lee and tortured her in front of Lee to make him talk.'' She shivered violently. ''They broke every bone in the poor thing's hands.''

Shelley had been only half listening as she watched the futility of the men's efforts. But Vo's story caught her attention. She had no idea the tiny woman had suffered such an ordeal, and when her gaze shifted to Vo she noticed that she kept her misshapen hands folded together.

''Glory be. Just look, Sister. I wonder how that scallywag has the nerve to show his face here?'' They all turned to see Glen "Tinkle" Ferris get out of his truck and walk toward the downed fence where he stopped to watch. "Louis! Where is that cowardly Sheriff Jones? He's not here yet?''

"No ma'am.''

Milly's back stiffened. "Then get my shotgun, Louis. I won't have him doing harm.''

The sound of an engine revving up turned everyone's attention from Tinkle. In silence they watched the fire truck start to pump water from the reservoir in a wide arch on the ground. While Shelley had been diverted by Milly, the fire had increased, eating up the dry grass, making the men run from the licking flames and smothering smoke. Their last hope was that the reservoir held enough water to extinguish the fire. Shelley shot a quick glance at Tinkle and stiffened, rage washing over her at the malicious smile that spread across the alcohol-red blotched face.

"Don't say anything, dear,'' Milly warned. "Let the men handle it. We'll all pray harder for rain.''

Though Shelley didn't intend to live on the farm much longer, she'd come to love the place and didn't want it destroyed. The heat from the fire and the burning sun made her eyes ache and her head spin.

"Louis! This child is about to faint. Bring my lawn chair and a cold compress. Sister, some lemonade. No, not tea. Lemonade is better for an upset stomach.'' Milly directed everyone. "Vo, help Sally May set up an umbrella in front of the car.''

After a minute under the shade and a cold cloth on her forehead, Shelley sighed and opened her eyes. "I guess the heat got to me.''

"Maybe.'' Milly frowned fiercely, her lined mouth

puckering with thought. Before she could continue her theory, a shout turned their attention toward the field.

"Praise be. The fire's out," Ruby exclaimed, and a loud cheer went up.

"Here be the sheriff." Louis, standing beside Shelley's chair, threw a quick glance over his shoulder. "Seems Mr. Nick's gonna talk his ear off."

With Milly's hand on her shoulder, keeping her seated, Shelley had to crane her neck to see what was happening. Once more she tried to rise.

"Sit, young lady. This is for the men to handle. Isn't it, Sister?"

"Yes, indeed. Why I can remember when Papa—"

"Never mind, Sister."

Too much time in the dear old ladies' company and she'd be a raving lunatic. Nick and the sheriff were talking some distance away, and though Shelley couldn't hear what was being said, she could at least see them.

"Louis," Milly said quietly, "mosey on over there and see what's happening."

They watched Nick hand Sheriff Jones something that looked to be a cartridge of some sort. A heated argument developed, then the sheriff called Tinkle Ferris over. Shelley leaned forward as did everyone, straining to hear, but only able to catch odd words.

Louis walked slowly back to them. "Mr. Nick's got a flare cartridge. He says he found it at the corner of the field where the fire started. Sheriff says Tinkle bought flares day before yesterday at Kasey's Hardware store."

"Is he going to arrest him?" Shelley demanded. Her gaze shifted back to the three men, but now the number had increased and she looked on as the crowd parted for Cord and Lee.

"Sheriff Jones will do his duty, Miss Shelley," Louis said. "No matter what Miss Milly says, he's a fair man. But he does believe in his own special brand of justice, too."

Shelley nodded, unable to take her eyes off Cord. He looked so exhausted, his handsome face smudged with soot, sweat and dirt. But as he listened to the men, his tiredness seemed to fall away and his eyes blazed to life with anger. Suddenly Shelley was on her feet watching as Tinkle began to shout at Lee. The sheriff turned his back and calmly strolled toward the spectators lining the road. She shook off Milly's restraining hold.

"Now child, just wait and see. Sometimes the law must turn its back."

"How dare you!" Shelley yelled at the sheriff, her gaze hot with anger at his cowardice. An excited yell from the crowd of men drew her attention away from the man calmly lighting a cigar, seemingly deaf to the confusion behind him. Tinkle punched Lee in the face and was taunting him cruelly. The men moved out of the way, and Nick grabbed Cord's shoulder to keep him from stepping in to help. As Lee recovered, Tinkle swung again, this time sending the much smaller man to the ground.

Lee scrambled to his feet, and before everyone's astounded gaze he politely bowed to Tinkle. Then he struck like a snake. His body became airborne, his arms and legs a blur as they pounded into the giant before him. Tinkle staggered under the blows, then was down, shaking his head like an enraged bull.

"Get up!" Ruby yelled, her frail hands clenched into balls. "Get up so Lee can knock your block off."

"Sister!"

Ruby blushed scarlet, glancing around furtively. When no one laughed at her she returned her attention to the warring men, moving her body, hissing and grunting with each blow.

Tinkle shot to his feet, his face bloody, his eyes wild with rage. But he didn't have time to charge before Lee was on him again.

Stunned and openmouthed, Shelley watched the gentle, soft-spoken Vietnamese defeat the bigger man, but the beating went much further than the physical blows he delivered. Lee was slowly humiliating the bully in front of the townspeople. She watched the last strike, and then everyone turned their backs on Tinkle. They would never forget nor forgive what he'd done. Because of his vengefulness and bigotry, he had started the fire that could have ruined them all. Small-town justice could be harsher than the law. Glen "Tinkle" Ferris would be arrested and fined for destroying private property, but, more importantly, the town where he'd grown up would shun him; his neighbors and friends would treat him like a stranger.

The crowd began to break up. Some of the men and women came over to Shelley to say a few encouraging words, and she thanked as many of them as she could. Then they began to circle around Lee, shaking his hand and thumping the small man on the back. With a lump in her throat Shelley watched the town's long-overdue acceptance of Lee and Vo.

She stepped away from Milly and Ruby and rushed into Cord's arms before either lady could protest her vulgar public display. He leaned down and kissed her quick and hard. As she pulled back, her nose wrinkled in distaste. "You smell awful, Cord." He laughed, a

deep rich rumbling sound that made her feel better just
to hear it.

"I'm out there fighting for your land—" he gave her
an extra squeeze "—and here you are lounging around
like a queen bee. Really, Shelley, an umbrella and lemonade to watch Rome burn?"

She grinned, her cheeks still pale, but her eyes sparkled with laughter. "Milly's doing, I promise you. I tell
you, Cord—"

Lee interrupted her with a deep bow, then he straightened and puffed out his chest with pride, though the
image was a little marred by a swelling eye and a lip
that was still bleeding. "I not lun anymore, Sherrey. Vo
and I, we earn light to fight back. We Texans now,
yes?"

"You most certainly are." She noticed that with the
return of his honor, Lee had ceased calling her Miss.
Heaven knew in the past she'd done everything possible
to make him stop addressing her so formally. She
smiled tenderly at the couple, then her smile slowly died
as she spied a white feathered head with small, beady
black eyes peek around from Lee's legs. Napoleon,
caked with mud from the empty reservoir, rubbed his
bill on Lee's loose pants, then fixed her with an un-
wavering stare. Shelley stiffened and began to ease back
as the gander's thick neck reached out toward her. He
hissed and snapped his bill, stopping only when Lee
nudged him with his foot.

"Such a nasty creature," Milly said, coming to stand
beside Shelley. She looked down her long nose at Napoleon. "Shoo, you arrogant, ornery beast, or I'll lend
our dear Shelley my Aloysius to take the starch out of
you."

They watched as Napoleon stalked off, and Shelley

mumbled "roasted goose," just loud enough for the
gander to hear. He instantly began to run across the field
toward the farm, his wings flapping as he went.

Cord told Milly of Shelley's feud with the big white
bird, and they were still laughing at her expense when
Nick strolled over.

Milly cut Nick's greeting short. "I recognize you
now, young man. You were Rex Harper's wild boy—
you lived over by the railroad tracks. A thoroughly dis-
agreeable man, your father. I remember you came back
ten years ago to bury him. Wasn't there some trouble
at the Flamingo Bar that night? Heard tell they kicked
you out for being disorderly."

The life suddenly drained out of Nick's eyes, then he
shook his head and shrugged. "I got disgustingly drunk
and made a fool of myself. I promise you, it's never
happened again."

Milly studied him a long, thoughtful moment. "Did
you by any chance meet up with anyone that night? Did
someone find you and help you?"

Nick stared at her, his expression peculiar. His
mouth, usually a firm straight line, softened around the
edges. "I...no. I don't think so. Why?"

"Just a thought, my boy, just a thought."

Shelley and Cord were easing away from the group,
praying that Milly wouldn't turn her attention on them.
From a distance she quickly thanked the Misses Randall, grabbed Cord's hand and headed across the charred
field to the truck.

"For a second there I thought Nick was going to tell
Milly to mind her own business. I've never seen such
a look. Have you noticed it only happens when someone
mentions his father or his past?" Shelley crawled up on

the seat, started the engine and waited for Cord to slam his door shut before taking off down the road.

"Don't go interfering there, Shelley."

"I wouldn't think of it."

Cord groaned, leaned his head back and closed his eyes. "God, I can't wait to get back to the house and take a shower." He opened one eye and stared at her. "You could use one, too."

Shelley shot him a quick glance and laughed as she turned onto another road. She saw Cord's look of puzzlement. "I want to swing by Robbie's house and reassure them that everything is under control." Cord groaned again, closed his eyes, and she grinned.

The small, red brick house nestled under huge spreading, pecan trees came into view, and Shelley immediately spotted Robbie sitting on the front porch. She reached out and poked Cord awake. "Look." Robbie was standing now, waiting for them to come to a stop. His red fireman's hat clashed with his bright yellow rain slicker and black rubber boots.

He was at the door of the truck before she could open it. "Have ya come to get me so I can help fight the fire?" He danced from one foot to the other, pushing the hard, red hat back so he could see them.

"Fire's out, buddy." Cord crawled out from the passenger side of the truck and stretched his tired muscles.

"Ah, crap." Robbie trudged back to the house, yanked off his hat and threw it on the ground.

"Robert Taylor, I'll wash your mouth out with soap if you say that word again."

"Hello, Sara," Shelley called out in greeting as Robbie's mother opened the front door and walked out to meet them. She turned to introduce Cord but swallowed her words when she saw his expression. She guessed

Sara was a shock to him. The woman hardly looked old enough to have a son Robbie's age, and she had an angelic face, with one of the sweetest smiles Shelley had ever seen.

Sara was small, delicate, with an abundance of silky blond hair and large blue eyes that were always laughing even when she had little to laugh about. Sara Taylor had had a hard life. As a very young, sheltered and pregnant eighteen-year-old, her parents had disowned her and kicked her out of the house.

Shelley had heard through the usual town gossip how Sara had gallantly kept her baby and stayed in the town that looked down on her. She had sustained the stares, the snickering and the slurs with a dignity far beyond her years. She had even managed to talk a cousin, a local bank executive, into hiring her and she started going to night school. It wasn't until Robbie, at age three, became sick that Sara, broke and devastated, and after much persuasion by Shelley's aunt and uncle, moved into the old farmhouse. Her pride demanded that Shelley's relatives accept a menial rent and allow her to have her own garden where she could grow and can her own produce.

"Antho...Cord." Shelley punched him in the ribs. "This is Sara, Robbie's mother."

Somewhat embarrassed for staring, Cord shook himself out of his tired stupor. He shook hands with Sara and could have been lulled asleep by her low husky voice, but Shelley was making their goodbyes and pulling him toward the truck.

"You didn't have to go into a trance. I know she's pretty, but really, Cord." Shelley stomped on the gas pedal, sending the truck bouncing down the rutted road.

"I thought any minute you were going to start drooling."

"You'll have to admit she's really something. The type a man thinks about protecting and hiding away so no one else can lust over his good luck."

Shelley's hands squeezed the steering wheel as she sped down the road, slowing only when she took the corner to the blacktop lane leading to the house. When she stepped on the brakes and the truck had squealed to a stop, she grabbed the door handle, shoved the door open and jumped out. "If you're so taken with her, then why don't you go back and let her cook for you?"

"Aw, Shelley, you know I didn't mean—" But his words were cut off as she slammed the front door. "Me and my big mouth." Cord slowly swung his legs out of the cab and climbed down, his body a mass of sore muscles. He glanced at the white Victorian house and sighed. She wasn't about to shower with him now. More than likely she'd kick him out of her bed, too. A slow sly smile touched his mouth. Her open display of jealousy made his blood sing through his veins in a familiar song. After dinner he'd see just how the wind blew.

A STORM WAS BREWING. Shelley invited Nick to dinner, then made the two men do the cooking. She sat with her feet propped up on a chair, giving orders, watching with a critical eye as they put together the meal. Nick, upon finding out he was going to have to help cook, opted for hot dogs. Cord, a little more in tune with Shelley's mood, decided on an omelet, country sausage, buttered toast and juice. He paid little attention to Nick's gripes that it was breakfast fare. Cord didn't even attempt to warn the man that he was treading on thin ice. Shelley's temper was about to explode, and it would be to his advantage for it to blow Nick's way instead of his. But Cord wasn't through taunting her. The thought of making love to an angry Shelley only added to his excitement.

"Nick, you should have come with us this afternoon to see Robbie. His mother was home."

Shelley stiffened, her sulky expression deepening.

"Yes, sir. She was something to see. All blond and blue-eyed. A small angel with the sweetest voice you've ever listened to—something right from heaven, I'd say." Cord's eyes cut in Shelley's direction.

Nick felt the tension in the room grow and looked up from his job of carefully chopping green pepper. He glanced from Shelley to Cord, wondering why the simmering anger.

Shelley gave Cord a cat's grin. "Sara Taylor wouldn't have you on a bet. She doesn't date...ever!"

The silence that had spread between them was suddenly broken as Nick cursed, crammed his finger into his mouth and swung around. His face was chalk white, his mouth somehow remaining a straight line even clamped around his cut finger. But it was the look in his eyes that shocked Shelley. She half rose from her chair. He wasn't hurt, not from the knife, yet he looked as if he would shatter into a million pieces.

"What did you say her name was?" His voice trembled and he blinked as if in a daze.

"Sara," Cord said, his attention now fully on Nick.

"And how old is Robbie?"

"Nine. Why, Nick? What's wrong?" Shelley stood and was walking toward Nick, concern etched in her lined brow.

"Why the hell didn't anyone tell me her name?" the

voice roared at them, stunning them with its volume and fierceness.

Gently, as if she were talking to a crazy man, Shelley said softly, rationally, "Why, Nick, we've always talked about Sara."

"You damn well did not mention her name. It was always Robbie's mom, Robbie's mother. Never Sara...." His voice trailed off. "Never Sara." He threw down the knife and stormed out of the house.

Shelley and Cord stood frozen to the spot, puzzled at Nick's behavior. "You better go after him, Cord, and find out what's wrong. He's sure acting strange."

Reluctantly Cord agreed. "You'll keep the bed warm?" He ducked the missile of a full glass of iced tea and rushed out the door. Nick Harper better have a damn good answer for his actions and for ruining the entertaining evening he'd planned.

CHAPTER TWELVE

SHELLEY LAY propped up in bed, waiting, thinking that any minute Cord would walk through the doorway. But her patience went unrewarded. She'd given up any hope of dinner hours ago. Her gaze lifted from the book in her lap, a new novel by Dorothy Dunnett that she'd asked Nick to pick up for her. She cocked her head, listening, but when the sound she'd thought she heard didn't come again, she sighed.

What in the world could be keeping him? She needed to talk with Cord, and what she had to say couldn't be put off another day. The specter of Anthony's notebook tucked away in the freezer was like a bad dream come to life, clutching at her heart whenever she least expected it. A noise from downstairs caught her attention, a sound she recognized as the back door being closed and locked.

With her clean-scrubbed face, and clothed in the ridiculous overlarge T-shirt Cord always made fun of, vanity forced her to push her hair into some order. She crossed her legs Indian fashion and pulled the cotton shirt over her knees. Slow, somewhat uneven footfalls up the stairs brought a perplexed frown. What the devil was taking so much time? Cord should have been up minutes ago. Her heart began to pound at the thought that whoever was treading carefully up those stairs might not be who she expected. Then he was there and she breathed a sigh of relief, biting her lip to keep her expression sober; it was evident Cord wasn't as he weaved a little in the doorway.

"You still up?" he asked, refusing to meet her gaze as he made his way toward the bathroom.

"Cord…"

He kept his back to her and said, "Let me take a cold shower first, Shelley. I smell like someone spilled a quart of bourbon on me."

The bathroom door thumped shut and Shelley smiled at just how precisely Cord had spaced his words to keep from slurring them. She hoped the shower did some good, because she certainly wasn't about to allow him to go to sleep without a detailed account of what had happened with Nick.

When Cord finally emerged he was steadier on his feet, naked except for a towel hanging around his neck and an apologetic smile. "For a man who can't tolerate alcohol, Nick Harper almost drank me under the table."

A tiny smile touched Shelley's lips as he sat down heavily on the edge of the bed and began to briskly towel-dry his hair. Why was it, she wondered, that a naked man without the strength of his passion looked so vulnerable? She got up on her knees and hobbled over the covers to him, took the towel from his hands and began drying his hair. "What happened? You've been gone all night." Tossing the damp towel on the floor, she began massaging his shoulders, working the knots out of his muscles.

Cord sighed and leaned back against Shelley, resting his weary body against hers. "You just wouldn't believe this night, Shelley. When I left here and caught up with Nick at the hired hand's house, he was walking the floor like a caged animal, talking to himself as he paced.'' He groaned softly as Shelley's strong fingers slid up into his hair and she began to massage his scalp and temples. "I thought he'd flipped out. He kept mumbling about a dream he'd had ten years ago. A dream about an angel of mercy with a voice that could calm the devil himself. Said that memory had haunted him for a decade, eating at him until sometimes he almost dreaded falling asleep. Then he told me that his angel of the night had a name—Sara. All blond hair and big, laughing blue eyes.''

Shelley gasped.

"My reaction exactly. Nick wouldn't say much more, but he did say he was going to retrace his steps. Shelley, the man was possessed, and I couldn't let him go off on his own.'' He lifted his head and looked at her over his shoulder.

Her hands were tired and she stopped massaging, slid her arms around his neck, resting her chin on Cord's shoulder. She nestled her cheek next to his. "From the way you weaved in here, I'd say you went to a local watering hole?''

Cord nodded. "The Flamingo Bar. The one Nick was in ten years ago. He really began to throw back the drinks. I should have tried to stop him, but he was so damn sure that if he was in the same place in the same condition all his memories would return.''

Cord rubbed his cheek against Shelley's in a slow, sleepy manner that made her chuckle.

"Sorry, Cord, but sleep is a long way off. Continue.''

"Nick remembers he was kicked out of the bar. He knew he couldn't drive so he began to walk home. Of course, his father's place was ten miles away, but what did he care—he was pickled to the gills. Then, he said his memory of the rest of the night comes and goes.

Suddenly, out of nowhere, a beautiful girl named Sara picked him up and drove him home. They talked all the way, he doesn't know about what. He even vaguely remembers her helping him to the house. And that's where he gets all screwed up in some sort of fantasy.''

Shelley felt suddenly cold and she shivered against him. "Cord. Nick didn't rape Sara, did he? If he was drunk, and as young and tiny as Sara was, it's a possibility, isn't it? As far as I've heard she's never dated anyone since her pregnancy, nor has she ever told who the father was. My God! If what Nick thinks is true, then Robbie is his son.''

"That's what Nick said when he'd worked out all the events of that night in his head. As to raping Sara, he didn't.''

Shelley's breath hissed out. "Now, knowing all this, I can see the resemblance. Robbie is a mixture of both Sara and Nick. Do you know what has always bothered me? I just could never make the connection. Robbie has Nick's smile—when you can get Nick to smile, that is. Maybe that's why I didn't notice it more; he's so damn solemn faced.''

"Well, about eleven o'clock he was all white teeth, idiot smiles and full of false courage. When we set off for Sara's house you would have thought the sun had risen in his face." Cord shook his head. "Frightening to see a man so hard and cold change before your very eyes. Like the reverse metamorphosis of a monster.''

"Cord!''

They both laughed and Cord leaned farther back into Shelley until they both tumbled backward.

"I have to lie down.''

"Yes, I see," she said breathlessly as she struggled

to get out from under his dead weight. "Don't you dare go to sleep."

"No, no. Wouldn't do that," he said groggily, and closed his eyes.

"Damn it, Cord." She reached over, prized one eyelid open and said, "I'll get a bucket of cold water. I swear I will. You can't do this to me, Cord Lowell." She dropped the eyelid and pounded her fist on his bare chest.

Cord grabbed her hand, sat up and shook his head like a wet dog shaking off water. "I'm awake. Where was I?"

"Going to Sara's."

"Oh, yeah. You should have seen that tiny angel lose her wings and halo, Shelley. When she opened the door and saw Nick standing there, she didn't faint as I expected. Oh no, she snatched up Robbie's baseball bat and came at us like an angry tigress. If the situation hadn't been so serious, I would have died laughing right there. But, Shelley, when Sara saw Nick and thought he was going to take Robbie away from her, she was ready to kill for her son. It was sad in a way. After Nick convinced her he hadn't come back to steal Robbie, they just stood there staring at each other like two strangers, totally at a loss at what to say, yet they couldn't seem to take their eyes off each other. Nick was scared—you could tell from his expression. He'd been haunted by her for ten years. He wanted her, but was afraid to reach out and take her. He left—ran was more like it—and I was stranded there."

Shelley stiffened, then relaxed when Cord chuckled.

"Sara had to drive me home," he said, sighing tiredly. "I'll tell you, Shelley, she's no fragile flower. She's as strong as iron. She's also in love with Nick and freely admitted it. Said the second she saw Nick in his full dress uniform walking along the roadside, she was lost. And no, it wasn't rape. Nick didn't force her or hurt her. I wanted to get that clear right away." Cord lifted his hands and rubbed his face roughly. He yawned hugely. "I'm bone tired, Shelley. I've got to get some sleep."

She didn't have the heart to say no and snuggled against his side. "What's going to happen, Cord? What will they do?

He yawned again. "Nick's going over tomorrow to talk with Sara." He chuckled lazily. "You're not going to believe this, but when Sara dropped me off here Nick was sitting on the porch waiting for me. She had no sooner driven down the lane than he was demanding to know what she'd said. He asked me to go with him tomorrow. Moral support, I guess." He yawned again.

"You didn't tell Nick that Sara was in love with him, did you?"

"I'm not stupid. That would give him an edge, and I think once Nick truly grasps the situation and gets over his shock, Sara won't have a chance. He can be charming, Shelley. And I can see where women might find that aloofness attractive."

She snorted in disbelief.

"I know it's hard to take in, but I saw some of his charm tonight as he calmed and reassured Sara he wasn't there to take Robbie away."

"Poor Sara." Shelley shook her head.

"Poor *Nick*. That little lady is going to tie him up in knots before he knows it. Poor Sara, indeed," Cord finished softly, his eyelids snapping shut.

Shelley absently ran her fingers lightly over Cord's

chest, playing with the springy hair as she wondered how on earth Sara could love a man as cold as Nick.

"Shelley, stop that! I've had too damn much to drink to do anything but talk about it, and I'm even too damn tired to talk."

Her fingers slipped lower, tracing the vee of short curls. "Did you ever give it a name? When we were young my brother used to call his—"

Cord half laughed, half groaned, and flipped over on his stomach, mumbling into the pillow. "For cripe's sake!"

She patted his tight behind, snuggled closer, telling herself she'd have her talk with him first thing in the morning.

But she woke up sooner than she expected, some time in the middle of the night. She squirmed, scooting closer to Cord's chest, floating in an erotic daze. Suddenly, her sensual dreams seemed to have fingers. One hand cupped her breast, a rough-tipped thumb rubbing her nipple until it was pebble hard. Another hand insinuated itself between her thighs, making her pulse race wildly.

"Cord," she murmured, then sucked in a startled gulp of air as his hard maleness slipped into her. "Cord!" Her eyes widened in surprise.

"Hmm?"

"Did you plan to wake me at all for this? Or just carry on on your own?" She couldn't catch her breath; her body was moving in tandem to his slow lazy thrusts as if she had no will or control.

"I thought you'd enjoy a surprise," he whispered against her ear, his breath stirring her hair, making her shiver.

"This isn't fair. I can't touch you."

"Good. Close your eyes, relax and enjoy it."

Suddenly she wanted to giggle. He was a sneaky, devious man, her midnight marauder, but she loved him anyway. Closing her eyes, she did as he suggested and drifted on a lethargic wave: the brush of his fingertips on her skin; the sound of his voice as he murmured his pleasure; the feel of his tongue, rough and moist, seeking out each sensitive spot on her body; and the scent of his damp skin rubbing against hers. Then the current of sensations changed, gaining momentum, forming a tidal wave of immense strength until it finally crashed around her. When her heart slowed to a normal beat and her pulse calmed down, she closed her eyes and slipped back into sleep as if Cord's lovemaking was simply a wonderful dream.

THE FAINT RUMBLING, a far-off murmur, tried to drag her from the depths of slumber. Shelley opened her eyes, amazed to see how dim the bedroom was. Rolling over, giving her mind time to catch up with her body, she stared at the ceiling and studied the shadows as they slithered across the walls like drifts of gray smoke. Why was it still dark? She glanced at the bedside clock and growled. No one in their right mind should be up at five o'clock, especially after a long night, but Cord was. She patted the cold, empty space beside her, shrugged, then rolled over, clutching the pillow to her breast as she tried to recapture her dreams.

No sooner had her eyelids met than the mysterious muted noise came again. More alert this time, she identified it. Thunder coughed in the distance. The sound brought Shelley upright and flying from the bed to the window. She yanked back the curtains and yelped in delight. Languorous dark clouds pushed one another across the misty sky, bringing with them a strong breeze that ruffled thirsty leaves. Shelley whipped around and charged to the bathroom. In fifteen minutes she was dancing down the stairs, pausing only a second as she heard the deep sound of men's voices.

"Did you two hear the thunder?" She shot the solemn-faced men a bright smile, picked up a cup and filled it with hot, fragrant coffee. "Do you think it will rain soon?" With the cup to her lips she turned, a little puzzled by the continued silence.

"Shelley, will you please tell Nick he can't go charging over to Sara's at five-thirty in the morning?" Cord looked at Nick, ignoring his stony, determined expression. "Think of Robbie, for heaven's sake."

Shelley pulled out a chair across from Nick and sat down. "Cord's right. Until you get this situation straightened out with Sara, you don't want to involve Robbie. It's going to be a real shock for him finding out you're his father." She gave him a rueful grin. "Besides, Sara and Robbie go to church early. Then she takes him to one of his friend's house to play until around three in the afternoon. If you wait, you can talk to Sara alone."

Nick nodded and relaxed. "You're right, of course."

It wasn't until she lifted the coffee cup to her lips once more that she noticed both men were dressed in slacks and dress shirts, not their usual casual clothes. Though it was evident from the weight of the coffeepot they'd been up for sometime, they both looked like hell. No amount of clean-shaven jaws or combed hair could disguise the pale cast to their skin. Nick's complexion actually appeared tinged with green. It was obvious that each had monumental hangovers. A mischievous grin touched the corners of her mouth.

Shelley's expression caught Cord's attention and he

winked, then winced dramatically, as if the movement had been painful.

Feeling that they each needed to be taught a lesson, she set down her cup and rose. "I'm starving."

Nick paled even more. Cord almost choked on his sip of coffee, knowing that the twinkle in her eye boded no good for him.

"How about...? No. I'll surprise you." She quickly rose, and without thinking headed for the utility room and the freezer. Not until she touched the latch did she remember what was inside. She simply had to find a moment alone to talk to Cord! But it seemed fate had been her enemy lately, and she shrugged and opened the freezer, retrieving a round plastic container. Then, deliberately ignoring the men as she walked back into the kitchen, she proceeded to pop the carton into the microwave. As the chili defrosted, then heated, she scrambled eggs, steamed corn tortillas and grated Cheddar cheese.

Once everything was done, she set hot, green jalapeño sauce and a milder red picante sauce on the table with frosty glasses of orange juice. She looked over her shoulder, satisfied that Cord and Nick were deep in conversation and completely unaware of what she was about to do. She assembled the food, placing the fluffy scrambled eggs on the plates, topping them with the rich chunky chili, then a dollop of sour cream and sprinkles of grated cheese. The aroma of the Eggs Rancheros was mouth watering, but the combination did look disgusting. Juggling the three plates in her best restaurant manner, she managed to rush to the table and quickly get Nick and Cord's plates down before she dropped them.

Nick glanced down, then up. As the scent of eggs, hot sauce and chili wafted upward, his nostrils flared, his skin turned sickly white and a fine sheen of perspiration broke out on his forehead. Suddenly he was standing, then he was gone and a moment later the nearest bathroom door slammed shut.

"Shelley!"

"Yes, Cord?"

"That was not funny."

"No? Then why are you laughing?"

"I don't know. Maybe I'm crazy. But he's not going to appreciate your little joke. Besides, it's cruel. Nick's got enough to worry about now."

"I'm sorry." She grinned crookedly.

Cord sighed wearily and picked up his fork. "No, you're not."

Shelley's stomach grumbled loudly and they both looked up and burst into laughter.

"I'm starved."

"So I hear." He glanced sideways at the mound of food before her and shook his head. "I can't face this, either." He set down his fork, pushed his plate aside, picked up the glass of orange juice and downed it, savoring the cold liquid as it quenched his incredible thirst.

"Cord, we have to talk. There's something important I have to tell you."

He eyed her over the rim of the empty glass, his gaze full of suspicion. But before he could comment, Nick staggered into the kitchen. The only sign of life in the bloodless damp face were his eyes, and that cold green stare was ablaze with fire directed at Shelley. Cord could sympathize with the man, he even felt sorry for him, but he wasn't about to let an enraged Nick lay into Shelley. He quickly rose, clasped Nick's arm and guided him out of the room before Shelley could open her mouth and start an all-out war. "Come on, Nick. Why don't you lie down on the couch in the living room for a while."

A smile slowly etched its way across Shelley's lips as she listened to Nick's mumbling and Cord's soothing "I knows". Nothing could humble a man faster than a bout of hanging his head in a commode bowl. She happily finished her breakfast and had begun to clear the table off when Cord strolled back.

"When he feels better, make yourself scarce. Nick promised me he was going to pay you back."

Looking over her shoulder, Shelley widened her eyes in innocence. "Oh."

Cord relieved her of the plates in her hands, setting them on the counter. "Now, just what is it that you wanted to talk to me about?" He led her to a chair. Sitting down, he patted his knee. When she grinned but made no move, he gave her arm a firm tug. "I haven't held you in my arms in…oh, say two hours."

"Yes, and I've been meaning to talk to you about that. Does alcohol usually affect you that way?"

"It's been known to do strange things to me, but I guess you're referring to the middle-of-the-night raid on your body? Didn't you enjoy it?"

She slipped an arm around his neck and brought her mouth to his to show him just how much. "Next time, wake me up; I might enjoy it more."

Cord ran his hand over her thigh, moving it up to the apex of her legs. He cursed under his breath at the denim barrier. "When we get away from here, I want you to wear nothing but dresses. These damn things were not made for easy access." Despite his headache and hangover, he wanted her more than ever.

Shelley put her forehead on his and closed her eyes.

"You said when *we* leave here…. Are we leaving together?"

"Of course."

She pulled back and stared at him, then dropped her gaze to his white-and-gray striped shirt. She fingered the material, suddenly at a loss as to how to make him say the words she wanted desperately to hear. "You're over your doubts?"

"No, Shelley, not entirely. But it looks like I'm stuck with you. How does it go…in sickness and in health?"

Her heart began to race, making her light-headed. "In craziness and laughter?"

"For richer, for poorer."

They smiled at each other.

"Forever," she said.

Cord's laughter faded. "Yes, Shelley." His fingers threaded through her silky thick hair, bringing her mouth to his.

When they parted, breathless and smiling like fools, she asked, "Is this a marriage proposal?" Then she added quickly, "I love you very much, Cord."

His hands cupped her face. "I love you, too, Shelley, and yes, it was a marriage proposal of sorts. I just hope to God you never regret not being able to have children. I'll never let you go."

"We've been over and over this. It will work out, Cord; just let it happen." She touched his face, wanting only to soothe away the lines of skepticism.

"It's all happened so fast, Shelley. I feel that I need to give you some breathing room before we make any final plans."

"Damn it! You're not still worried that I'm confusing you with Anthony, are you? Cord, quit making problems for us."

"I can't help it. As I've said, it's all happened so fast. You were so confused and hurt. And about Anthony...no. I don't know how it happened, but I finally realized when you look at me you really don't see any part of Anthony, do you?"

"Absolutely not!"

"You're sure this is what you want? What if staying home palls? What if—"

She kissed him to make him shut up. "What if the world stops tomorrow. You could 'what if' our way into old age."

"I guess you're right." His hands slipped around from her back and gently covered her breasts. "I'm thinking Nick and his problems can go to the devil. Want to venture upstairs and see if the midnight marauder can strike again?"

"Come on. Nick will be asleep for hours." She slid off Cord's lap, stood, then froze. Her gaze collided with Nick's as he leaned against the kitchen doorframe.

"Hate to disappoint you, but as you can see, I'm up." He headed for the coffeepot, the shaking in his hands only a slight tremble now. With more bravado than he felt, he pulled out a chair and sat down, forcing a smile he was far from feeling. "I've been thinking."

"A very dangerous habit," Shelley mumbled under her breath.

Cord yanked her back down on his lap, giving her a threatening squeeze to shut her up.

Nick clasped the coffee mug with both hands and brought the hot liquid to his lips. After a big swallow he closed his eyes and sighed, thankful the brew had stayed down. "Shelley, were you serious about selling Pecangrove Plantation?"

A sarcastic retort was on the tip of her tongue, but

she bit it off. She'd harassed Nick enough, and he *had* begun to change. That hard edge that both scared and angered her was gone. "I'd like to sell, but it would have to be to the right person. Why?"

"I'd like to buy the place."

She straightened on Cord's lap, shrugged off his hold, rose and moved to a nearby chair. "I find that hard to believe, Nick." She found it more than hard to believe; she was dumbfounded. "What on earth would you do with a pecan plantation and with the added responsibility of Lee and Vo? I would never even consider selling to anyone who wouldn't agree to keep them on and continue to lease Lee the produce fields."

"I'm aware—"

"And there are other conditions that my aunt and uncle made that would have to be agreed to."

"I'll—"

"Like Sara and Robbie. They don't know it yet, but in another year their house and a small acreage will go to them, per my uncle's will." Her eyes narrowed. "No, I don't see you, a Navy man, particularly in your job, giving up your career for farming."

Nick looked at Cord for help. "Does she never shut up?"

Cord grinned, watching the two spar before he realized they actually liked each other and enjoyed their verbal fights.

"Shelley," Nick said, frustration tinging his voice, "I'm going to retire from the navy and I want this place for my family."

Shelley frowned. "What family? You don't have one."

Now it was Nick's turn to scowl. "Sara and Robbie,

of course. What the hell do you think I've been agonizing about for the past twelve hours?''

She was shocked to the marrow of her bones at the man's tenacity. ''You're buying this place for Sara, Robbie and yourself?''

''Right.'' He relaxed a little as she seemed to understand what was going on.

''And just how in the hell do you think you'll get Sara here?''

''Marry her, of course.''

The arrogance of the statement took her breath away. Shelley stood, put both hands on the table and leaned toward Nick. ''Just like that!'' She raised her hand and snapped her fingers before his eyes. ''After ten years of what she's been through?'' She snapped her fingers again. ''Just like that, you'll marry her. What if she doesn't want you? Have you even considered her feelings? From what I've heard she ran you off last night.'' She was pleased to see color stain his pale cheeks. ''If you go over there with that attitude, I wouldn't give you a nickel for your chances. You need help, Nick, lots of it, if you think Sara's a naive, submissive woman. She's tough. She's had to be to put up with some of the things she has in this town. But everyone respects her, Nick. She didn't run when the going got tough. She stayed and faced people till they accepted her.''

The color that had touched his face drained away, then returned brighter than ever. Shelley bet it was the first time in his adult life that he'd given in to his emotions in such a way.

Nick's eyes blazed, then the life died away and his shoulders slumped some. ''I have to make her understand that I never forgot her, even if she was only a beautiful dream.''

There was so much desperation and unhappiness and, yes, a lost little boy quality in his voice, that Cord winced. Seeing a man like Nick who for years had hidden behind an emotional wall now being stripped bare of his shield brought back his own pain. He was thankful for Shelley in more ways than one. She would never allow him to retreat behind his own poorly constructed shell again. He was free and alive. "Shelley, I don't think Nick meant his statement about Sara and Robbie to sound as self-centered and arrogant as you thought."

"Well, I hope not!" She sat down and stared at Nick's white face. There was so much emotional turmoil in those green eyes that she felt rather sorry for him. "I don't know what happened ten years ago. Maybe someday you or Sara will tell me, maybe not. But whatever you do, don't you dare hurt Robbie. If you do, I'll see to it that this town hangs you from the tallest tree."

"He's my son," Nick whispered, his voice ragged. "I'd never deliberately do anything to hurt him or Sara." He glanced at his watch, took a deep breath as if to brace himself, then looked up at Cord. "I can't wait any longer. I think we should go now. You are coming with me?"

Cord came to his feet, clasping Shelley by her arm and turning her to face him.

"Do you have to go?"

"Yes, I promised."

She dropped her voice to a low murmur. "What are you going to do, hold his hand?"

"If he needs it, yes," he whispered. "Stop being so hard on him, Shelley. The man's an emotional wreck."

She nodded and he kissed her. "I'm just worried about Sara and Robbie."

"Shelley...."

She spun around to face Nick, realizing he must have heard her.

"I know what pain and anger is. I suffered the first sixteen years of my life with a father who drank and beat his wife till she ran off, leaving both of us. Then he turned his meanness on me. I know how important love and tenderness is to anyone, but especially to a child. If I had stuck around ten years ago, I would have been different. But I didn't. I was due back at the base, had a hangover, and I couldn't separate fact from fantasy. Ten years ago, if only for a few dazed hours, I had a taste of what love and tenderness truly was. I want it again. I need someone to love me for what I am." He gave her one of his crocodile grins, then he was gone.

She was deeply ashamed. He was entitled to happiness just as she was. She looked at Cord with tears sparkling on her cheeks. "I'm a selfish bitch."

He folded her in his arms, laughed and patted her on the back. "No, you're not. I think you saw something in Nick that no one else did, and you were determined to release him from his personal hell. You've made the first incision. I hope Sara and Robbie will heal the rest for him." He kissed her again, torn between keeping his promise to Nick and staying to comfort her. A car horn honked impatiently a couple of times and he let her go.

Shelley watched the door close behind him. Though she was troubled over Nick's and Sara's situation, she couldn't help feeling elated that she and Cord had worked out their own problems. There was absolutely nothing to interfere with her happiness from now on.

CHAPTER THIRTEEN

LIKE MANNA FROM HEAVEN, rain pelted the parched ground in pea-size pebbles. Puffs of dust clouds rose with each drop, then disappeared as the rain began to fall in sheets of silver. Lightning stabbed at the earth, brilliant in its slashing forked jabs.

Shelley stood at the open kitchen window inhaling deeply as the air took on the pungent fragrance of renewed life. The cool breeze ruffled the curtains and teased her hair around her face. She rubbed the goose bumps on her arms and smiled with contentment. Taking another deep breath, she sighed. Damp air mingled with the enticing aromas of freshly baked bread and a peach cobbler just pulled out of the oven.

Forcing her attention from the window and back to what she was doing, she picked up a knife and started to shave paper-thin slices of veal from the thick roast. Shaved ham and turkey and grated Swiss cheese lay in aromatic heaps as she mentally ticked off the ingredients for Veal Savanna, one of her mother's famous specialities. Asparagus in a delicate white sauce and lightly sautéed julienne vegetables were going to make tonight a special dinner—just she and Cord. And now that all their problems were settled, he'd be in a better frame of mind to forgive her for squirreling away Anthony's notebook.

A moment later her sweet serenity was shattered. Napoleon, that damnable gander, was raising hell. His insistent honking grated on her nerves to the point that she couldn't ignore the racket any longer. Throwing down the knife, she spun and was stomping through the house to the front door before the blade had stopped quivering. She didn't even stop to think that with Cord and Nick at Sara's, and Lee and Vo having left earlier to take their day's crop to the market, she was totally alone.

Though determined to get rid of the feathered menace, she was cautious enough that when she yanked open the wooden door she made sure the screen door was securely closed by grabbing for the handle. But the handle was wrenched from her hand, and Shelley found herself staring into exotically slanted dark eyes. The eyes slitted.

"Dee!"

"Shell, call that damn *thing* off. What is it, anyway?"

"Our guard. Dee!" She stepped aside as her friend rushed past her to evade Napoleon's snapping. She pulled the screen door shut on the beady black gaze and the clicking bill. "Dee?"

"Well, yes, of course it's me, silly." She jammed her fists on her hips and flipped the cloud of black hair over her shoulder. "Look at my shoes—ruined!" She held out one mud-caked black-and-white Ferragamo pump and cursed.

"Dee, what are you doing here?"

She looked up, shrugged and stepped out of her shoes. "Now just what the hell do you think? My best friend disappears—runs off without a word to anyone..." she said reproachfully, her sensuous lower lip pouting pertly.

Shelley could only stare as her friend shook the drops of moisture from her trench coat, tossed it on the brass coatrack and turned to face her again. Dee Radford hadn't changed and never would. A small voluptuous woman with a cynical sense of humor who absolutely loved expensive clothes, possessions…and men. Shelley wasn't sure in which order her preferences ran, either. Dee devoured men. She dazzled and dumbfounded them by turning their own philosophy on them. She taunted them, teased them, fought with them and loved them until she was tired of the game, then she dropped them without explanation or regret. And if any man was stubborn enough to pursue or pester her with retribution in mind, Shelley had seen and heard Dee rip them apart with her cutting tongue.

One dark, delicately arched eyebrow rose haughtily. Suddenly they were in each other's arms, crying, laughing and trying to talk all at once. Dee grabbed Shelley by the shoulders and held her away from her. "I expected you to be a mere shadow of your former self, but I actually believe you've put on some needed weight." Shelley took another step back, gave a watery chuckle, pulled up her loose yellow cotton blouse and showed Dee the unfastened snap on her jeans.

"Disgusting. But you look so much better than when I last saw you. What the hell has been going on? Where's that no-account Anthony? Have you come to your senses and kicked the two-timing bastard out of your life for good?"

"Dee, Dee, please. One question at a time." She hugged her friend again. "Oh, it's so wonderful to see you. You just can't imagine what's been happening. Why…" A tiny warning bell went off in her head, and as hard as she tried to ignore it, it only rang louder. She wasn't supposed to disclose anything about Anthony or the trouble she was in. But surely, she argued with herself, it wouldn't hurt for Dee to know now that she was here. Yet, when she tried to start to explain again, nothing came out.

Dee must have thought Shelley was overwhelmed by the reunion and choked with emotion; she took her in her arms again. Shelley couldn't hold back the tears that welled up in her eyes and spilled down her cheeks. Dee had been a part of her life with Anthony, and though she wanted desperately to forget most of those events, there were still some happy memories worth remembering.

Dee straightened her bottle-green silk shirtwaist dress, checking it carefully for water spots, talking all the while. "Everyone has been asking questions about you. First you disappear, then Anthony vanishes." She glanced up and smiled, showing pearly white teeth. "There were bets going on all over the accounting department. I had to put a halt to it because of the rumors that were flying with the bets. All crazy talk of course, but some said you'd divorced Anthony and left town for good. Others said Anthony kicked you out because he had another woman. We both know that was nothing new to you, don't we, darling? Anthony always had a woman. Then there was the rumor that you were pregnant." She gave Shelley a sympathetic look. "We both know that's wrong, don't we?"

Shelley couldn't help smiling at the way Dee stood there trying to second-guess her, wanting desperately to know without asking outright. Dee was sharp and liked to maneuver her friends and co-workers into confiding in her and revealing information she needed. In fact, there was little, if anything, within Martin Aviation that

Dee wasn't aware of. Shelley began to feel uneasy. Dee
was head of the accounting department at Martin. Eventually, every expenditure came under her scrutiny. And,
of course, all cash distribution was handled by the accounting department, too. What if... She stopped. She
was being ridiculous. "Dee, how did you find me?"

The dark head was thrown back and Dee laughed.
"You know me. If you'll let me sit down and give me
some coffee, I'll tell all."

Shelley laughed and shook her head, trying to rid
herself of her distrustful thoughts. Dee was...Dee.
There was nothing faintly resembling Mata Hari in her
nature. "Come into—"

"For heaven's sake, don't ask me to sit in the
kitchen. I haven't changed, Shell. I absolutely hate the
place. Besides, I smell fresh-baked bread and something
else that's making my mouth water. You know I'm always on a diet, and the temptation will be too great to
resist. You get the coffee and I'll—" she looked
around, spotted the living room and began walking toward it "—I'll plant my tired body on that overstuffed
pillow with legs." She stopped, glanced over her shoulder and said with raised eyebrows, "What in the world
do you call this decor? It's—positively sweet and so
homey."

Shelley spun away, laughing as she left Dee inspect-
ing the Early American furniture, chintz and ruffles.
"So it's not plastic and chrome; it's comfortable." She
heard a long sigh as Dee settled down.

A few minutes later Shelley returned to the living
room, but Dee was nowhere in sight. She heard a low
curse, set the tray of coffee and cookies down and followed the sound to the library. Dee was standing in the

middle of the box-filled room, hands on hips, her expression one of frustration.

"One of your neighbors told me they'd seen a moving van parked in front of your place, but I just wouldn't believe them." She shot Shelley an angry glance. "Looks as if they were right. You and Anthony moved out bag and baggage. He is with you, isn't he?"

"Come on, Dee. Let's go sit down." Shelley walked into the living room and began to pour them each a cup of coffee, all the while trying to think of some version of the truth. She didn't want to lie, not to Dee, yet she knew she couldn't tell her what had actually happened, either.

"I'm waiting, Shell."

"Yes, I can see that you are. But I just don't know where to start. Maybe the end of my marriage came when Anthony told me he had a vasectomy. You know how badly I wanted children?"

"Yes, and he said he did, too, the bastard."

"Everything seemed to snowball after that. I told him I wanted a divorce and he agreed to sign the papers."

"I wish you had come to talk to me, Shell. After all, I am your best friend."

"I couldn't, Dee." That wasn't a lie, either. After she'd found Anthony in her boss's office with his camera and the plans for the VS-1 prototype, she couldn't have talked to anyone.

"But you didn't get the divorce?"

"Yes, actually I did."

"Well, hallelujah. You have more guts and smarts than I gave you credit for. So—" she dragged out the word thoughtfully "—you and Anthony aren't married any longer?"

"Well, yes and no. Legally we're not, morally we

are." Now came all the lies, and she hated herself for them. "Anthony followed me here and talked me into considering a reconciliation."

"And you fell for it! Really, Shell."

Shelley frowned, suddenly realizing just how much she hated Dee's habit of shortening her name.

"No! I did not fall for anything he said. I made him prove he wanted to work things out."

"You're a bigger fool than I thought. It's a damn good thing I came here or he'd have you talked into marrying him all over again. Have you forgotten the other women? Or the endless lies? The way he treated your family? What about the humiliation he caused you?"

Shelley didn't like the turn the conversation had taken. Dee, though her questions were honest enough and showed concern, seemed to be taking a sadistic pleasure in dragging up the past. There was an underlying viciousness in her tone and she appeared to be enjoying herself. Studying her friend's features carefully, Shelley noticed that worry had turned the sensuous lips downward, but didn't extend to the bright eyes. They were clear, cold and full of malice. It suddenly registered that Dee seemed to have aged a good ten years since Shelley had seen her last.

"We have problems, but we're trying." She picked up her coffee cup and glanced at Dee over the rim. "How did you find us?"

"Well, you used to tell me I was a witch."

"That was bitch, Dee. You were always good at purposely misunderstanding or twisting my words to suit you."

Dee eyed the small crescent-shaped cookies sprinkled generously with powdered sugar. She gave Shelley a quick scowl, sighed, then added three cookies to her saucer. "You've changed."

"Have I? But we're digressing. You haven't answered my question. How did you find me?"

Like a finicky cat grooming her whiskers, Dee licked the white powder off her lips slowly. "Did you know that after you left and Anthony skipped, Mr. Martin nearly went crazy? Then all of a sudden he just calmed right down and went about his business as if he'd never lost his assistant or his best test pilot. Strange, don't you think?"

"Dee! The answer."

"I'm coming to it, Shell, just be patient. Your family didn't know what was happening or where you were, either." She gazed at Shelley with a reproachful pout, her full lips wet and shining, eyes glassy with coldness.

Something was terribly wrong. Shelley felt the fine hairs on the back of her neck rise and goose bumps creep up her spine. She couldn't figure out if Dee was just carrying her teasing too far, or if she was truly enraged because she and Anthony had slipped away without telling her. Dee, she realized, had always been involved in their lives one way or the other. She must have really been hurt to react so strongly. As badly as she wanted to tell her friend all that happened, she knew she couldn't, so she hardened her voice. "How, Dee?"

"I don't understand what all the secrecy is about anyway. No one knew where you and Anthony were, but I suspected Mr. Martin did. He and his wife always treated you like a daughter." There was a long pause, then Dee smiled sweetly. "Did you ever shack up with the dear old gentleman, Shell?"

Shelley had just taken a sip of coffee and almost strangled. Finally, after catching her breath and getting a grip on her rising anger, she said, "That's a disgusting thing to ask." Her feeling of unease persisted.

"Where's Anthony, by the way?"

"He's out in the pecan grove with one of the hands." She glanced at her watch, noting how late it had become.

"It'll be nice to see him again," murmured Dee.

Shelley's head snapped up. "I thought you hated him."

"Hate's such a strong word, Shell. I feel nothing but contempt for Anthony, but he's a good sparring partner. I haven't had a satisfying fight with anyone in weeks."

Dee and Anthony had consistently been at each other's throats, though they were always very civilized and sophisticated about it. She'd just been thankful that they never turned their sarcastic needling and cruel little digs and thrusts on her. They never raised their voices, never lost their tempers, but sometimes they got so ugly that she'd leave the room. Later she would be amazed to hear laughter, but in no time they'd be at each other again.

Shelley glanced at Dee, knowing that once again she had deliberately distracted her from her original question. Folding her arms across her chest, Shelley leaned back against the chintz-covered couch and just stared.

"Oh! Very well. If you're going to be that way until you find out. I was in Mr. Martin's office when he received a call from your father. You know how Liz always screens his calls. Lord, you fussed at her enough to stop it. Anyway, it was lunchtime, so I slipped into your office and picked up the receiver." She grinned, a satisfying turn of her lips as if the action itself rid her of any guilt. "All I heard was something about you and Texas and pecans before I had to hang up. But I remembered you going to your aunt's and uncle's funeral, then later you mentioned something about inheriting the pecan plantation. It wasn't hard to trace you after that. I simply checked out travel records for airline and rental-car receipts.'' She spread her arms, smiling like a Cheshire cat. ''Abracadabra. I flew to Houston, picked up a map, rented a car and here I am. By the way, my overnight bag is in the car, and I'm not about to get wet or face that feathered beast again.'' She shivered delicately.

Shelley sympathized with her feelings about Napoleon, so it took her a minute to realize that Dee actually intended to stay at the farm tonight. She felt her cheeks redden in a mixture of injustice at how easily Dee had found them and how Nick's silly rules and precautions had obviously been for nothing. Then her color drained away and she cleared her throat. ''Listen, Dee, I hope you'll understand....'' Dear God, what excuse could she give her for not wanting Dee to stay the night? It was a hell of an evening, what with the rain looking as if it never intended letting up. Who would send a friend out in weather such as this? ''You can't stay here tonight.''

''You must be joking, Shell? Of course I can.''

''I'm sorry. Stay for dinner. I've cooked one of mother's specialities, the one you like so much. Then I'll call a hotel in Houston and get you a room.'' At that very moment she hated both Nick and Cord for putting her in such an embarrassing and awkward situation.

Dee looked around, her sharp gaze taking in everything. ''Come on, Shell. It's not as if you don't have the room.''

''It's Anthony, Dee. We made a promise to each other that we would settle all our problems by ourselves

without any interference from family or friends.'' She
was talking fast and lying freely, trying to cover up her
inhospitality and guilt. "We're working on this marriage, Dee." Dee gave a derisive expletive and Shelley
flinched, but continued. "It's only an hour's drive back
to Houston and the rain's slowing some. I…" She
trailed off as if her voice had slowly run out of power.
"I'm sorry, but that's the way it has to be."

"I guess I don't have a choice, do I?"

"No."

"What I do in the name of love." Dee sighed, then
gave Shelley a wink and they were both laughing. "Just
when is this new paragon of virtue coming in from la-
boring in the fields? Lord! Anthony actually getting his
hands dirty!''

Shelley was in another fix. She couldn't have Dee in
too close contact with Cord. Granted, he and Anthony
were identical twins, but there were subtle differences:
Cord's scar over his eyebrow; the small hump that on
too close inspection would reveal a once broken nose;
his more muscular build; his deeper voice, and probably
the most telling of all was the genuine compassion that
showed so clearly from his navy blue eyes. Dee, if allowed to get too close, would eventually discern a difference and ask questions. Questions she couldn't answer—not yet.

"You're not angry, are you Dee? You know at any
other time you'd be more than welcome to stay, just not
now. We need the privacy. Anthony, for the first time,
has admitted he has some real problems."

"He certainly does," said Dee angrily, giving a jerky
flip of her head, sending the dark hair bouncing over
her shoulder. "But I think you're a fool. The man's not
going to change." She held up her hand to stay Shel-

ley's retort. "Sorry. But, damn it, Shell, I don't want to see you hurt anymore, and... Oh, never mind."

Both women jerked upright as they heard the shutting of the back door. Shelley set down her coffee cup. "Cor...Anthony," she said unnecessarily, suddenly at a loss as to how to handle the situation. When she caught Dee's puzzled expression at her uncertainty, she could have kicked herself. "Let me tell him you're here." Panic caused Shelley to immediately surge to her feet when Dee set down her cup and looked as if she was going to join her. "Dee, please. Anthony and I *did* make promises to each other. Your being here will look as if I've broken mine."

Dee sat, crossed her shapely legs and sighed. "Very well. Go tell him the wicked witch has arrived."

Shelley smiled. "It's bitch, Dee. You keep conveniently forgetting." The last was said over her shoulder as she quickly left the room.

Cord wasn't hard to find. Barefoot, his slacks and shirt damp and clinging to his frame, his tie obviously forgotten somewhere, he was standing beside the table, spoon in hand as he helped himself to a huge bite of peach cobbler. Shelley rushed in and he looked up, smiled lovingly, then returned his attention to the cooling cobbler.

Wondering if that endearing grin was for her, or the fact that she'd cooked one of his favorite desserts, she tried to frown but her mouth wouldn't cooperate. "Put that down." She plucked the spoon from his hand as he was about to dig out a crunchy corner. "Why are you so wet? Where are your shoes? And," she continued, "where the hell have you been all day?"

Cord reached out, attempting to snatch the spoon. "I walked home from Sara's. And as to why I've been gone so long…'' He shrugged, then gave her a helpless look that defied the sparkle in his eyes. ''Nick lost his courage this morning, and we drove around for what seemed days before he regained enough backbone to face Sara again.'' Cord grinned. ''By the way, he blames his weakened condition on you and…'' What he would have said next died in his throat as he took a good look at Shelley's strained face for the first time since he'd come in. There was a sudden sinking feeling in the pit of his stomach. He knew he shouldn't have left her alone. ''What's wrong?''

''Dee's here.''

He cursed low and fluently, then paused only to stare at her accusingly. ''You called her?''

''Of course not.''

''How could you after all Nick's warnings?''

''I didn't,'' she snarled quietly as she took a quick look behind her. ''Dee found us, Cord. And just how in the bloody hell are we to handle this? Where's Nick when you need him? You're so quick to accuse—you think of something.''

He picked up a napkin and wiped his mouth in an angry gesture, still gazing hard at Shelley, trying to decide whether she was being straight with him.

But neither had time to think of a plan as a husky voice spoke from the doorway.

''As I live and breathe, the happy couple—so touching.'' Dee strolled into the kitchen. ''Anthony, I do believe country air agrees with you; you've put on some weight.'' She laughed. ''You both have.''

Cord froze and watched Dee like a hawk would a tiny field mouse. This was no helpless innocent creature. As far as he was concerned and no matter what Shelley said, this was a dangerous woman. A self-centered, self-indulgent, exotic woman with the morals of an alley cat. He had an unexplainable insight into people; perhaps that's what made him a top-notch photojournalist. Put a camera in his hand and he could capture the uncapturable—a look, a gesture that would reveal what the subject usually wished to hide. Now, all his senses were screaming that Dee was nothing but trouble and definitely no friend of Shelley's. Her relationship with Anthony? He didn't know *yet*, but he had his suspicions.

He knew he couldn't stand there and allow the devouring dark eyes to inspect every inch of him. His radar already told him she sensed something amiss. He had to leave before she put two and two together and exposed him for what he was. Bringing the paper napkin he had wadded in his fist to his mouth, he sneezed. Not a quiet sneeze, either, but a huge one that shook his large frame. "Dee," he asked soggily, "what broom did you fly in on?"

Shelley started visibly. It was something Anthony would say to needle Dee and had just the right amount of sarcasm and contempt. She shivered. Damn, it was eerie to hear it coming from Cord. All she wanted to do now was get Cord out of the room, but she didn't even have a chance to open her mouth.

"I could ask you how you got here, too, Anthony…dear. You've stopped running? Or is it that you've run out of places to hide?"

There seemed to be much more to the question than Cord understood, or if the truth be known, more than he wanted to. He was sure that at some time Dee and Anthony had had an affair. Whether it was before his brother married Shelley, he didn't know. "I never *run*. Like you, Dee, I fly."

Shelley smiled.

Dee frowned. Cord brought the napkin to his mouth and faked another mammoth sneeze. "Shelley, I'm coming down with a damn cold. I'm going to take a hot shower, some aspirin and lie down." He would have to pass very close to Dee as he left the room, so he sneezed again.

This time he didn't cover his mouth and it had the desired effect. Dee stepped back a couple of paces and turned her head slightly away from him.

"I know your heart's broken that I won't be able to stay and chat. Oh, sorry. I forgot, you don't have a heart."

"That's right. You and I are two of a kind. You've said it often enough, but I'll survive without you and we'll talk another day."

Dee's tone had an ominous ring to it. Shelley opened her mouth to say something, then shut it immediately, deciding to drop the subject. Her gaze went to Dee, then to Cord's retreating back.

"Shelley, he hasn't changed at all. And you are an even bigger fool than I first thought." Dee walked out of the kitchen with a tight-lipped Shelley following at her heels. Snatching up her purse from the corner of the couch, she headed for the brass coatrack and jerked down her trench coat.

"I thought you were going to stay for dinner." Dee didn't answer, but struggled into her coat. "Don't leave like this. At least let me call a hotel in Houston and get you a room."

"No thanks, Shell. If I hurry I can catch the eight-o'clock flight back to Seattle."

This was her best friend. Shelley felt wretched, rid-dled with guilt at being unable to tell Dee why she was acting so standoffish. Something she couldn't grasp or understand had subtly changed between them. "I'm sorry, Dee. Truly I am." And even though Dee tried to avoid her, she reached out and hugged her.

Silk-clad shoulders stiffened for a moment, then Dee returned the embrace. There were tears in the dark, cynical eyes as she forced Shelley to arm's length. "I'm sorry, too. More sorry than you'll ever know. You were a good friend."

"Were, Dee?" She wanted to laugh, but the sound hung in her throat. "Nothing's changed, we're still friends."

"Yes, of course." Dee opened the front door, gave a disgusted grimace at the drizzling rain and started to run for the car parked in front of the house. "Take care of yourself, Shell."

With a limp wave and without a backward look, Dee was in the car and starting down the driveway. Shelley stood with the door open, shivering from the damp air and a sudden feeling of apprehension. The red eyes of Dee's taillights soon disappeared into the dark, gloomy night, but still she watched. She'd lost a friend. She knew it in her heart just as surely as night turned into day, but she couldn't figure out why. What possibly could have sent Dee away as if she had a burr in her backside? Shelley sighed, closed the door and glanced at the stairs leading to her bedroom. She smiled suddenly, pushing away the unpleasantness of the day as she thought of Cord's fine bit of acting. Her smile grew as she bounded up the stairs, wondering what interesting bits of information he had to tell about *his* day.

CHAPTER FOURTEEN

LIKE SHELLEY, CORD STOOD at a window in the bedroom watching the the taillights of Dee's car being swallowed up by the rain and darkness. There was a queasy feeling in the pit of his stomach about her visit. He felt sure Dee had had an affair with Anthony. He was equally sure that Shelley didn't even suspect them. Why else would Dee come all the way to Texas? Friendship? He didn't think so. More than likely she was anxious about Shelley and Anthony's disappearance and a possible reconciliation.

His eyes traced the weighty drops running in ribbons down the outside of the glass. A deep frown puckered his forehead, pleating his eyebrows together as a new, rather outrageous thought persisted to nag him. What if…? No, that was too wild to contemplate. Besides, Nick would have thoroughly checked out Dee and her background. If there was even the remotest chance that she was involved in Anthony's treasonous act, he would have told him. Wouldn't he? Damn! Nick was a sneaky bastard. He probably wouldn't have warned him once he realized how close he and Shelley had become.

Nick was smart enough to know he would have discussed Dee's possible involvement with Shelley, and Shelley would have laughed in both their faces. The frown deepened. What if his theory was right? That meant they were in real trouble. Where was Nick? Still at Sara's trying to put his personal life together? He needed to phone and tell him about Dee's arrival right away. Cord swung around, only to stop as he caught sight of Shelley staring at him from the doorway.

She leaned against the doorframe and gazed at Cord. The short robe he was wearing hid very little. Even with all the problems of the past couple of hours and the headache that was a dull throb behind her eyes, she still had a genuine smile for the sight of Cord and his long, muscular legs. Loving someone was the easy part, she realized. It was the daily maintenance of the relationship that truly mattered. The smile blossomed like an opening rose in spring.

Cord's mouth stretched into a grave and determined line. "No evasions, no sidestepping, no dithering. How did that woman find us?"

Shelley strolled past him, sat down on the edge of the bed and sighed, closed her eyes, then flopped back. "Would you bring me an aspirin, please?" The room's quiet pounded with every beat of her heart, and she didn't stir until the bed gave way to Cord's weight. Barely opening her eyes, she accepted the glass of water and two tablets and propped up on her elbow to take them, then lay back down.

"Shelley, we have to call Nick and tell him that Dee found us and how."

"Yes, I know. Just let me rest a minute so I can gather my wits."

"How, Shelley?"

She repeated what Dee had told her and rather enjoyed the silence that followed her explanation.

"If it was that easy for Dee, then the people after me—Anthony—hell!" He fanned stiff fingers through his damp hair. "I've become so caught up in this deception I think I'm losing my identity."

"No you're not. You're nothing like your brother."

"Tell me again how she found us."

She did, slowly this time so she could remember every word Dee had spoken.

"I don't like it, Shelley. It doesn't hold together. Why didn't she simply phone? If she knew where you were, she could have just as easily looked up the phone number. Why take the trouble, time and money to come all the way out here?"

Shelley opened one eye and studied his worried expression. "That's just Dee."

"I don't like it. I've got bad vibes."

"I like your vibes." She rolled over to face him, letting her fingers straighten his ruffled hair.

Cord grabbed her hand. "This is not the time." He tried to scowl fiercely, but his sparkling dark blue eyes gave him away. "If Dee is head of accounting that means she eventually sees all expenditures, right?"

Shelley closed her eyes and grimaced. "Yes."

"How did Martin pay the designer of the new jet-fighter prototype? Would payment have gone through the accounting department, or does Mr. Martin pay them out of a special fund?"

"Accounting pays the bills." Her heart began to pound at his line of questioning. "But the expenditures are disguised with false names. The checks don't go directly to the designer per se, but first to a dummy company set up and headed by Mr. Martin. He then issues a check to the designer."

"Is that customary among independent aviation companies?"

"I think so. They all have to have ways of hiding their secrets."

"So someone who was familiar with the general procedure would know where to look and when to spot a dummy corporation?"

"Cord, I know where this is leading, and you're wrong. Dee is not mixed up in this business of treason."

"How do you know? From what I remember, she worked at the same company Anthony did, and she had only been with Martin a short while before Anthony joined her. And I do know something about current fashions and the cost of women's clothes. That was one expensively dressed woman who left here a while ago."

"Dee has an outside income, Cord, from a deceased relative—" She broke off trying to remember which member of Dee's family had left her money. "I think it was an uncle or great-uncle. I don't know, but someone left her an inheritance, which she invested wisely."

"She told you all this?"

"Yes."

"I see."

"Well, I sure as hell don't. Do you really think Dee is involved in this mess?" She rolled over on her back, not wanting to see the confirmation in his eyes. She didn't want to argue with him any longer, either, because it was ridiculous to think of Dee as... But it wasn't hard, she admitted suddenly. Dee, with her exotic looks, daring and aggressive personality, certainly had what it took to be a spy. Dee liked the darker side of life, the thrill and suspense of a hunt.

Could she have so misjudged her? Making an ass of herself over Anthony was bad enough, but to think that she'd been fooled by Dee, another woman, her best friend. They'd shared secrets only women share. There was supposed to be an honesty, a bond… Lord, if it was true, then what did that have to say for her ability to judge people?

Shelley was so lost in her thoughts that she was jerked back to the present when Cord slammed down the telephone.

"There's no one at Sara's. Damn it! Nick needs to know what's happening, and I don't dare call Milly's."

Her eyes popped open. "Milly? What has Milly to do with Nick and Sara?"

Cord reached out and drew her into his arms, disregarding the way his robe gaped open and exposed an enticing expanse of flesh. Shelley was distracted by the sight as her eyes traveled down hard muscles, prominent blue veins that lay just under the surface of smooth tan skin, a soft pelt of hair and long legs. She almost laughed at herself. Here she was in the middle of a serious conversation and she wanted Cord to shut up and make love to her. But she'd asked the question and waited for an answer.

"Sara has almost agreed to marry Nick. By the way, you should see him; you wouldn't recognize him. He's happy, Shelley, really happy, and it shows, too." She snuggled closer and he tried to ignore the quickening throb in his groin. "Anyway, Sara told him if they were to marry and live here she was going to have to let the town know that Nick is really Robbie's father. She said Milly and Ruby were the best ones to consult about how to handle the town gossip, which is inevitable, so as not to hurt Robbie."

"They've told Robbie, then? How did he take the news?"

"They haven't told him. Just before I left there Robbie's friend called to ask if he could stay for dinner, so he hasn't been home yet.''

Like a magnet her hand seemed drawn to the hair on his chest, and she absently wrapped tiny coils around the tips of her finger. ''They're in for a rough time, Cord. Even with Milly's and Ruby's help, this is still a small town and a piece of gossip of this magnitude is rare. It will go on for a long time.''

''Maybe, but Milly will help soften the blows somehow. The old dragon will soon have everyone feeling sorry for the star-crossed lovers. I know that old girl, Shelley. She won't lie—that's beyond a lady like Milly—but she'll have this town believing that Nick and Sara were parted by something outrageous enough to be believed and accepted.''

He eased her from his warm side as he reached for the telephone and dialed. When he turned and stretched, the robe rose up and over his body to reveal an arousal he'd been trying to conceal. Shelley chuckled to herself, her eyes gleaming wickedly.

Cord almost dropped the receiver as he felt her hands on him. He quickly hung up and rolled over, capturing her hands and prying them away from his body. ''No, no. No you don't. We're still having a rational conversation and I want to continue. Then I want to go downstairs and eat—dinner, Shelley.'' His deep voice roughened as her head dipped and he had to restrain her efforts. They were both laughing over the struggle, and he sighed dramatically when she finally gave up. ''Tell me about the VS-1, Shelley.''

To go from lust to an airplane was a shock to her system and it took a few seconds for Shelley to gather her thoughts. She frowned and Cord misinterpreted it.

''Damn it, my life is probably on the line because of

the thing. The least you can do is tell me about it. Besides, I'm cleared by Nick and the admiral. One of the perks to induce me to come here was an exclusive story about the plane when the navy is ready to release the proven prototype to the public. Come on, Shelley. I know it's more than a jet fighter capable of obliterating its own image on radar.''

"You're right; it is more, much more. The VS-1—incidentally, the VS stands for Vapor Septer—is not only a small deadly fighter, it's a phenomenon! The jet is so revolutionary, Cord, that its value to American defense is mind-boggling.''

She could see he was becoming impatient, yet she didn't want to rush. She needed to explain the innovative engine and fuel system thoroughly. "The jet runs on a relatively cheap form of fuel that is reduced to vapor by the specially designed engine. The vapor is recycled and allows for continuous refueling. Think of it, Cord, the aircraft has a constant supply of fuel. No midair refueling mishaps, no quarrel with foreign countries for permission to land, fly over or take off as we did with Spain and France during the Libyan incident. The VS-1 can conceivably fly from anywhere in the U.S. to say, Russia, and back without landing or refueling.''

She had absolutely stunned him. His staring silence lasted so long she began to get uneasy. "Cord?"

"That aircraft is a weapon even our *allies* would like to get their hands on—right?''

She hadn't looked at it from that angle. "Well, yes, I guess they would.''

"Shelley, some of our so-called allies are not so friendly. They have spies everywhere. My God, now anybody and everybody could be after us! If we're found here we're dead. Do you hear me, Shelley? They, whoever they are, are after Anthony's notebook or the plans they think he—I—have. They won't hesitate to kill for the information.''

He was quiet a moment as another thought struck him. ''They'll think I'm Anthony and probably won't kill me right off.... Oh, crap. I could end up in Russia, in Lubyanka Prison before anyone even realizes I'm gone. I doubt I'd ever be able to convince them I'm not Anthony.... This whole scheme was outrageously wild from its inception!''

His fear and the reality of just what kind of danger they were exposed to transmitted itself to her with the same stunning blow. ''This isn't a game, is it, Cord?''

''You can bet your life on it, sweetheart. The stakes just changed and old Nicholas is going to have to find someone new to play out his deadly charade. We're out as of this second. Dee found us and others won't be far behind. They're smart enough to have put a tail on your best friend.''

He reached for the phone, fumbling in his dread. Finally he yanked the receiver from its cradle and began to punch out Sara's number. When no one answered, he cursed, then hit the numbers that Shelley called out for Milly and Ruby's home. The line continued its empty ringing as he held the instrument so Shelley could listen. It was obvious to them both they were alone—and totally on their own.

THEY BARELY SLEPT that night. At least that's what Shelley thought until she was roughly shaken awake. The room was in total darkness, and she could just make out the silhouette of Cord leaning over her. ''What?''

''Shh.''

A wad of material landed in her face.

"Get up and get dressed."

She could sense the urgency in his every word. Catching the anxiety and fear and, yes, there was an edge of excitement in his voice, she whispered, "What's happening?"

"Quietly, Shelley. Get dressed." His shadow left the side of the bed and moved to the window facing the front of the house and the lane.

She swung out of bed, stepped into her jeans, then yanked on the dark blue shirt he'd picked out. As she buttoned it, she moved to the window, stopping only when Cord grasped her arm and pulled her to the side where he had made a tiny crack in the curtains.

"Take a good look. There are three cars blocking the lane down by the road." He shifted her body in front of him so they could both see. "I count five men getting out. That's not a posse, Shelley, and those guns they're carrying are for real. Let's get the hell out of here." He didn't give her time to open her mouth before he was shoving her jogging shoes at her and whispering roughly for her to hurry.

They sped down the stairs and were out the back door before the five men had made two furtive steps toward the house.

Cord eased the screen door shut so it wouldn't alert the men that they'd been spotted. As he turned he stopped and looked around. "Where the hell do we go?"

Moonlight caught the glitter of excitement in his eyes, and she realized Cord wasn't even going to give her time to freeze up with fright.

"Where, Shelley? You know this place better than I do."

"We could hide in the windbreak."

"What's that?"

Shelley raised her hand and pointed to the north beyond the pecan groves. "That jungle you once asked me about and obviously weren't listening when I explained. The trees and thick vegetation were planted to break the winter's north wind and protect the pecan trees. It's a jungle in there, Cord. We could hide, at least until morning, then go for help."

"Good thinking." He snatched her hand, holding it firmly in his as they took off across the yard.

Thick, humid air made breathing hard, or was it fear that forced her lungs to overwork? Shelley pondered the question as she ran, gasping for breath. She could jog five miles a day without too much trouble, yet here she was, struggling for air after what seemed only a few steps. She stumbled on a mud-slick patch of ground and would have fallen to her knees if Cord hadn't quickly yanked on her arm and pulled her upright.

He slowed, wrapped an arm around her shoulders and whispered, "You all right?" Just barely making out her nod, he led her to the corner of the big machinery barn and stopped. "We have an open field to cross before we hit the shelter of the pecan grove." He glanced up at the sky. Dawn was about an hour and a half away and the sky was beginning to lighten. But there were clouds starting to move like ghosts across the surface of the full moon, disguising the land below in a false darkness. "We'll wait for another series of clouds before we try for the open. Damn!" A soft rain began to fall. Shelley shivered hard next to him and he said, "What a hell of a time to be out in the rain."

She tried to smile but her teeth began to chatter, and she forced her lips tight to keep them still. She didn't

want to tell Cord it wasn't the weather making her tremble, but fear. "Cord, I have something to tell you—
something important you should know if I don't make
it out of here." She admitted her imagination was running wild, but she couldn't help it. She'd never been in
a life-and-death situation before.

With his attention on the sky and the house behind
them, he almost missed what she was saying and the
guilt in her voice. "Of course we'll get out of here.
Don't even doubt it for a second."

Confessions of wrongdoing never came easy for her,
but she gritted her chattering teeth. "I found Anthony's
notebook."

"What!" He almost yelled but caught himself just in
time. He didn't have a chance to continue as the ebony
darkness fell once more over them. "Run," he growled
angrily, grabbing her hand and taking off across row
after row of strawberry plants.

Fingers of light began to peek out from the tattered
clouds just as they reached the first line of pecan trees
and stopped to catch their breath. Moonbeams and the
rain that had settled on the leaves made the grove a
fairy-tale place; the trees looked as if they were covered
in a veil of gossamer silver. A soft breeze rustled rain-
drenched leaves, sending down a shower of pearly
drops.

Cord and Shelley looked at each other, soaked to the
skin, hair plastered to their heads and water dripping off
their noses. They blinked drops of moisture from their
eyes, wanting to laugh out loud despite their fears.

"I hope the sky and trees dumping on us isn't a sign
of what's to come."

Cord grinned, and in the strange glow of the moon
his teeth took on an eerie brightness, a jack-o'-lantern

smile, that made Shelley want to laugh all over again. His fingers intertwined with hers and they stepped out from under the weeping trees. Then they ran, or walked as fast as they could. Once again Mother Nature seemed determined to put obstacles in their path. The once hard-packed ground was now a mire of mud, saturated with the torrential rain. Hand in hand, sometimes arm in arm, they slipped and slid through the center of the grove.

Shelley's feet almost flew out from under her and she grabbed Cord's arm in panic. He grimaced at her vise-like hold. If the situation hadn't been so serious, she would have flopped down in the mud and rain and laughed herself silly. But as they continued to struggle out of the grove, and with Cord looking over his shoulder every other second, their predicament didn't amuse her. All she wanted to do was get to the thick jungle shelter beyond, find a place to sit and rest.

Out of the night a sound reached them, a sound like a firecracker exploding. The noise froze Cord in his steps, and he pulled Shelley to a sliding stop, also.

"What was that?" She could feel the muscles in his arm grow rigid and became alarmed by the tension that emanated from him. "Cord?"

The muffled popping came again and Cord cursed. "Gunfire."

"Lee and Vo!" She felt a deep bite of guilt that she'd never once given a thought to the Oriental couple. "Cord, what have we done? We have to go back, they might be hurt." She turned, carefully placing her feet in the slimy mud, then found herself yanked back around sharply. She teetered, lost her footing, grabbed for Cord and pulled him down as he tried to catch her.

Cord ignored the ooze of mud sucking at his body

and hauled a sobbing Shelley into his arms. "They'll be all right, Shelley. Now get up, honey."

She sniveled, feeling suddenly beaten, as if the whole world were against her. Her attitude amazed her. She'd always been strong, in control of every situation and never overly emotional. Now, sitting in a puddle of mud, wet and cold, she was falling apart. "Why didn't we warn them? We could have."

"No!" Cord growled. "We didn't have time." He grabbed her shoulders, gave her a tiny shake and said, "Whoever those people are, they're not going to hurt Lee and Vo. Shelley, they can't afford to have dead bodies scattered all over the place. If they had caught us, we would simply disappear. Taking two people is far easier than taking four. If they do anything to Lee and Vo, they'll only tie them up and make it look like robbery. Come on, sweetheart. Get up. We have to get out of here."

He managed to stand, then grasping her upper arms, hauled her to her feet. "Shelley, stop crying." He reached out to wipe away her tears and stopped after the first touch. A wide streak of mud adorned her cheek. With a glint of mischief, he duplicated the mark on the other side of her face, then placed a stripe across her forehead.

Shelley stood perfectly still, trying to get hold of herself. She sniffed. "Why'd you do that?" She knew she looked ridiculous, painted for war and as bedraggled as a wet dog. She sniffed again.

Cord chuckled. "Hell, I don't know. Just seemed the right thing to do. It stopped your crying and feeling sorry for yourself, didn't it? Come on, sweetheart, let's go."

For some unexplainable, silly reason, she felt better.

Wet, muddy, exhausted, but her spirits were revived. She carefully walked beside Cord toward the windbreak.

The smell of rotting vegetation, rich dirt and pine reached them before they entered the tangled jungle. Cord held back a web of wild blackberry vines and Shelley, on hands and knees, crawled through. They moved a few yards on all fours before the berry and ivy vines thinned out, and they were suddenly able to stand under a canopy of tall pine trees. The ground was damp and spongy beneath their feet. Moonlight filtered through the tree limbs in sharp spikes of light.

After her eyes became adjusted, Shelley spied a fallen log and made her way toward it. She was almost out of the shaft of light and into the gloomy darkness when she stumbled, cursed, then felt her way to the decaying stump. Just as she turned around and her body began to sag downward, she was suddenly hauled back to her feet.

"We can't stop here. It's too close to the edge." Shelley groaned. Cord ignored her, but sympathized. He was cold and tired, too, and remembering a warm bed and body he'd been driven from. With the urgency to run and hide fading in the thickness of their cover, he began to remember the bomb she'd laid on him and became angry. "We'll make our way in a little deeper, and as we go you can tell me how and where you found Anthony's notebook...and where it is now."

Shelley groaned again, but for a different reason this time. Cord was not pleased with her tidbit of news. Why hadn't she told him before now? *Because,* she answered herself, *I was afraid he'd leave before we'd worked out our problems.* With that reasoning in mind, she really didn't feel so bad. After all, she'd done it for them.

Abruptly Shelley pulled her arm from Cord's grasp and peered at the trees in all directions. "Somewhere in here Robbie has a tree house. Sara found out about it and nearly threw a fit until he promised not to come alone again. If we could find it we could at least have some shelter."

Cord followed the circle of her gaze and scowled. "Which direction?"

She shrugged and murmured, "I wish Lee was here, he'd know. Robbie never brought me—I'm a *girl*."

His scowl deepened, then he shook his head. "We could roam around in here for days and never find his fort. And you changing the subject won't make me forget my question. Why on earth didn't you tell me you'd found Anthony's notebook?"

As they walked through the gloomy jungle, breathing in the damp pungent air and shivering from their wet and muddy clothes, Shelley began to explain all her reasons for keeping quiet. When she finally finished and her explanations met only silence, she glanced over at Cord. "Well?"

"Where did you hide it?" He didn't want to let go of his anger just yet, but he was touched with her reasoning.

"The freezer, labeled 'Lamb Chops.'"

A short bark of laughter bounced around them in a muffled echo. "I guess it's as safe a place as any."

"You're not still angry?"

"No. I should be, but I'm not." He stopped suddenly, alerted by sounds that were foreign to those he'd become accustomed to. They weren't the noises of the night, but human sounds. "Listen. We have company."

CHAPTER FIFTEEN

SHIFTING SHADOWS seemed to close in around them. Even though dawn was beginning to highlight the night in shades of violet, the sky still appeared angry, as if the dark clouds were bruises on the surface of the moon. Cord drew Shelley deeper into the shadows between two towering pine trees. The intrusive sounds stopped, then started again, growing louder with their gradual advancement. "I think it's just a small animal," he whispered next to her ear. "But we'll wait here until we're sure."

Shelley felt the warmth of Cord's chest against her back, the security of his arms around her, and was grateful he was there. She could feel the heavy pounding of his heart—or was it hers? Both, more likely. Then, over the noise of her own breathing, she heard the stomping of feet, the snapping of limbs and a low muttering punctuated every so often by a sob. As the intruder drew closer, Shelley's mouth went dry. She grabbed one of Cord's hands, squeezed hard and closed her eyes.

It was a combination of Cord's chuckles, the feel of his body relaxing and the increasing volume of a small boy's pitiful sobs that snapped her eyes open. Robbie was walking slowly toward the clearing, kicking anything within reach of his foot and crying profusely. Every once in a while he'd swipe at his nose with the sleeve of his blue Superman T-shirt, mumble, sniff, then begin crying again.

Simultaneously Shelley and Cord stepped forward, bringing the boy to a watery, wide-eyed stop. It was then that Shelley noticed the ingenious little fella had used his superman cape as a makeshift backpack. Bulging to overflowing, it left angry red marks on the child's neck. It didn't take a detective to figure out that for whatever reason, Robbie was running away from home.

"Robbie…" she said softly, and in a shot his thin arms were wrapped around her waist and his head buried in her middle. His narrow shoulders shook in her embrace. Tears welled up in her eyes and spilled over, running down unchecked on her cheeks. She couldn't stand to see Robbie hurt and glanced over at Cord. He wasn't unaffected by the wretched sobs, either. Reaching behind her, she pried Robbie's viselike grip loose, grasped his shoulders and held him at arm's length. "Have you run away from home?"

The boy's gaze fell to the ground. He sniffed, took a deep, half-sobbing breath and said, "Yes, ma'am."

Shelley placed a finger under his trembling chin and raised his blotched face. "Why?"

"'Cause…'cause." He hiccuped, sobbed, then dug in the hip pocket of his jeans, pulled out a mangled red-and-white checkered handkerchief and blew his nose with a loud honking that made Shelley and Cord laugh and even brought a twisted smile to Robbie's lips. "He's my real dad," he burst out. "I told all my friends my dad was dead." Another sob escaped his lips and he squeezed his eyes shut.

Shelley waited, knowing that the real reason for this little boy's outburst was not that Nick was his father or what he'd told his friends.

"I came home from Jeff's and my mom was crying, see. So…I kicked *him* in the leg like I did that Tinkle man. My mom…" His chin began to wobble. "My mom spanked me." He hung his head and dropped his gaze to the leafy ground between his feet. "She never walloped me like that before and…I hate him, and he's not my father, neither. He made my mom mad at me…and, and…" Robbie glanced up, his expression bewildered. "She let him sleep in the house, all night long."

"Oh, Robbie." Shelley gathered the crying boy into her arms and shot Cord a helpless glance. If this wasn't so serious she'd laugh. Here they were, running from killers and having to deal with a little boy's problems first. There was no knowing how far away their hunters were, or where they were, for that matter.

Cord squatted, took hold of Robbie and tried to shift the child around to face him, but Shelley tightened her hold, and for a second they frowned at each other over the boy's head. "Come on, my man, you used to like Nick."

"Did not."

"Now, I know better. Be honest, Robbie, you did and I bet you still do."

"Don't." His small square chin was stubbornly stuck out, the hazel eyes were full of hurt and the lips mutinous.

"Yes, you do. Think of all the things he's done for you. You're just mad because you're used to having your mom to yourself, and now you'll have to share her. But, Robbie, you'll have Nick around all the time, too. Think of all the things you can do with him that you couldn't do with your mom. Or, if you did, it wouldn't be as much fun as it would be with another man. You love your mother, don't you?''

"Yes." The chin began to tremble again.

"And your mom loves you, but she also loves Nick in a different way. She has a special love for you, Robbie. You're her only son." Cord could see the thoughts spinning about behind the boy's bright eyes. Robbie looked skeptical and hopeful and frightened all at the same time.

"Do you think Nick would teach me to fight like Lee?''

Shelley fought back a smile. "I'm sure he would if you asked." Robbie's worried gaze shifted from one to the other for reassurance, then it suddenly struck him where they were and how strange his friends looked. "Shelley, why are you all muddy and painted up like an Indian on the warpath?''

Cord answered before Shelley could reply. "Robbie, we need your help. There are some bad men after us, and we need to find a hiding place.''

Robbie threw back his shoulders and sucked in an excited breath, his tears immediately drying. "Some men came to the house just when I was sneaking out the back door. They woke Mom up. Said they wanted to use the phone, then Nick gets up and..." His face screwed up as if he was going to break out crying again, but he managed to pull himself together. "I don't know no more 'cause I left so they wouldn't see me.''

Shelley quickly placed both hands over the boy's ears and whispered to Cord, "Do you think those men are the same ones who were at my house?''

Robbie struggled out of her hold and glared up at her. "That's not fair," he said indignantly, his voice coming out a raspy croak as his bundle of provisions shifted and the weight around his neck began to choke him.

Cord helped Robbie out of his predicament, heaved the load in his hand experimentally and shook his head in amazement before he slung it over his shoulder. "Where's this hideout or fort of yours, kid? I think it's time we found some shelter."

Robbie gave a hushed whoop, waved them to follow and took off.

Shelley tried hard not to laugh at the child's bubbling excitement.

Cord took up the end of the line, his eyes on Shelley's rear end, loving the way she moved and the way the damp denim clung to her every curve and crevice. Somewhere deep inside his mind a little voice scolded him for enjoying this excursion; he should be more alert, more careful, but the way things were turning out, somehow he just couldn't keep his thoughts in a serious mode.

He'd been through wars, bombing raids, been held hostage, beaten up. Those were the rough times. He'd been in every stressful situation imaginable as a photo-journalist, and he'd always succeeded in coming out unscathed, but this time he had the lives of the woman he loved and a young boy to consider. Still, he couldn't repress a chuckle. He was actually having fun, and so was Shelley. Usually he was alone in his escapades, and he found that having someone to share the funnier, lighter side of adventure with was more appealing.

They came to a gloomy clearing not unlike the one they'd just left, except this one was deeper in the over-grown windbreak. In the center of the area was a bench built around a huge pecan tree. Boards serving as steps were neatly nailed up the trunk to the first intersection of the long spreading limbs. In those limbs was a tree house of mammoth proportions. Obviously Lee had given Robbie more than a little help. The hideout was well constructed and painted green, black and brown to camouflage it from prying eyes.

Cord came to a stop, threw his head back and whistled.

Shelley, at his side, had her hands in Robbie's makeshift backpack and was foraging for something to eat. She jerked her head up at his sound of appreciation and stared, too.

Robbie preened at their admiring silence. "Lee helped me some. Come on up." Like an agile monkey he was up the steps and swallowed by the leaves and branches.

Shelley pulled out a chocolate bar and a jar of peanut butter, glanced at the steep climb and shook her head. "Not me, folks. I never liked heights. I'll just sit down here and eat."

Cord snatched the candy and jar from her hands, stuffed them back in the pack and waited. "After you."

"Cord, I want to stay here where it's safer. There's no telling how sturdy that tree house is or what's crawling around in there."

Robbie, his eyes now a luminous leaf green as they gazed down at her from a round window opening, scolded, "Aw, Shelley, don't be a sissy."

Cord pulled her to her feet, turned her around by her shoulders, then gave her a none too gentle push.

"Okay, okay." It was plain to see she was going to have no say in the matter, so she stepped on the bench, grasped the first wooden slat and began to climb, keeping a wary eye on Cord to make sure he was close enough to catch her if she lost her precarious footing.

Two hours later the sun made itself felt on the land by turning the windbreak into a steam bath. Shelley thought she was going to smother, and was sure she was wetter now than when she'd first arrived. She complained repeatedly and Cord finally agreed to chance leaving their hideout and have a look around the farm to see what was happening. A long, heated argument delayed them as Robbie dug in his heels when they suggested he return home.

"I don't got to go," he mumbled, kicking the ground with the toe of his much abused sneaker. Giving a long-suffering sigh, he sat down on the bench, put his elbows on his knees, jammed his chin on his fists and said mournfully, "No one lets me have any fun. What if those bad men are at my house? I might get captured and taken far, far away." He looked from Cord to Shelley. "I'd never see my mom or Nick or you guys again." He was upsetting himself rather than them and gulped out the rest. "They'll think I'm a spy. Th-they'll…"

"Enough," Cord growled, fighting a smile. "You can come with us, young man, but you're to stay behind Shelley and at the first sign of danger you'd better run like hell for help. Got that?"

They left the hideout, walking single file through the steaming vegetation, breathing in the pungent smell of rotting leaves, decaying insects and dark, moist soil. Shelley knew it was best not to think about what she was stepping on or what creatures were watching their passage. Even for a rural farm area they had animals living among them that Shelley had only seen in the zoo. She'd just as soon not meet them face-to-face anytime soon, either.

She was complaining for the hundredth time about

the steam and her wet clothes when Cord stopped in front of her and she realized they had reached the edge of the windbreak.

"It's a damn good thing those men aren't anywhere nearby. All your bitching and talking would give us away."

Shelley ignored him rather huffily and looked around. From where they stood, she could see through part of the pecan grove to the side of the house and the lane. The road appeared deserted. Sighing with relief, she saw that no cars blocked the lane leading to the house. Cord relaxed, also, and she knew by the lessening of tension in his shoulders that he felt it was safe to venture a little farther afield.

The relief she felt made her light-headed, and she rested her head on Cord's back for a second. "I wonder what happened to the beast? He's not here when he's needed and he didn't warn us earlier, either. Lazy damn devil."

"Napoleon's not lazy," Robbie defended stoutly as he trudged through the gluelike mud to catch up with them.

"Maybe one of those men ate him."

"Aw, Shelley," Robbie said, giggling.

"Feathers and all. Do you think that's how we'll catch the man? He'll have white feathers stuck to his lips?" She was getting giddy.

"Hush, you two." Cord motioned for them to begin to move along as he surveyed their position. The only thing that moved were the leaves. Cord was suddenly suspicious of the stillness around them. A warning bell went off in his head and he spun around, scanning the land as far as he could see. He held out his hand for them to halt. Everything looked okay, yet his instincts were telling him something was not as it should be.

Shelley paid no attention to Cord's tenseness, and instead of standing still as he was, she squatted, picked up a broken tree limb, leaned against the nearest tree and began to scrape off the globs of mud that had collected on her jogging shoes. "What I wouldn't give for a nice hot bath. Will you just look at all this mud? I must be carrying around an extra three pounds. No wonder I'm exhausted."

"But then you always were an exercise nut, weren't you, Shell?"

Cord placed his hands on Shelley's shoulders and slowly walked the three of them backward, thinking that if they could only make it to the edge of the windbreak... But his hopes were dashed with Dee's next words.

"Can't do it, Anthony," Dee taunted as she stepped out from behind the wide trunk of a pecan tree.

"What the hell's going on?" Shelley couldn't believe her ears, then as her friend walked farther into the open, she couldn't believe her eyes. Dressed almost identically to the men who had come up the lane earlier, Dee was now holding a small, deadly gun on her.

"Dee, if this is a joke it's in extremely poor taste and not the least bit funny. Now, put that thing down."

"Shut up, Shell. You never knew when I was serious, did you? It always amused me to see how far I could go before you'd realize I hated your guts. So just keep your mouth shut, or I'll be more than happy to shut it for you." Her eyes glittered as she swung her gaze toward Cord. "Where is it, Anthony?"

Cord calculated his chances of getting to Dee and the gun. He knew he would get shot, but maybe it would

buy Shelley and Robbie enough time to get away. He
tensed his muscles and was about to spring forward
when a dry twig, probably the only one for miles that
had evaded the rain, popped like a pistol shot in the
hushed silence of the grove. His head snapped around
to the sound behind him and, though defeated, he was
thankful he'd stopped just short of making a crucial
error in judgment. Dee was not alone. Three men were
moving up fast; their guns, unlike Dee's handgun, had
long barrels and were equipped with silencers. Cord
wrapped his arm around Shelley, bringing her close to
his side. He glanced down at Robbie's small blond head
and felt a deep sense of anger and injustice that this
innocent child might have to suffer.

"I asked you a question, Anthony. Answer me, damn
you. Where is the coded notebook you keep all your
secrets in?"

Cord shrugged. "Well hidden, Dee. Did you think
I'd leave it lying around?" He knew he had to play this
particular game out as long as he could.

"I don't understand." Shelley could only stare at
Dee. "Are you mixed up in this, Dee? How—why?"
Not believing what she was seeing or hearing, she
wanted to roll back the past years in her mind so she
could examine Dee's behavior. But she couldn't, not
now. She had to be alert or Cord and Robbie could end
up dead. "Why? God, why Dee? Surely not for the
money?"

"Well, yes, Shell, that was an incentive, but the excitement was the real lure. Now, I see that my friends
are growing impatient. Anthony, I'll give you one minute to tell me where the notebook on the VS-1 is. If
you don't start talking, I'll shoot that boy Shell seems
so attached to."

"You're a bad woman and I don't like you," muttered Robbie.

"My heart's breaking, kid." Dee moved closer, her gun now pointed directly at Robbie. She glanced at one of the men and said, "Get him away from her. I wouldn't want anything to happen to Shell...just yet."

Cord froze.

Shelley screamed as a dark shadow moved to her side. She felt a jab of cold steel in her ribs but wouldn't let go of Robbie. A hard object tapped the side of her head, not enough to knock her out, yet enough to make her knees go weak for a second and force her to release the boy.

Cord made a lunge for the man but was immediately hauled back by the two thugs behind him. He tried to reach out for Shelley but the men stopped him from doing that, too. "Touch her again," he ground out between clenched teeth as he was dragged farther away, "and I'll see you dead."

"What's this?" Dee said, sneering. "Why, I actually believe you care for her, Anthony."

Shelley paid no attention to Dee and Cord as they traded insults. Her attention was on Robbie as he yelled, kicked and then screamed at the top of his lungs as the man who had struck her struggled to keep him out of her reach. Robbie's shrill voice cut through the quiet like a knife. Then his screams stopped sharply when a gloved hand cuffed him on the side of the head. Shelley had to admire Robbie. He didn't cry, instead he glared up at his captor with all the hate a nine-year-old could muster.

"Wait till my daddy finds out you hit me. He'll give you a chop across the throat." Robbie demonstrated his words with his free hand. "You'll be really sorry, mister."

Shelley saw Cord stiffen and knew what he was worried about. Robbie's words were more true than anyone would ever know. If anything happened to the boy, Nick would search until he found those responsible, then he'd simply dispose of them as the vermin they were. But now was not the time for Robbie to reveal that his father was a navy intelligence officer.

Shelley decided to take a chance and move the focus off Robbie. "Dee, Anthony's dead. There are intelligence agents all over this place. Probably the CIA and the FBI, too, if these men with you are Russians, as I suspect. You might as well give up."

"You're a scream, Shell, but then you always were. Anthony and I used to laugh at your naïveté all the time." She glanced at Cord. "Didn't we?"

Cord had let the two women talk, trying hard to think of a plan of action. The one he'd come up with was faulty, but it was better than the three of them just standing there and getting executed one by one. "She's right, Dee. I'm not Anthony. I'm Cord Lowell, Anthony's twin brother."

Dee's laugh echoed through the trees. Even the men with her laughed softly at the joke. She cocked the gun, took aim at Robbie's head and asked, "Where, Anthony?"

"At the house." Cord answered, purposely letting his shoulders slump to show defeat. There were only three men here with Dee. Five figures had come up the drive. That meant one man was more than likely at the house. He'd allowed himself a quick glance at the farmhouse and saw a light in the living room; it had flickered off, then on, then off again. It was a signal, and obviously not for these four. Someone was waiting for them to return. He had to get Dee to take them all in.

"Stop playing games. Where in the house?"

"Ahh...I'm tired and wet and my memory doesn't function properly under these conditions." He held his breath as he watched Dee take careful aim once more at Robbie. "And if you hurt that boy or Shelley, I'll never tell you where it is."

"You never change, do you? Always had to have total control over every operation. Well, I'll let you have your way one last time. Now move—all of you."

Robbie was shoved into Shelley's arms, and she cuddled him close to her side before they moved off. Her mind was numb with the implications of Dee's last words. Anthony and Dee must have been in it together. All this time they'd planned to steal the plans for the VS-1. She'd trusted them, loved them, and they had lied to her, stolen from her and used her. Worst of all, she had never suspected their corrupt duplicity. Never! "How long have you and Anthony known each other, Dee? Was the job with Martin Aviation the beginning?"

She stumbled over a protruding tree root and was immediately hauled upright by the man who walked beside her. Dee was on her other side next to Robbie. Cord was in the lead, walking between two men.

"You might as well know, Shell. I mean, what harm will it do me now?" She leaned closer, pressing Robbie into her side as she whispered over his head. "I promise you, you're not going to live to tell anyone. Anthony and I have known each other for years. We've always worked together. We were lovers, Shell, even after he married you. Didn't you ever want to know who the women were he was seeing? There was only one woman—me. We excited each other in a way you'll never know. He's been fighting that attraction lately. I'm like a drug to him. He may do without me for a while, but eventually he'll come back for more.''

Shelley was devastated by Dee's revelation, but pushed her feelings aside as an obsessive need to know all the ugly truth made her ask, "Then why did he follow me here?" It was a stab in the dark, a way to needle Dee. It worked only too well as a hand shot out and slapped her cheek.

With a great deal of satisfaction Dee watched Cord struggle as he heard the slap. "He—" she nodded toward Cord "—got scared. Didn't you, Anthony? When the people we're dealing with heard about some of the features of the VS-1, they began to play a different, more deadly game. You see, Shell, that precious airplane secret leaked out. Not much, you understand, but enough to put the pressure on us. Moscow wants those plans, and they're willing to do whatever it takes to get them." She prodded Shelley on with the barrel of her gun. "When they found out Anthony was about to get hold of the plans, and then he just suddenly disappeared...well, they went berserk. Now I'm afraid there's no hope for any of you. We can't have you talking to the authorities after we've gone."

They were almost at the house and the white Victorian building had never looked so good to Shelley. She hoped Cord had some sort of plan or they were indeed dead. "You don't really think you can get away with this, do you Dee? You'll be hunted down."

"I'll get away, Shell, the same way Anthony planned to. We have passports and bank accounts in several different countries. Dee Radford just disappears as if she never existed," she said, snapping her fingers.

Robbie had kept quiet long enough. "You're an evil lady and my dad's a good spy and he's gonna kill you dead. You just wait and see!"

"Bloodthirsty little kid. I'm from the old school and believe you should be seen and not heard, so shut up."

Shelley quickly wrapped her fingers over Robbie's mouth. Dee, she could tell as they had stepped out of the grove and into the sunlight, had been pushed far enough. There were dark circles under the exotic eyes. She wondered why she hadn't noticed them yesterday. Then she remembered how expert Dee had always been with makeup. Still, the woman looked haggard, and it was best to let well enough alone. There was no telling what could trigger her off. Dee might lose what control she had and start shooting. She couldn't take the chance of Robbie or Cord getting hurt because of her needling.

"Nothing else to ask?"

Shelley shook her head, watching the back door of the house grow closer and closer. But as they rounded the side of the machinery barn they stopped. There were two bodies spread out on the ground. Shelley swayed and groaned in horror. It took both a sobbing Robbie and a laughing Dee to hold her up. Lee and Vo lay lifeless on the damp grass. Closing her eyes, Shelley cursed Anthony for the millionth time for the hurt and misery he'd brought to everyone. Two innocent people killed because of their friendship with her.

A sob rose in her throat, only to be abruptly cut off in wonder. The man closest to Lee and Vo reached down and pulled them to their feet. Gagged and trussed like chickens for market, both glared with small black eyes at the thug. Lee had a dark, swelling bruise on his forehead and Vo's neat bun had come undone, spilling her straight blue-black hair in a curtain around her waist. Both looked very alive and very angry.

The relief that swept over Shelley was only a momentary comfort as she was almost thrown off her feet when Dee shoved her forward.

"Don't get your hopes up," she whispered roughly. "Like you and Anthony, everyone here is expendable. These men aren't going to leave any witnesses behind."

"I can't believe I've known you for so long and never once suspected anything. You're a good actress, Dee, but do you really have the nerve to kill these people in cold blood? Have you ever killed before?"

"There's always a first time."

Shelley detected a note of questionable bravado in the voice and wondered when Dee had realized she'd gotten in way over her head. For all her faults, Dee was not a killer. At least, not the Dee she'd known, and she didn't believe she could have hidden the icy streak it took to take another human life. It was there in Nick; she'd seen it and knew he'd killed before and probably wouldn't hesitate to kill again if he was forced to. "It's still not too late, Dee. Help us. Please!"

"Are you kidding? And do what after I save your necks? Go to jail? Because that's what would happen. I'd rather be dead than rot in a drab, dreary prison." She smiled maliciously at Shelley. "Besides, Shell, you know I'd go crazy without men."

They had reached the steps to the back porch. Shelley glanced up, watching as the two men ushered in Cord, Lee and Vo, then she and Robbie. Dee followed. Her heart began to pound as she saw the back door open and they filed into the kitchen. What was she going to do now? If she gave them Anthony's notebook, they were dead. If they knew Anthony's code and realized that he didn't have the information they thought he did about the VS-1, they were dead—except for Cord. He'd end up in Russia somewhere trying to convince them he wasn't who they thought.

She looked at Cord for guidance or some sign of what to do and caught a waiting expectancy in his eyes. When he realized she had noticed, his expression quickly warned her to be ready. But ready for what? Surely he wasn't going to try something on his own?

"Now, Anthony, where's the notebook?"

"You'll have to ask Shelley, Dee. She hid it from me."

Dee was distracted as the three men spoke softly behind her. She turned, her gun still pointed at the circle of prisoners, and demanded to know what her cohorts were talking about. One of them, a small dark man with mean eyes, asked in accented English, "Where's Ivan?"

Suddenly, and without warning, the kitchen was filled with men and drawn guns. Shelley screamed and Robbie cried out in terror. Before she could collect her wits she was on the floor with Robbie clutched to her side, and Cord was trying to cover them both with his body. The startling sound of a gunshot pierced the scene, and gruff male voices called out for the intruders to surrender their weapons.

An eerie silence permeated the kitchen, making the hammering of Shelley's heart excruciatingly loud in her ears. Robbie wiggled and shoved, trying to get a better look at what was going on around them. His shrill welcoming cry for Nick brought Shelley's eyes open. She tried to glance around, but saw nothing but legs as she squirmed. Then Cord was helping her to her feet and she was able to take in the complete scene.

There were men everywhere—Nick's men by the way they handled Dee and the others. Shelley quickly counted six before spotting the local sheriff and some of his deputies. Stunned, she leaned against the wall and watched as Dee and her accomplices were herded together. Cord left her side and she experienced the first jolt of real emotions since they'd entered the kitchen. She'd never seen Cord in a rage...until now.

Cord grabbed Dee by the front of her blouse, and as everyone watched, too shocked by his quick move to stop him, he dragged her to stand under the kitchen's overhead light. "Take a good look at me, bitch." Dee turned her head away, but Cord clamped her face in one hand and forced her to look. "See the scar bisecting my eyebrow? See the hump in the bridge of my nose?" He waited until he had her undivided attention, then smiled grimly as her eyes began to frantically search his face. She shook her head as if to deny what she was seeing. "I'm not Anthony Rayburn. I'm Cord Lowell. Your partner and lover is dead, and you're going to take this rap all by yourself."

Dee began to realize the truth and magnitude of Cord's words. Now she had no one to blame for her actions. There would be no throwing herself on the mercy of any court, no claiming that she'd been taken in by a man and used without knowing what she was getting into. She began to cry, something she thought she'd forgotten how to do.

"I hope you like your own company. Because you'll have it for a very long time in some maximum security prison." Cord let her go, bringing his hand away from her as if she were dirt. He stepped back, nodded to one of the men and watched as the officer clamped handcuffs on her.

Shelley could only shake her head as another scene played out in front of her. Lee and Vo were set free and their high, indignant Vietnamese voices filled the room. How had all of this happened? she wondered, but a noise from the doorway put a stop to her questions.

She saw Sara materialize, then Robbie was in his mother's arms. Suddenly, beside Sara were Milly and Ruby. Then Louis appeared carrying a lethal-looking shotgun perched in the crook of his arm. He looked directly at her and smiled, his white eyebrows wriggling questioningly on his brown forehead. It was all too much. For the second time in her life, Shelley fainted.

She came back to reality on the living room couch amid a gaggle of voices all striving to outdo one another. But it was the touch of Cord's hands, one holding hers and the other patting her cheek, that made her open her eyes. "Tell me I've been dreaming and none of this happened."

"Sorry, love."

She sighed. "Where are Dee and her men?"

"Gone. Are you feeling better, Shelley? You scared the hell out of me when you keeled over."

"I'm fine, just hungry."

He laughed. "Me, too, but I didn't think it would look right to leave you lying on the floor while I stuffed my face with Robbie's goodies."

She smiled, then bit her lips as they began to tremble. "Is it all over?"

Cord brushed back a silken strand of hair from her forehead and glanced over his shoulder. "All but rehashing the events—for the third time, I might add."

Shelley looked around and spotted a crowd of people at the opposite end of the living room. "What happened? How did Nick know we were in trouble?"

"Maybe you ought to let everyone tell their own story."

"I haven't got the strength. You tell me."

"It seems that Dee was followed by navy intelligence to Houston, then to the farm. When she returned to the city they stayed right with her. She met four men. By the way, the fourth, Ivan, was tied up in the living room while everything was going on. Anyway, Nick's men tried to call him here. When they couldn't reach him, they got very concerned. Half of them followed Dee, the others stayed in Houston to see if Dee had any more reinforcements coming. You remember Robbie telling us some men came to his house? They were Nick's agents. They'd tailed Dee here but couldn't locate Nick, and scared the operation was falling apart, they called in their backups. The ones that were already here split up. Some watched Dee, a few others went to the first house they came to—Sara's—to use the phone. It was pure luck they found Nick."

He cupped his hand to her cheek, letting his fingers stroke the soft skin. "You'll get a real kick out of this. The rest of Nick's men went to Milly and Ruby's house. You know how the old ladies can smell a story? Well, they had Louis drive them over to Sara's early this morning, saw the lights on and decided Nick couldn't do his job properly without their advice. When Nick got ready to come here he ordered the ladies to stay with Sara, saying he would call and tell them if anything was happening at your house. They all showed up here, Shelley." He chuckled at the scene that must have met Nick as he opened the door. "To add insult to injury, the sisters called the sheriff and told him to make himself useful for once and come help. From what I understand, Nick came close to shooting the lot."

"But how did they know where we were or that we were headed back to the house?" She was feeling better and sat up, only to be spotted by Milly who immediately rushed to her side.

"Here, dear Shelley, have a nice cup of hot tea. It will restore both the body and spirit." She handed Shelley a cup. "You'd best see a doctor, dear. My papa always said fainting wasn't natural for a person, even as much as women like to do it…to get attention, mind you. So unladylike to fall on the floor, though." She clucked her tongue reprovingly, gave Shelley a reassuring pat on the shoulder and headed back to the group to hold court.

Shelley looked at Cord over the rim of the cup, wanting desperately to laugh but not daring to hurt the old lady's feelings.

Cord wrapped his arm around her, brought her to his side and leaned back to relax for the first time that day.

"The whole time we were making our way back to the house this morning, Nick's men were there. They were watching us being led by Dee and the others and had witnessed Lee and Vo's predicament, but knew, though bruised and shaken, they were okay. Nick told me that if there had been the slightest hint that they might hurt us, he would have had his men intervene. Dee and her men were after Anthony's notebook and would bring us back to the house. Nick's hands were tied. He couldn't step in and help or he would have given his presence away. He had to have everyone together before he made his move. By the way, the thug that manhandled Robbie is sporting a couple of broken ribs and maybe a busted jaw. Nick was not gentle."

"Good!" She was feeling better and snuggled closer to Cord. "I take it that Nick and Robbie have resolved their differences?'' Her gaze wandered over the group of people in the room and spotted Nick and Sara. Robbie seemed glued to his father's side.

"I'd say they are about as close as can be expected. Robbie will still have some problems at times dealing with another man in his mother's life, but eventually everything will work out, I'm sure.''

Shelley closed her eyes and sighed deeply. "I just can't believe it, Cord. Dee and Anthony. They always acted like they hated each other. How could I have been so blind? Why didn't I see what was happening—at least between them?''

The crowd at the other end of the room seemed to be breaking up, and none too soon for Cord. He wanted to shake Shelley for blaming herself again, but he didn't have the chance; they were suddenly swamped with people.

THE NIGHT QUIETED and Cord and Shelley were finally alone in bed together. Shelley reached out and touched him, and he quickly drew her closer.

"What were you thinking about?''

"Us. Shelley, I have to return to San Francisco tomorrow.''

"No!" she wailed. "Not tomorrow. Wait until I can come with you.''

He rolled over to face her. "You have the sale and closing of the farm to work out with Nick and Sara. You'll have to be here to sign papers. Besides, Shelley, you need some time alone, time away from me to make damn sure you want to spend the rest of your life with a man who can't give you children.''

Shelley pushed away from him and flopped over on her back. "For God's sake! Not that again? I love you.

We can adopt children." She covered her eyes with her arm. "I thought we had gone through this and resolved it together, Cord. Don't put this on me now, not with everything else I've been through today. Now you're saying you're leaving tomorrow. Just why in the hell do you have to leave so soon, anyway?"

He wasn't going to let her put any physical distance between them and pulled her back into his embrace. "I've been away from my magazine for weeks, Shelley. My sister's good, but there are some decisions only I can make. I promise you, I'll only be gone a week. It's enough time for you to finish what you have to take care of, then we can leave together."

She didn't want to give in. The events of the day still pressed in on her and her old insecurities had returned. Then she realized what Cord was doing. "You bastard." She grabbed a handful of hair on his chest and gave it a tug. "You're leaving because you know I've lost some of my self-confidence. That's stupid, Cord. I need you here to help me, not take off."

He winced and removed her grasping fingers. The tone of her voice, the desperation she couldn't hide, made him frown. "You have to help yourself this time, Shelley. That way you'll never question your decisions again." He kissed her eyelids, her cheeks, then her lips. "I'll be back. I know it and you know it, but somewhere in that brain of yours you have too many doubts."

He was right, of course. Anthony and Dee had done a thorough job of damaging her self-confidence once again, and it was up to her to get it back. If she didn't, she would never trust her judgment or her instincts again. What was worse, she realized, at some point she might even begin to question and doubt Cord. She couldn't let that happen. "I don't like it, but if you have to go, okay.'' She wound her arms around his neck. ''I might cry a lot, though.'' Her foot rubbed along his calf and up his thigh. He was tough, male, scarred, and he could take her to heaven and make her feel all soft and feminine…and strong, too. Cord knew how to make her feel whole again.

CHAPTER SIXTEEN

A WEEK, Cord had said.

How long could seven days be? Yet, when a week and a half crawled by, Shelley realized all too painfully how time could turn enemy and drag. There were moments when she felt so lonely she thought she'd lose her mind.

Even though Cord called twice a day, it didn't make up for his extended absence. But she understood. At least, that's what she kept telling herself. Her problem was that all her business had been taken care of and she could no longer bury her excitement and her secret in constant work.

Shelley paced before the big bay window in the living room watching for Cord's car to turn up the lane. Today. He'd be here today, she'd told herself when she awakened at dawn. Way before his phone call, she knew he was returning and had risen early, washed her hair, planned what she would wear and rehearsed what she was going to say.

There would be no jeans today. She stopped her pacing and smoothed the skirt of the yellow linen dress. Then she worried with the exaggerated shoulder pads, trying to adjust them so they wouldn't ride back. Was the wide alligator belt too big? She sucked in a breath and tucked in her behind. Was the skirt too tight? Lord knows, she'd gained a little weight.

Everything had to be perfect. Turning her gaze toward the windows she smiled, a silly twist of her mouth. The weather was cooperating, the day was...perfect. The sun shone like a bright yellow diamond in the sky that was filled with cotton clouds. The breeze was cool and sweet and the parched earth had finally quenched its thirst, turning the leaves and grass a brilliant green. Perfect.

Now, all she had to do was wait. That was the hardest part. She'd packed all her belongings with the help of Nick, Sara, Lee and Vo. And of course Robbie. The boxes stood scattered throughout the house waiting to be transported to San Francisco. To Cord's home—and hers.

She tore her gaze from the landscape and began pacing again. What would Cord say? She clamped her hands together, stopped in her tracks and stared off into space. She'd done that a lot the past few days. Shocked, numb, elated, her moods swung back and forth like a pendulum. What would Cord do?

The sound of a car door slamming jerked her from her trance. She swung around and stared as Cord unfolded his tall frame from the car. Why would he rent one so small? she wondered, then giggled. What difference did it make? All that mattered was that he was back. A sudden light-headedness made her aware that she'd been holding her breath and she exhaled slowly, allowing herself the pleasure of watching Cord as he stretched his cramped muscles. He looked as fit and happy as she felt. Her eyes widened in surprise as her gaze took in the way he was dressed.

Wow! she thought, and grinned. She'd imagined him a conservative dresser, but the black pleated slacks and the charcoal, chalk-stripe sport coat that was obviously of Italian design denied his conservatism. Only the Italians could make the unconstructed coat with its loose fit appear so elegant. There was still a lot about Cord that she didn't know and would have fun discovering. He took her breath away; he was beautiful.

When Cord turned toward the porch Shelley flew out of the house and was down the stairs and in his arms before he could take a step. And just as quickly he was kissing her wildly, laughing and trying to talk all at the same time.

"I missed you like hell," he said, and held her away from him. "You look good enough to eat."

"I love you, Cord." It sounded so inept, but it was the only thing she could think of to say. After all the days and hours she'd planned his homecoming and what she would say, now she was tongue-tied.

He groaned and kissed her with a passion that neither could deny or ignore.

After a long time Shelley broke away and framed his beloved face in her hands. "Stop this, Cord." She shook his head and kissed her again. "Cord, please." She laughed. "I have something to tell you."

"What could be more important than this?" His mouth captured hers and this time the kiss was different; hard, searching, confirming the fact that she'd missed him as much as he'd missed her.

Shelley collapsed against him, her bones like jelly, but she was smiling hugely as she backed away. "Come into the house." She turned, then glanced over her shoulder, giving him a look that immediately set him in motion. He walked toward her, his expression set and determined, and she began to run. She laughed wildly when he caught up with her, scooped her into his arms and carried her over the threshold. Knowing where he was headed, she began to squirm. "Let me down." She had to talk to Cord before they got to the bedroom. "Cord, put me down this minute. Please."

He did so reluctantly, but instead of setting her away from him he hugged her close.

Shelley's happiness all but bubbled over as she backed out of his reach. "Listen carefully now."

"What? Damn it, hurry up. I have much more interesting plans for us than standing here and talking all afternoon."

She laughed. "Cord, you're not going to believe this."

"What?"

"Cord…Cord. *I'm pregnant.*"

He went deadly still, saying nothing, his face slowly losing all its color as he stared at her.

Shelley shifted from one foot to the other, stunned by his reaction. His face, the pain and yes, rage, that were displayed made her reach out for him.

Cord took a step backward. "Whose?" He nearly strangled on the question. Flashes of his first marriage rushed back with an unreal clarity. The thought of Shelley in bed with another man was a blow he couldn't accept, one that would surely fell him on the very spot where he stood. He shook his head like a wounded bull, trying hard to collect his thoughts, but he couldn't think straight. "Whose?" He couldn't disguise the anguish in his voice and because of it, he lashed out, grabbed Shelley by the shoulders and began to shake her. Never in all his life had he wanted to strike someone so badly.

"Cord, stop. Please."

"Nick. It's Nick's, isn't it?"

"No! God, no. Cord listen to me." She gazed up at him, her eyes huge in her pale face. She was so shocked by his rage she couldn't think. He'd let go of her and was walking past her before she realized that he was going to leave. Sprinting past him, she planted her back against the door, blocking his exit.

"Get the hell out of my way."

"Cord, sweetheart," she pleaded softly. "If you'll just calm down and listen." His eyes wandered over her with so much contempt she shivered, but she remained where she was. How had everything gone so wrong? She'd had this meeting planned in her head for days, and it wasn't happening as she had envisioned.

"Surely you're not going to try to convince me that a miracle happened and it's mine? We both know better. Besides, while I was in San Francisco I had some tests done just to see if maybe there had been a change and some hope for us. There's not, Shelley." He swallowed, his throat aching with the finality of their situation. "I'm sterile. The kid isn't mine."

At that moment she believed she loved him more than she'd ever loved anyone in her life. To think he'd gone through those tests again just for her....

"Move, Shelley."

"It's not Nick's, Cord." He reached out to physically remove her from his path but she slapped his hands away. "Think, Cord! It couldn't be Nick's. You've only been gone a week and a half. That would be too soon for me to even suspect anything unusual." She had to keep talking to calm him down or else he was liable to walk right through her and tear Nick apart before he heard the truth. "The baby is Anthony's, darling. I'm a little more than two months pregnant."

Cord jerked back as if he'd been slapped across the face. Nick or another man he could kill, but Anthony!

His brother's baby! He shook his head, trying to comprehend what she was saying.

"I know it's silly, but I really didn't have any idea I was pregnant. The last time Anthony and I made love was just prior to his vasectomy, and that was only a couple of days before I found him in Mr. Martin's office. Then with everything that's happened it never occurred to me that I hadn't started my period. But with Nick, Mr. Martin, the FBI and you showing up and telling me Anthony was dead, I wasn't concerned. It never crossed my mind I might be pregnant till after you left and Milly advised me that I ought to see her doctor. You can imagine…"

He couldn't accept the fact that she was going to have another man's child. Never his, dear God, never his. How could he raise *this* child and love it as his own? She was going to destroy him. Without knowing, she was killing him, making him realize how much he wanted a child of his own. He could take in a stranger's baby, but not his brother's. He couldn't explain the revulsion, but it was there. How inadequate it made him feel. She'd never understand that his pain was all wrapped up in knowing that by her having Anthony's child he would have to acknowledge the fact that there had been an intimate side to her marriage, a side he'd attempted to blank from his mind.

His thoughts didn't make any sense, and he was even more confused. Taking a backward step, he said, "I want nothing to do with that child. Damn you, Shelley." He spun around before she could say anything and walked through the kitchen, out the back door and around the side of the house to his car. His route was impeded only by the blur of tears that he angrily blinked away. He felt dead inside.

The slamming of the car door brought Shelley out of her shocked state. The sound of the engine starting made her whip around, yank on the doorknob and fly down the porch steps. She stopped, her chest aching as she watched the car turn off the lane onto the road.

A breeze dried the tears on her cheeks as she stood in the front yard long after Cord had disappeared from view. Suddenly chilled, she wrapped her arms around herself, hunched over as if the pain was too much to bear, then walked slowly into the house. When she found herself in the living room, she pulled a comfortable chair up to the window and sat down to wait. *He'll be back,* she told herself. *He'll be back.*

IT WAS SUNSET, the shank of the day, when night descends slowly and gossamer threads of ebony darkness inch their way across the landscape. A shadow touched the kitchen window, slipped over the sill and spilled into the sink, filling it to overflowing before it ran over the rim and onto the floor. The same shadow crept across the room and into the hall as if it were a thief on stockinged feet, silent in its coming, devastating in its melancholy gloominess. A breeze, like a hushed breath, picked up the shadow, split it into searching fingers and sent them dancing across the living room toward the woman sitting motionless in a wing chair. Somewhere in the depths of the house a door shut quietly.

Nick found her alone in a pool of defused light, her eyes too big for her wan face, her lips a tight, white line against her teeth to keep them from chattering. Her hands with their delicate bones gripped the curved arms of the chair. He leaned closer to catch the rustling of her words.

"He'll be back…he has to come back."

"Shelley…who'll be back? What's happened here?"

She told him, her voice a husky monotone as she stared off in the distance.

Nick hunched down beside the chair, afraid to touch her, scared that with everything she'd been through this one last shock might send her over the edge. He'd sure like to get his hands on Cord.

Keeping his own voice level, unemotional, he said, "That doesn't sound like Cord, Shelley. He loves children, and from what you just told me he was even willing to adopt. Why wouldn't he want the child you're carrying?" Nick wanted to do something to comfort her, but didn't know how, so he just kept talking. "Think, Shelley. Through everything that's happened he's never changed toward you. Why now? Don't you see it's not you, but himself." He liked what he was saying, it made sense, and better still he was getting through to her. "For whatever reasons, for whatever haunts him, Cord has to conquer his own devils before he can help himself."

Shelley listened to Nick's words, letting them wash over her without really comprehending what he was saying. But gradually they began to soak through and Cord's recent scolding came back to her. She had to regain her self-respect, and trust her own judgment. No matter what was making Cord run now, she knew he would be back. "Thanks, Nick. I guess this means we're friends and I can't fight with you anymore?"

She smiled, but to Nick it seemed a sad smile.

"You and I will always argue, Shelley. You're too outspoken to keep your mouth shut for long." He laughed, something that was coming easier these days, and rose to his feet. "I have to take Robbie to a baseball tryout. Would you like me to send Sara over to stay with you?''

"No, I'll be fine now." He frowned and she laughed softly. "I just had a temporary collapse, but really, I'm okay."

"You're sure?"

She rose shakily to her feet, then straightened her spine and gave Nick a convincing smile. "Absolutely. When are you and Sara getting married?"

"Just as soon as those two old bats decree it's the proper time." He shook his head and laughed again. "No, really, they're right. For Robbie's sake, we don't want to rush things. Milly and Ruby tell me it will be a couple of weeks yet. You know, I've planned missions, life and death situations, but I'm not allowed to have any say in my own wedding." He gave a disgusted snort.

Shelley walked him to the door, wanting to tell him that he was in for a real shock if he thought he was ever going to be master of his life again.

"You're sure you don't need Sara?" he offered. She shook her head and still he hesitated. "Cord will come to his senses, Shelley, just be patient."

"I will." She shut the door behind him, leaned against it and closed her eyes but immediately opened them. Anything was better than being locked behind the black backside of her eyelids with only her thoughts. He was right, of course. All she had to do was wait. Cord loved her, of that she had no doubt. She would just have to be patient until he came to terms with the fact that she was having his brother's baby. She turned her eyes toward heaven and said, "Anthony, you're not going to ruin this for me, not this time. You're the past. The future is somewhere out there hurting and trying to come to terms with you having existed and the life you left behind. But...he'll be back and then you'll only be a picture in an album.''

CORD GUIDED THE RENTAL CAR down the dirt road at a slow speed, avoiding the potholes when he could, trying to figure out what he was going to say to Shelley. Mentally he edited his speech, tore it up and started again. A low curse issued from parched lips. He pushed his sunglasses back up the bridge of his nose, cutting off any chance of the glaring sun finding his sensitive eyes. Lord, he felt like he'd wrestled with demons and barely won. In fact, he reminded himself, he'd done just that. Two days in a Houston hotel with a fifth of Scotch and his thoughts. What a hell of a combination.

Cord lifted his heavy-lidded gaze from the rutted road and studied the distance ahead of him. He squinted at his watch, realized it was five in the morning, then raised his eyes once more to the far end of the road and the dot of white. Shelley was out for her morning jog. His mouth, if possible, went drier. What if she wouldn't listen to him? What if she told him to get out of her life? What if...? A frown thundered across his forehead, and he winced at the pain it caused. Should she be jogging in her condition?

SHELLEY SPOTTED the strange car coming down the road. Her pulses leaped and her senses clamored, telling her it was Cord. Yet, as excited as she was, she neither slowed her pace nor stopped as the car pulled up beside her. He needed to suffer a little before she forgave him.

Cord slammed on the brakes, shoved open the door, stepped out and yelled, ''Are you crazy? Jogging in your condition!''

She took a sideways glance at him as she loped past the car and grinned. From what little she saw he looked awful. Good!

"Hello to you, too," she called out without turning around.

Cord held on to the doorframe grimly, knowing this wasn't going to be easy. He sighed mournfully and sprinted to her side, unable to stop the groan that escaped his lips as the hammering in his head grew louder with each footfall. Like an eel she evaded his restraining hand and forced him to run next to her.

"I'm sorry, Shelley." His vision blurred, not from any tender emotions, but from the fact that he actually hurt all over. "Please stop, sweetheart." He huffed beside her, totally out of breath now. "I know you're very angry with me, but Shelley, don't kill me before I can made amends. What good would I be then?"

The question deserved some thought, and after a couple more steps she stopped, but she continued to jog in place even though the sight of him close up almost made her freeze. Cord was a wreck. He obviously hadn't shaved in the past two days, his hair defied description, his beautiful navy blue eyes were obscured by red puffy lids and bloodshot whites. And his clothes, those expensive Italian linens, looked as if someone had wadded them in a ball. She fought a smile as she caught a whiff of the alcohol that reeked from him.

Waving her hand before her face, she moved backward and said, "A person could get high just standing too close to you."

He had the grace to look shamefaced. "I've had a few," he snapped defensively. *More like a fifth in two days,* an inner voice mocked him. He was getting dizzy and his eyeballs hurt from watching her move up and down. Angrily he grabbed her arms. "Be still, damn it, you're making me sick to my stomach." Then he was immediately contrite. "Shelley...Shelley, can you ever forgive me? I know I hurt you. Lord knows I wish I hadn't. What can I say? It was just...your news hit me hard and where it hurt the most—in my ego."

The sun beat down on him and he began to sweat. Letting go of her arms, he slipped out of his sport coat. The minute he let go of her she started to jog in place again.

He scowled and grumbled, "What's with you this morning?" He was more than a little miffed that she wasn't in tears at his humble return. But then, Shelley never did the expected.

"It's not healthy to stop jogging all of a sudden. I need to cool down." She fought the smile again but lost the battle.

"Yes, I'm sorry. I forget about the baby. I mean..." He was tongue-tied. Damn her, she looked as if she were enjoying this. "Get in the car, Shelley."

"Can't."

He closed his eyes and turned his face to heaven. *What now, God?* His patience was wearing thin. She was delighting in torturing him. "Why not?"

"I'm waiting for someone."

His scowl quickly changed into a deepening frown. She wasn't going to cooperate at all, and he figured he deserved the punishment. He sighed again, stumbled on a rut and cursed. She needn't look so damn pleased with herself, though. "This is impossible, you know? I had what I was going to say to you all planned out. But now it doesn't matter. I love you more than life. That's what counts."

"It's not everything." She continued to jog in place.

His gaze dropped to her bouncing breasts and an inner spark almost ignited the alcohol into a raging fire. "No, I know. I had no idea how deeply the pain and insecurity of my sterility went until you told me you were going to have a baby. Not mine, never mine, Shelley. It almost killed me. And so is your bouncing. Stop!"

He took a breath. "Thank you." He wiped his sweaty brow and unbuttoned his shirt. "You'll think I'm a little crazy, but I never associated you and Anthony and intimacy. I didn't want to admit you ever made love to him even though you were his wife. I was jealous—jealous of a dead man who gave you something you wanted so much that I never could."

She wanted to wrap her arms around him and hold him, but she kept her distance, knowing it was more important for them to get all their problems worked out now while their emotions were still raw and new.

"And the baby?" She held her breath. "How do you feel about the baby now?"

Cord hauled her to him, enfolded her in a tight embrace and buried his face in her damp hair. Someday he'd tell her of the agony he'd gone through as he came to terms with himself. How at the lowest moment of his life he'd been given a miracle as he recognized the true relationship between himself and the baby.

"It's mine."

"What?" She jerked back and gaped at him.

"The baby, Shelley, is really mine."

"No! Now Cord, don't try and lie to yourself and—"

"No, you don't understand. I spent hours working it out, and when it finally came to me it sobered me immediately. Shelley, Anthony was my brother, my identical twin. Biologically, the child *is* part mine."

As hard as she tried not to, she burst into tears.

"Aw, Shelley, please don't." His own voice shook. He had to clear his throat several times before he could speak again. "You didn't really think I would leave you, did you?"

She sniffed. "No. I knew you loved me. Surprisingly, that's the one thing I was sure about. Oh, I had a bad time when you walked out, but I remembered what you said about believing in myself, and I never doubted that you would be back. I just didn't know how you were going to come to terms with the baby."

She felt so good in his arms, so right. He could have stood there holding her forever, but the morning sun was making itself felt on the top of his aching head. "Come on. Let's go to the house and finish this discussion where it's cool and I can take some aspirin."

Shelley laughed at his hopeful, hangdog expression and said, "Sorry, but I really am meeting someone." She grabbed his wrist and glanced at his watch.

"Shelley, what are you up to?" He didn't like the way her eyes glinted all of a sudden.

"You'll see." They both turned as the sun reflected off the hood of a brightly polished car. Milly and Ruby's vintage Cadillac purred down the road and came to a gliding stop beside them.

Louis stepped out slowly. "Morning, Miss Shelley." He regarded Cord coldly for a second, then dismissed him totally.

"Is there anything the old ladies and this town don't know?" Cord murmured to Shelley, but Louis heard and smiled. "I'll humbly make my apologies to the ladies for the way I've treated Shelley, Louis."

"That'll be the right thing to do." Louis nodded. "You're in deep water with the sisters right now so you'd best go over there to let them chew you out. Get it over with before they think of something else. It'll make them feel better." His dark eyes were sparkling as he opened the back door and pulled out an orange and black bundle. "Here's Aloysius like the ladies promised, Miss Shelley. Now, you do just what I said, and never mind about finding him. He'll come home soon enough." Louis transferred the yellow-eyed cat to Shelley's arms, then he crawled slowly back behind the wheel, shut the door and drove away.

"I can't believe this! We have our lives to plan and you're playing with a cat."

Shifting the limp feline in her arms, Shelley half turned and stuck out her leg to show Cord four dime-size bruises on her calf. "Napoleon caught me yesterday. Now I'm going to pay the beast back—in full." She straightened her shoulders and heaved her load. "It's either this or I'm going to kill him, Cord. But Lee and Robbie would never forgive me." She whipped the towel from around her neck and covered the cat as it hung over her arm.

"Shelley, the cat is a natural predator of our feathered friend."

"Yes." She smiled evilly. "I know that, but Aloysius doesn't." She took off before he could stop her.

"What do you mean Aloysius doesn't?" Cord asked, keeping up with her as best he could. "He'll tear the gander to pieces."

"Not him. Milly would never allow a cat of hers to eat birds." She jogged on. "Why, Milly told me Aloysius's best friend is their parakeet, Zeus. This cat will scare the hell out of Napoleon, yes, but he won't hurt him. More's the pity," she mumbled.

Shelley stopped at the corner leading to the blacktop

lane and peeked around the fence post. Cord did the same. Sure enough, Napoleon squatted halfway up, waiting for Shelley. Cord glanced at her, caught the elation in her expression and began to chuckle. Aloysius, sensing her excitement, began to squirm under the towel. "You best hurry," he said on hearing a muffled snarl.

"Stay here. If that devil sees you, he'll just waddle away."

Cord nodded as she took off down the lane, then smiled. The towel didn't completely cover the cat, and his orange-and-black tail hung down her legs, twitching between her knees.

The tail tickled Shelley and she almost lost her stride several times. As she ran, her eyes narrowed to slits and her heart swelled with revenge.

Napoleon rose, shook his pointed tail, stretched his long neck and flapped his wings threateningly at Shelley. Then, with a few hissing honks he ran straight for her.

Shelley waited until he was almost upon her, then whipped off the towel and threw twenty pounds of overly playful cat who spied a potential new friend.

The gander shot up in the air and took off across the field with the cat on its tail feathers. Shelley was laughing so hard she didn't hear Cord come up behind her, but when she saw him she grasped his arm for support. "Look!" She pointed to Napoleon, a white blur. He half flew, half ran from his tormentor, squawking all the way as Aloysius trotted behind him. All they could see of the cat was the tip of his tail as he meowed plaintively while his new friend managed to evade him.

Shelley had never heard such a racket and leaned

against Cord, laughing harder than she could remember. "Revenge *is* sweet, Cord."

He had to admit he'd enjoyed the sight himself, but he had more important things on his mind. "Come on, let's go up to the house. There are a few things that need to be straightened out between us." He waggled his eyebrows, winced and touched his forehead as another needle-sharp pain shot through his brain.

By the time they reached the house, any romantic thoughts Cord had had disappeared like empty words on the wind. He was hung over to his very toes, he admitted freely.

Shelley smiled sweetly, took his coat from the crook of his arm and flung it in the direction of the brass coatrack.

Cord's gaze followed the expensive coat, saw it catch on the curved hook and hang limply. "Neat," he said, and glanced back at Shelley. That glint in her eye was still there, but it was no longer directed at Napoleon. "Shelley, I need a couple of hours' sleep." He chuckled grimly and began to back away. She followed.

"What happened to the infamous midnight marauder?" she mocked.

"He did battle with a bottle and lost. I've had too much to drink in the past two days."

She yanked his shirt from the waist of his slacks.

"Shelley! Come on, sweetheart, be reasonable." He stepped away from her hands. "You'll only make me embarrass myself."

"I doubt that." The look she gave him was full of promise and the tips of his ears actually turned pink.

"I'm exhausted." His heels slammed into the bottom of the staircase, and he slipped a fraction on the hardwood floor. Shelley was down on her knees before he could protest. She pulled off his shoes and tossed them one by one over her shoulder. As she stood she ran her hands up his legs, and every nerve in his body screamed no, then yes. His system was like a sluggish engine being jump-started. Miraculously his headache receded only to be replaced by another ache. Suddenly he was a willing participant in her game. "I'll disappoint you."

"I'll help." She grinned, her eyes sparkling with laughter as she unsnapped the waist of his slacks.

"I don't have much strength."

"Do you love me?" She pushed his shirt off his shoulders, down his arms, then pitched it behind her.

"Of course I love you."

"Then you'll find the strength."

He began backing up the stairs, and when she reached for his zipper he grabbed her hands. "I have a head-ache." He dropped her hands and took a few more steps up the stairs.

"I know a sure way to get rid of it." She grinned again, this time holding the smile and showing all her white teeth. She took two steps, then stopped.

The grin got to him. It reminded him of cannibals he'd seen in the jungles. They showed their pearlies just before they had you for dinner. He swallowed hard, fighting to keep from laughing. "You'll be gentle?" He took another step and found himself on the landing.

Shelley gave him a sweet smile. "Of course." She advanced.

"Will you respect me in the morning?"

She couldn't keep a straight face any longer and be-gan to laugh. But laughter didn't deter her from her mission. "Only if your performance is what it should be." The slacks dropped in a dark pool around his feet.

She glanced at the tight jockey underwear and raised an eyebrow. "You don't look exhausted to me."

"A flash of hope. It won't last long."

"We'll see." She was in his embrace without knowing who'd actually made the first move. "Love me, Cord."

His hangover was immediately forgotten, his lack of sleep a memory as he scooped her into his arms. "I do love you, Shelley, never doubt that, ever." He swung around and headed for her bedroom.

Shelley glanced over his shoulder to the trail of clothes on the stairs and began to laugh. There would never be a dull moment in their lives—she'd see to that. For one brief second she thought of Anthony and pitied him for all he'd missed in life. Then she let go of him, along with the resentment and the hatred she'd harbored for too long. She was finally where she was supposed to be—in Cord's arms. For all she'd been through, she thought dreamily, there was a happy ending, after all.

Harlequin Romance ®

Delightful
Affectionate
Romantic
Emotional

Tender
Original

Daring
Riveting
Enchanting
Adventurous
Moving

Harlequin Romance ® —
capturing the world you dream of...

HARLEQUIN®
Makes any time special ®

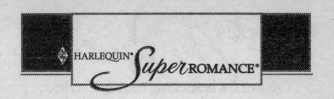

HARLEQUIN *Presents*

**The world's bestselling romance series...
The series that brings you your favorite authors,
month after month:**

Helen Bianchin...Emma Darcy
Lynne Graham...Penny Jordan
Miranda Lee...Sandra Marton
Anne Mather...Carole Mortimer
Susan Napier...Michelle Reid

and many more uniquely talented authors!

Wealthy, powerful, gorgeous men...
Women who have feelings just like your own...
The stories you love, set in exotic, glamorous locations...

HARLEQUIN *Presents*

Seduction and passion guaranteed!

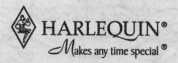

Harlequin® Historical

From rugged lawmen and valiant knights to defiant heiresses and spirited frontierswomen, Harlequin Historicals will capture your imagination with their dramatic scope, passion and adventure.

Harlequin Historicals . . . they're too good to miss!